MADEMOISELLE
AT ARMS

ELIZABETH BAILEY

Contents

CHAPTER ONE

In the quiet of an autumn afternoon, the deserted mansion slept. Or appeared to do so. Concealed among the trees that edged the estate grounds, the watchers paused.

There were two of them. Men of action by the scarlet coats with their grey facings—insignia of the county militia. Cocked hats and buckled swords spoke of rank. Officers were these. Too skilled to advertise their presence by a show of arms and men. The spy—if there was one hiding out in the late Jarvis Remenham's empty house—would be taken unawares.

Wary they might be. Sanguine they were not. In fact, one of them was downright sceptical.

'Seems quiet enough,' observed the junior officer, his gaze raking the shuttered windows of the building's grey stone frontage.

'Don't be too sure,' responded Major Gerald Alderley on a dry note. 'I am expecting a huge rat to emerge any second. Waving a white flag, naturally.'

Captain Roding grinned. 'Why not a French flag?'

'Because I don't believe that fool Pottiswick could tell French from Arabic, even if he heard it as he says he did—which I take leave to doubt.'

The lodgekeeper had been in fine fettle by the time Major Alderley had produced his investigatory force at the gates.

'Gabbling and muttering in a foreign tongue, that's what I heard, sir,' had declared the gap-toothed ancient, when he told them of the initial foray he had made, sneaking around the house in the dark. 'One of they Frenchies, that's what I say —if it ain't a ghost.'

'A French ghost?'

'Well, it ain't a rat this time, Major, I can promise you that,' Pottiswick had rejoined, his tone affronted.

'It had better not be, by God,' had barked Captain Hilary Roding.

Gerald sympathised with his friend's irritation. The last time Pottiswick had called out the militia on suspicion of intruders in Remenham House, a large rodent had been all the spoil. It had certainly caused some havoc in the uninhabited mansion, chewing through Holland covers to get at the furniture beneath, and knocking down a fire guard and a couple of wooden stands. Truth to tell, more damage had been done in the enthusiastic chase carried out by the militiamen detailed to catch it.

'I never met a rat what wandered about the place with a lantern, I didn't,' grumbled the old lodge-keeper aggrievedly.

'Did you see the man?' Gerald asked.

'No, but I seen the light, sir. Moving room to room it was.' He added pointedly, 'Early this morning that were. I sent a message straight.'

'We had other matters on hand this morning,' Roding told him sharply.

Fiercely defensive, as usual. It both pleased and amused Gerald that Hilary adhered rigidly to protocol before the men, no matter what he might say to his major on other occasions. Besides, it was not the lodgekeeper's business to know that "other matters" included a reluctance on Gerald's part to allow his little company to conduct the search without him, and he'd had an engagement this morning.

'I suppose you think I can't manage it myself,' had complained Captain Roding sarcastically.

'Nothing of the sort,' argued Gerald. 'But on the off chance—slim, I grant you—that there is a spy down there, I don't want to miss the fun.'

The possibility was indeed remote, for there had been no trouble with France since the Peace of Versailles had been signed six years ago. But the current rumblings of internal discontent across the Channel were productive of unease in certain quarters. Even an unlikely episode such as this could not be ignored. Besides, Gerald would not for the world have passed up the chance of a little excitement.

It seemed at this moment, however, that there was not going to be any "fun", and Captain Roding said so.

'How disappointing,' mourned Gerald. 'Ah, well, we'll check the back and then go home.'

'Don't tell me,' exploded his second-in-command. 'I know you, Gerald. We won't drag you away until you've been through the place from top to bottom.'

Alderley laughed. 'Just around it, Hilary, that's all.' He added on a teasing note, 'Though if there's anything suspicious we can always get the key from Pottiswick.'

Hilary Roding groaned, but obediently followed Gerald as he began to make his way through the trees towards the back to a vantage point from where they might examine the rear of Remenham House. One glance swept across the place and it was immediately apparent that Pottiswick had not, this time, been mistaken.

'Aha,' grunted Gerald with satisfaction, squinting up at the two open shutters on the second floor. 'A French rat with exceedingly long arms, I see.'

'Gad, there is someone there,' exclaimed Hilary beside him, shading his eyes with one hand. The warm September sun fell strongly on this part of the grounds, uninterrupted by trees, its light bouncing off the glass in the mansion's walls. He added succinctly, 'Windows are open.'

Even as they watched, a shadow passed across one of the apertures.

'I'll get the key,' said Roding, turning abruptly.

Gerald stayed him. 'Wait! No time for that. We're going in.'

Hilary eyed him. 'And how do you propose to get in?'

'Scullery window.'

'You're going to break into the house? You're mad.'

'Nonsense, it'll give Pottiswick something genuine to complain about,' said Gerald cheerfully, moving to the edge of the trees. 'Besides, I don't want the men blundering in here and frightening off our spy. Come on.'

'You're incorrigible,' scolded Hilary, beginning to follow. 'No one would credit that you are three years older than I.'

'You always were an old sobersides, even as a boy,' retorted the major, who was close on thirty now, yet as ripe for excitement as he had been on receiving his first commission at sixteen. Ten years of military life had taught him caution, but only strengthened a fearless zest for diving into any promising adventure with unalloyed enjoyment.

Out of sight of that tell-tale window, the two officers darted across the grounds, speedily gaining the lee of the mansion walls. Hugging them, they crept stealthily around the house, Major Alderley leading, and wasting—so his captain acidly commented—a deal of time checking the windows and doors. When he tried the scullery door, and would have moved on, Hilary intervened.

'Thought you were going to break in here,' he said, in an impatient whisper.

'We may have to,' Gerald answered thoughtfully, staring at the window to one side.

'But you said—'

Gerald tutted. 'Housebreaking, Hilary? I take the matter of housebreaking very seriously, I'll have you know.' He quirked an eyebrow. 'I thought, you see, that we might as well enter by the same way our intruder had done.'

Roding looked struck. 'You mean there isn't any evidence of a break-in.'

'Precisely.'

'That's odd.'

'Precisely,' Gerald repeated. He glanced up. The open windows were above them now and, unless the intruder were to lean out, they could not possibly be seen. 'Let's check the rest of it and then I suppose we will have to break in.'

'For God's sake,' protested his junior. 'I thought you said you take housebreaking very seriously.'

'I do. I intend to remain very serious indeed while I'm doing it.'

'Dunderhead. Why don't I just go and get the key from Pottiswick?'

Alderley flicked a glance back at him over his shoulder. 'You can if you like.'

'Yes, and leave you to break in on your own. No, I thank you.'

Hilary Roding, despite the fact that he was both a younger and slighter man than his friend—although wiry and tough with an attractive countenance that had won him the heart of an extremely eligible young lady—had a rooted conviction, as Gerald well knew, that it was not safe to leave Alderley to his own reckless devices. It occasionally troubled the major that Hilary's staunch loyalty had led him into hair-raising exploits at Gerald's side, for he was perfectly aware that Hilary would not have dreamed of deserting him.

They had completed a circuit of the mansion before Roding's frustration burst out. 'How in God's name did the wretched fellow get in then?'

'Dug a tunnel?' suggested Gerald, halting next to a pair of French windows at the front. 'Or flew in by balloon, perhaps.'

'Oh yes, or walked through the walls, I dare say. And if you mean to use that dagger to slip the lock, you'll make enough noise to bring ten spies down on us.'

But Major Alderley might have been an expert for all the sound he made as he forced the lock with the heavy blade.

Darkness closed in on them as the officers stepped inside the musty interior. Gerald stood quite still for a moment or two, listening intently. Utter silence answered him. Then he could hear Hilary breathing beside him, and from outside the muted twittering of birds.

As his eyes adjusted, he was able to make out the great shrouded shapes of the furniture. A brief feeling of empathy with Pottiswick passed through him. There was an eerie sense of brooding menace about an uninhabited establishment. No one had lived here since old man Remenham had died some eighteen months ago, for the heir, so it was rumoured, was a relative with property of his own.

Someone, it appeared, was trying to profit from that fact. Gerald's task was to stop him from doing so. In this spy theory, however, he had no faith whatsoever. It was his belief that the French had enough troubles of their own in these difficult times without bothering to nose out British business.

Noiselessly, his booted feet stepping with careful restraint, he started forward, signalling to Roding to follow. Together they crept through the erstwhile drawing room and entered the massive flagged hall.

'No sense in snooping about down here,' Gerald whispered.

'Of course the fellow has doubtless stayed put to wait for you,' retorted Hilary.

'Maybe not,' Gerald conceded, 'but I'm damned if I herald my approach with a lot of unnecessary blundering about in the dark.'

Roding allowed that he had a point, and followed him as he began to mount the stairs. The odd creak was not to be avoided in an old house such as this. But it seemed that their presence was not even suspected. For on reaching the second floor, a swishing sound came to Gerald's ears, as of someone moving about.

He halted and put out a hand to stop Hilary. Finger to his lips, Gerald pointed in the direction of the noise. Listening on the dimlit landing, he saw Roding's face muscles tighten. He was conscious of a quickening of his heartbeat and the familiar rise of adrenalin that sent his senses soaring in anticipation.

This was what he missed. This was the reason he had raised his little independent Company of Light Infantry and joined the West Kent Militia. Selling out of the Army to take up his inheritance had spelled boredom to Gerald Alderley. The militia offered little in the way of relief. This was just what he needed. God send the fellow did turn out to be a spy!

Beckoning Roding on, Gerald crept down the corridor towards the source of the swishing he had heard. It had ceased now, but as he closed in on the area, a faint muttering came to his ears. Pottiswick had mentioned muttering. Perhaps the old fool was not as fanciful as they had thought.

The door to the room in question was closed. Gerald pressed against the wall, and signalled Roding to go to the other side of the door. His hand went to his pocket and extracted a neat silver-mounted pistol. Like most officers, he'd had it especially made, for a man who loved danger had need of a precision instrument of defence.

Hilary Roding was all soldier now, his earlier grievances laid aside. His fingers cherished the hilt of his sword and his eyes were on his friend and superior, ready at his back to do whatever was needed.

Very gently indeed, Alderley grasped the handle of the door and stealthily turned it. A minute pressure inwards showed him that it was not locked.

He glanced up at Roding and met his eyes. A nod was exchanged. Taking a firm grasp of his pistol, Gerald eased back, let go the handle of the door, and at the same instant, swung his booted foot.

The door crashed back against the wall inside and both men hurtled into the room, weapons at the ready—and stopped dead.

Standing before a mirror set on a dresser between the windows, two hands frozen in the act of adjusting a wide-brimmed hat on her head, stood a lady in a dark riding habit, her startled features turned towards the door.

For a moment or two Gerald stood in the total silence of amazement, his pistol up and pointing, aware that Hilary was likewise stunned, standing with half-drawn sword. And then amusement crept into Alderley's chest and he let his pistol hand fall.

'So this is Pottiswick's French spy.'

'Gad, but she's a beauty,' gasped Hilary, and slammed his sword back in its scabbard.

The lady, who was indeed stunning, Gerald suddenly realised, said never a word. A pair of long-lashed blue eyes studied them both as she slowly brought her hands down to rest by her sides. The pouting cherry lips were slightly parted and the very faintest of panting breaths, together with the quick rise and fall of an alluring bosom, betrayed her fear. Raven locks fell to her shoulders from under the feathered beaver hat, and curled away down her back.

It struck the major that she was very young. But although startled and clearly afraid, there was no self-consciousness in her gaze and she was standing her ground. A tinge of admiration rose in his breast.

Gerald raised his cockaded hat, and smiled. 'Forgive this intrusion, ma'am, I beg. We were expecting rather to find a male antagonist.'

Still the girl said nothing.

'Perhaps she don't understand English,' suggested Roding.

Gerald switched to French. '*Étes-vous Francais?*'

Her eyes, he noted, followed from himself to Hilary and back again, but she did not speak. Her gaze flickered down to his pistol. Gerald caught the look and slipped the weapon into his pocket. One did not use pistols against a female.

'We mean you no harm,' he said reassuringly. 'You have no need to be afraid of us.'

Still no response. Gerald exchanged a puzzled glance with his friend. Was she so fearful still?

Roding shrugged and grimaced. 'What do we do now?'

Gerald took a pace towards the girl. She moved then, fast, taking refuge behind a Chinese screen that was set beside the four-poster at the back of the room.

Gerald swore. 'She's terrified.'

Hilary's gaze was raking the room. 'She ought to be. Been making herself at home all right.'

Alderley glanced round the bedchamber. Strewn across the bed was a multitude of jumbled garments. A long chest under one of the windows was open, some of its contents dragged out and spilling onto the floor. He drew an awed breath.

'Was she planning to make away with all this stuff?'

'What's this?'

Hilary pounced on a black item slung on the floor by the dresser. His gaze drawn, Gerald watched him dip to pick up a crushed square of white linen and a starched object that resembled a helmet. Then he lifted the black cloak-like garment from the floor.

'Gerald, this is a nun's habit.'

Before the major could verify this, the lady re-appeared. To his consternation, she was holding an unwieldy, ugly-looking pistol, all wood and tarnished steel, with both hands about the butt. Coldly she spoke, in a distinctly accented voice.

'Do not move, *messieurs*, or I shall be compelled to blow off your head.'

Hilary's jaw dropped open, and he stood stupidly staring, the nun's clothing dangling from his hand.

Gerald lifted an eyebrow. 'Odd sort of a nun.'

The lady uttered a scornful sound. 'Certainly I am not a nun. But one must disguise oneself. To be *jeune demoiselle*, it is not always convenient.'

Gerald controlled a quivering lip. 'So it would appear.' He nodded in the direction of her pistol.

The lady grasped it more firmly and turned it upon Hilary. 'Move, you. Back, that you may be close together.'

'I should do as she says if I were you, Hilary,' observed Gerald, noting the fierce determination in the girl's lovely face.

'Never trust a gun in female hands,' grumbled Hilary, dropping the nun's habit and backing to join his friend. 'That's what comes of disarming yourself.'

'A mistake, I agree.' Gerald's eyes never left the girl. 'What are the chances, do you think, of that thing being already cocked?'

'Probably not even loaded,' suggested Hilary hopefully.

'*Parbleu*,' came indignantly from the lady. 'Am I a fool? Can I blow off a head with a pistol which is not loaded?'

'She has a point,' conceded Alderley, relaxing a little as amusement burgeoned again

'Ten to one she is a French spy,' burst from Roding.

The pistol was lowered slightly. 'I find you excessively rude, both of you,' said the lady crossly. 'You talk together of me as if I am not there. "She", you say. But I am here.'

'You are perfectly correct,' agreed Gerald at once. 'You are there. Why, is the question I would like answered.'

'I do not tell you why,' the lady uttered flatly. 'But a spy I am not.'

'Can you prove it?' demanded Hilary.

'Certainly I can prove it. That is easy. I am not French in the least.'

'Not French?' echoed Hilary. 'That's a loud one.'

'It is true,' insisted the lady. 'I am entirely English.'

'Entirely *English*,' said Gerald as one making a discovery. 'Of course. Why did I not realise it at once? It just shows how one should not judge by appearances. The little matter of an accent may be misleading, I grant you, but—'

He was interrupted, and with impatience. '*Alors*, you make a game with me, I see that. It is better that you go away now, I think.'

'Ah, but there's the little matter of your presence here,' said Gerald on a note of apology.

'This is a private house,' Hilary said severely, 'and you are trespassing.'

'Also stealing,' added Gerald, with a gesture at the clothes on the bed.

'I do not steal,' declared the lady hotly. '*Parbleu*, but what a person you make me! One who spies. One who steals. One who——who——tres...' She paused, struggling for the word.

'Trespasses,' supplied Gerald.

'And, if this was not enough,' went on the lady furiously, 'you dare to say I am French. Pah!'

She flounced about and, crossing to the bed, plonked down on it, pointedly averting her face and resting the large pistol in her lap.

Hilary made a movement as if he would seize the opportunity to disarm the girl, but Gerald stopped him.

'I think,' he said pleasantly, 'that it would be as well if you, Hilary, were to go and fetch the troops. And Pottiswick, of course. He will wish to have his fears laid to rest.'

The lady's face came round, a puzzled frown on her brow. 'Troops?'

'Go, man,' urged the major in an undervoice. 'I'll handle her better alone.'

'You certain? She's a thought too volatile for my money.'

'*She* once more,' came in disgust from the girl on the bed. Her heavy pistol came up again, although she did not rise. 'What do you say of these troops?'

'You see, we're militia. *Milice*,' Gerald translated. 'Civilian peace-keeping forces, you know. That's why we are here.'

A scowl crossed the lady's face. 'You will arrest me? For—for—'

'Trespass, theft and spying,' snapped Hilary.

'And housebreaking,' added Gerald calmly.

At that, the girl jumped up. '*Parbleu*, the house, is it broken in the least? I do not think so.'

'As a matter of fact, it isn't,' conceded Gerald. 'We were wondering about that.' With an air of real interest, he asked, 'I suppose you did not dig a tunnel or fly in by balloon?'

The lady gazed at him blankly. 'That is *imbecile*.'

'Well, she didn't walk through the walls, that's certain,' said Hilary acidly. 'How did you get in? The house is all locked up.'

The lady looked unexpectedly smug. 'Assuredly it is locked up. *Alors*, how did *you* get in?'

'Oh, we broke in,' Gerald told her cheerfully.

She stared. Then her eyes flashed. 'And it is me you dare accuse? It is yourself you should arrest.'

Gerald could not resist. He looked at Hilary and nodded. 'She's perfectly right.' He threw one arm across his own chest and clapped himself on the shoulder. 'Major Gerald Alderley, I arrest you in the name of the King.'

A peal of laughter came from the girl. 'It is *imbecile* that you are. You cannot arrest yourself.'

'Will you have done, Gerald?' demanded Hilary, exasperated. 'What in God's name do you think you're playing at?'

'Let me alone, man,' Gerald muttered under his breath. 'I told you I could handle her.'

'Well, don't blame me if you get your head blown off.'

'It is you who will get the head blown off,' threatened the young lady fiercely. 'It will suit me very well that you go away, because you are a person without sense and I do not wish to talk to you.'

'Eh?'

Gerald grinned at Hilary's blank expression, and was gratified when the girl turned a brilliant smile upon himself.

'But you,' she said in the friendliest way imaginable, 'are a person *tout à fait sympathique*, I think. I will permit you to rescue me.'

'It will give me the greatest of pleasure,' Gerald said at once, making an elegant leg. 'Only perhaps I can more readily do so if you will put down that pistol.'

The lady frowned suspiciously. 'I think it is better if I hold the pistol. Then, if you are bad to me, I can more easily blow off your head.'

'You see? Not to be trusted,' Hilary uttered disgustedly. 'And what is it you're to rescue her from, I should like to know.'

'From you,' the lady threw at him furiously. 'You are stubborn like a mule. Why do you not go away?'

'Yes, do go away,' begged Gerald. 'You are really not helping matters, my friend.'

Captain Roding looked frowningly from one to the other. The lady reseated herself, watching him expectantly. He shrugged and, to Gerald's relief, made to leave at last.

'You're as mad as she is, Gerald. I'll be waiting for you outside.'

'No, no, go and fetch the men to the house. And tell Pottiswick to mend that lock we broke.'

'We!' said Hilary witheringly, and went off as Gerald laughed and turned back to the lady.

She was frowning, but it was evident that her initial fright had left her. The ruffled chemise-front under the wide lapels of her waistcoat and jacket no longer quivered, and her pose, with the full cloth petticoat spreading about her, was relaxed. Only her ungloved fingers, and the arms in their long tight sleeves as she held the heavy gun aloft, bore any sign of stiffness.

She addressed him in a tone of puzzlement. 'Why does this person say you are mad?'

'Because I am risking having my head blown off,' Gerald answered cheerfully.

The girl nodded sagely. 'And me?'

'Oh, you're mad because you wish to blow off my head.'

A radiant smile dawned. 'Then I am not mad in the least. I do not wish to blow off a head, you understand.'

'I am relieved to hear it.'

The smile vanished. 'But to do only what one wishes, it is not always convenient.'

'Consider me warned,' said Gerald solemnly. He removed his cocked hat and came towards her. 'You don't mind if I sit down?'

She considered him a moment, her head a little on one side. 'You are, I think, a gentleman, no?'

Gerald bowed. 'I try to be.'

'Ah, that is good,' sighed the lady. 'You do not say, "I am a gentleman born." Frenchmen, they are different.' She released the pistol which lay in her lap and gestured expressively with her hands. 'They hold their nose up, so. And look down, so. Englishmen also certainly. But only inside, you understand, that one cannot see it.'

Her conversation was wonderful, Gerald decided. And she was as shrewd as they come. 'You seem to understand the gentry very well.'

'You see, I am of them,' she said seriously, 'but not with them—yet.' With pretty imperiousness, she gestured to the bed beside her. 'Please to sit, monsieur. I am not afraid that you may try to make love to me.'

'What?' uttered Gerald, startled.

The thought had not even occurred to him. He was not, in truth, much of a ladies' man. Which was not to say that ladies were not interested in him. But Gerald took it for the routine interest in an eligible bachelor, although he was aware many females had an eye for scarlet regimentals. He spoke the automatic thought that entered his mind.

'I should not dream of forcing my attentions on you.'

'No, you are a gentleman,' she agreed. 'And me, I am a lady. *Voilà tout.*'

Such simple faith touched Gerald. He refrained from pointing out that the case would be exactly the same if she was not a lady. He sat on the bed, throwing aside his hat.

'That is settled then. May I know your name?'

The lady eyed him. He waited. She frowned, appearing to think for a moment. Then she shrugged.

'*Eh bien.* It is Thérèse. Ah, no, I have it wrong.' With care, she gave it an English pronunciation. 'Tee-ree-sa.'

Gerald tutted. 'You must think me a fool, mademoiselle.'

The eyes flashed momentarily. Then the long lashes sank demurely over them. 'You do not like it?'

'That is hardly the point.'

She looked up again and smiled sweetly. 'You do not think it is enough English. I will endeavour.' She bit her lip and thought deeply. Something seemed to dredge up from the recesses of her memory and she brightened. 'How is this? Prooden-ss.'

Gerald gazed at her without expression. 'Very inventive.'

'But it is a very good English name,' she protested.

'Very. But it is not your name. Nor is Theresa, or even Thérèse.'

The lady opened her eyes very wide indeed. 'You do not believe me?'

'I do not.'

'Pah!'

'Precisely.'

She let out a peal of laughter. 'You are not at all stupid. Even if you pretend sometimes to be without sense.'

'Well, let us leave your name for the present. From what do you wish to be rescued?'

The girl fluttered her eyelashes, sighed dramatically and spread her hands. 'I escape from a fate entirely *misérable*, you understand.'

'Indeed?' Gerald said politely. 'What is this fate?'

'*Un mariage* of no distinction. My husband, he is cruel and wicked, and—and entirely undistinguished. It is very bad.'

'Your husband?' Gerald tutted. 'I agree with you. That is very bad indeed. I shall be delighted to rescue you. Where is this undistinguished husband?' Leaping to his feet he seized his sword hilt and partly withdrew it from its sheath, saying dramatically, 'I shall kill him immediately!'

Her eyes widened, but she did not move. 'Kill him? Oh.' The lady's gaze dwelled thoughtfully on the half-drawn sword and then came up to meet his, an odd look in her eyes. 'He is not in England, you understand. I have—run away.'

'That I do not doubt,' Gerald muttered drily, but added in a tone of intense satisfaction, 'Then this husband is still in France? Excellent.' The sword was released to slide back into its scabbard. 'In that case, he is probably already dead, and you have nothing to worry about.'

Her face fell. 'Oh, you are making a game with me. You do not believe me.'

'When you begin to tell the truth,' Gerald told her severely, 'I shall be happy to believe you.'

'*Parbleu*,' exclaimed the girl, jumping up in some dudgeon. 'You are not *sympathique* in the very least.' She raised the pistol.

'If you shoot me,' Gerald said quickly, throwing out a hand, 'I shan't be able to rescue you.'

'I do not need the rescue from such as you. And I think I will indeed blow off your *imbecile* head.'

'In that case, I ought to warn you that my friend, Captain Hilary Roding, who is even less *sympathique* than myself, you remember, will undoubtedly arrest you for murder.'

The lady stamped her foot. '*Alors*, now I am also a murderer. This is altogether insupportable. Take, if you please, your own pistol. Take it, I tell you. From your pocket there.'

'What for?' asked Gerald, half laughing, as he put his hand in his pocket and brought out his elegant pistol. 'Now what?'

The girl's voice was shaking, and there were, he saw now, angry tears in her eyes.

'At me,' she uttered, holding her own pistol high and aiming it steadily. 'Point it at me.'

'Like this?'

'*Parfait.*' She sniffed and swallowed. 'I am not a murderer. The chance it is the same for both. It is no more a murder, but a duel, you understand.'

She was backing across the room, moving towards the screen. *Cocking the gun*. He was damned if he knew what to do. Was the girl seriously expecting him to pull the trigger? Lord, but she had courage!

'Shoot, then,' urged the lady. 'And we shall see which of us is more quick.'

'There is no need for this,' he ventured mildly, and lifted his finger to show his own pistol was not cocked. 'I cannot possibly shoot a lady, you know. I am far too much the gentleman.'

She halted, her pistol still held firm and straight, both hands gripping it, her expressive features at once determined and uncertain.

'If, in truth, you are a gentleman,' she said in a trembling tone, 'you will move to the side that I may leave this room.'

'And where do you propose to go?' enquired Gerald carefully.

She lifted her shoulders in an eloquent shrug. 'Where is there that I can go?'

All at once Alderley felt acutely suspicious. What was the wench at? Yet he could not maintain this stand off forever. He was by no means certain that she would not in fact attempt to blow off his head as she had threatened.

'Very well,' he said, lowering his own weapon. After all, Hilary must be near returned by now. Where was the harm in letting her go? She could not get far.

He moved to one side, bowing and gesturing to the door. 'Mademoiselle.'

The lady hesitated a moment, her eyes seeming to measure the distance between where he stood and the door. He stepped back further. Slowly she released the hammer on the pistol, uncocking it, and Gerald became conscious that he had been holding his breath.

Giving him a wide berth, and keeping her pistol high, she made her way to the door and warily peered through it. A glance down the passage—to see that Roding was not lurking?—and her face came back to Gerald, triumph in her eyes.

'*Adieu, imbecile*,' she threw at him gleefully. Then she was out of the door and running, fast.

The sound of her flying feet brought Gerald leaping for the door. He was into the passage in time to see her slip into another chamber at the end. A door slammed. Racing, he reached it perhaps a moment or two later. He thought he heard a scraping sound as he turned the handle.

He flung open the door and cast a quick glance round. The place was gloomy, with its darkly panelled walls, but it was sparsely furnished. A dresser, a washstand, and a clothes press. No window.

A dressing-room then. But where in the world was the girl? A door led to another chamber beyond. Gerald tried it. Locked! He sped out to the corridor and went swiftly into the next room. Wasting no time, he crossed straight to the shutters and opened them.

Light flooded the place. It was bare of any furnishings. And empty. The young lady—if she had come in here at all—had vanished.

CHAPTER TWO

'Our French friends are beginning to form quite a little coterie,' remarked Gerald, covertly studying the group gathered in an alcove at the other side of Lady Bicknacre's ballroom.

The vast mirrored chamber, with its four little square window bays, two either side of the large raised dais that led to the French doors, was very full of company for the start of the Little Season. The clever hostess having let fall that several distinguished guests from France would be present, the world had flocked to her doors to catch, like the gossip-hungry vultures they were, a glimpse of them.

Few approached the *émigrés* directly, preferring to stare covertly from behind their fans, while pretending to admire the simple elegance of Lady Bicknacre's neo-classical refurbishments. To Gerald's eye, the refugees therefore presented a rather forlorn little group, almost huddling together and chattering in low tones in their own tongue.

The future Mrs Roding turned bright, laughing eyes on the major. 'Dare I guess at the reason for your sudden interest in *émigrés*, Gerald?'

'Lucilla,' barked Hilary warningly. 'Not here.'

'Don't be stuffy, Hilary,' admonished his betrothed.

She was a small blonde, not handsome, but with a flair for fashion demonstrated by her elegant chemise gown in the very latest Canterbury muslin, with its low décolletage barely concealed under a fine lawn handkerchief set about her shoulders, and decorated with a mauve satin sash at the waist. She had a warm, fun-loving personality, and an unflattering disrespect for her future husband's authority. Gerald liked her enormously.

'If you did not want me to talk of it,' she told him with characteristic insouciance, 'you should not have mentioned the matter to me.'

'Are we to infer that he had a choice?' enquired Gerald.

'Of course not,' snapped his friend. 'She wormed it out of me, the little fiend.'

Gerald tutted. 'The cat's foot, Hilary. You're going to live under the cat's foot.'

'Fiddle,' scoffed Miss Froxfield. 'I am perfectly devoted to him, as well he knows.'

She bestowed a dazzling smile on Roding, who had reddened to the gills at these words. Which were perfectly true, as Gerald was aware. Lucilla clearly adored her betrothed, anyone could see that. If there was such a thing as love at first sight, these two must epitomise it. And his scarlet coat had nothing to do with it, as Hilary was fond of recounting, for he had been in civilian clothes when they met, as he was tonight. Neither he nor Gerald chose to attire themselves in full military rig on fashionable occasions such as this. Alderley's company of militia being his own, he was able to choose duty periods convenient to himself and his captain, and was under no obligation to wear dress uniform.

With a rustle of her full lilac petticoats, Miss Froxfield turned back to Alderley. 'Would you like me to enquire for your mystery lady, Gerald? I know the Comte and Comtesse de St Erme quite well.'

'How can you possibly enquire for her?' demanded Hilary acidly. 'We don't know who she is.' He threw a fulminating glance at Gerald. 'Though we might have done, if a certain addlepated clothhead hadn't let her get away.'

'Addlepated imbecile, Hilary,' corrected Gerald calmly.

'Did she call you that?' asked Lucilla, amused. 'How famous. I shall borrow it and apply it to you, Hilary.'

'Don't you dare. In any event, I would not have let her escape me so easily.'

'Yes, she duped me finely,' agreed Gerald.

'And then vanished into thin air,' rejoined Hilary on a sardonic note.

'No, no, I am convinced your very first theory was right. She walked through the walls.'

Lucilla Froxfield laughed gaily. 'Fiddle, Gerald. Hilary could not have suggested such a thing.'

'He did, you know,' grinned Gerald. 'Though he didn't mean it. I do, however.'

'Are you mad?'

'Gerald is convinced there is a secret passage into the house,' explained Roding. 'And since the entire company and Pottiswick himself were unable to find hide nor hair of the infernal French female —'

'English, Hilary,' Gerald reminded him.

'Gammon. She is no more English than that set of beggars over there.'

'For shame, Hilary,' admonished his fiancée, casting a pitying glance at the refugees. 'They cannot help it. But, Gerald, do you believe there is a secret passage indeed?'

'Well, we covered every inch of the house and grounds, and I swear she never left that room by way of the door. I would have heard her.'

'How exciting.' A sudden thought brought a frown to her brow. 'But if there is one, how in the world did this mystery lady of yours know of it?'

'That, Lucy, is precisely the point that has been exercising my mind,' Gerald said, turning his eyes once more to the group of French exiles in the alcove.

'Can't have been a common housebreaker, you see,' Hilary explained to Lucilla, quite unnecessarily.

'Of course I see that,' she said impatiently. 'Could she have been a spy, after all?'

'Oh, she's not a spy,' Gerald answered, almost absently.

'How do you know?'

'Exactly,' pounced Roding bitterly. 'Ask him. All he will say is that she said so—as if anyone could believe a word the girl said.'

Gerald grinned. 'Difficult, I grant you. But though she lied about pretty much everything else, she didn't lie about that.'

'How do you know?' Lucilla repeated, almost as sceptical as her intended spouse.

'If you had met her, you'd understand.' With an unexpected flush of pleasure, he recalled the girl's antics. 'When she lies outright, she thinks about it. It's the feinting tricks you have to watch for. Wily little devil she is.'

Miss Froxfield regarded him in some interest. 'You speak as if you expected to meet her again, Gerald.'

Hilary exploded. 'Expect? He's had a twenty-four hour watch on Remenham House these two days. The men have never had so much work to do since they banded. You'd think he wanted to meet the wretch again.'

'To be sure I do,' said Gerald swiftly. 'I haven't been so much entertained since I left the Army.'

'Entertained, he says!'

'Intrigued, then,' amended Gerald equably, although truth to tell he was enjoying the mystery enormously. He grasped Lucilla's elbow. 'What you can do, Lucy, rather than make enquiries, is introduce me to this comte and comtesse.'

'By all means,' agreed Lucy at once, and ignoring the automatic protest that issued from Roding's lips, she threw a command over her shoulder as she turned to go. 'Come on, Hilary. You don't want to miss the sport.'

'Sport!' grumbled her betrothed, but he accompanied them across the ballroom all the same.

Madame la Comtesse de St Erme regarded the English major with a lacklustre eye, Gerald thought. Did she suppose him a possible pretender to her daughter's hand? The girl—Dorothée, if memory served—was clearly marriageable, but he imagined most of these unhappy exiles were all but penniless. Gerald doubted there would be many eager suitors, even assuming the comtesse was keen to marry off her daughter to a foreign protestant.

According to Lucilla, this comtesse had constituted herself something of a social leader in the rapidly growing assemblage of refugees, and would undoubtedly be ready to introduce an eligible bachelor appropriately.

Mesdames Thierry and Poussaint appeared delighted to meet Gerald, and he was obliged to do the pretty to their daughters too. If the young ladies were dowerless, which seemed likely, their attire at least—so Lucilla assured him in a whisper—was of the first stare. Silken open robes over full tiffany petticoats in a contrasting colour were, Lucy assured him, of the very latest Parisian design, cut by the finest French tailors.

Gerald, whose French was adequate from his military service abroad, was able to respond suitably to such remarks as the ladies addressed to him, but was less exercised by their fashionable dress than their decidedly careworn appearance. Both girls looked pale and listless. There was little fighting spirit here. He could not see these two shrinking misses capering about in a nun's habit and brandishing a defiant pistol.

There was a third lady among the younger set. A buxom piece, who looked, Gerald decided, as if she would be more at home in an amorous engagement in a hayloft than sitting demurely in a ballroom. She occupied a small sofa, a little apart, a ruddy-complexioned gentleman some years her senior beside her, and glanced about with an air of considerable unease.

Briefly, with a careless wave towards the couple, the comtesse presented them as Monsieur and Madame Valade.

'Who have lately joined us,' she said, adding *sotto voce*, 'A very great tragedy. The entire family massacred. Wiped out, but for these. A lucky escape.'

'Lucky indeed,' answered Gerald, glancing at the pair again.

Such stories were increasingly heard in English society. There were some deepseated fears of the rot spreading to England, if the simmering discontent of the peasantry of France were to erupt any further. The gulf between rich and poor was perhaps greater in France, but by all accounts it was not the *canaille* who were responsible for the present turmoil. It was the incendiary intellectuals of the bourgeoisie, with their militant ideas of revolution, who had raised the populace to a pitch of violence resulting in cases of wholesale slaughter—such as had overtaken the Valades. Families had seen their lands seized, their chateaux ransacked or burned, and those unlucky enough to have failed to anticipate disaster, had been murdered or dragged away to gaol. In Paris, in July, a raging mob had stormed the Bastille, provoking circumspect aristocrats to uproot themselves and take refuge abroad. Also from the capital came news of grave fears for the safety of the royal family, who had moved there from Versailles.

These things were common knowledge among the *bon ton*, who were generously welcoming these unfortunate escapees. They had not so far been of much personal interest to Gerald, but tonight was different.

He eyed the young couple with the tragic history behind them, and could only suppose that familiarity had dulled their senses. The man had favoured him with a brief nod, but the girl had gone so far as to offer a tiny smile, and a look under her lashes with which not even Gerald, for all his scant interest in female society, could fail to be familiar. It was a look that accorded very well with the hayloft setting that had come to mind.

Now, however, as Gerald watched them, their heads were together and they were murmuring in French. The female's words caught at his attention, and he no longer heard what the young Poussaint girl was saying to him.

'I was not born to this. I am not comfortable,' complained Madame Valade.

'Courage,' urged her spouse.

'It is not easy.'

'It will be worth the pain, you will see. Hist!' he added, as he turned his head and noticed Alderley's glance.

Gerald smiled and excused himself with the Poussaint girl, whose mouth pinched together as she threw a dagger glance at the voluptuous Madame Valade. Gerald, intent on his trail, ignored it.

'I understand you have not been in England very long,' he said in English, noting that Madame raised her fan and lowered her gaze demurely.

'But a week and some days,' answered Valade.

'It must seem strange to you at first.'

'*Oui, mais*—safe. It is safe.'

'I imagine it must be a relief to you, after so lucky an escape.' Gerald infused sympathy into his voice, and deliberately addressed himself to Madame. 'I am sorry to hear of your misfortunes.'

Madame ventured a glance up at his face, and fluttered her lashes. Her English was halting. 'But we—*mon mari* and myself—we have the *bonne chance*. The rest...' She shrugged fatalistically.

Monsieur Valade heaved a gusty sigh, and Gerald, with heavy diplomacy and a forced heartiness of manner, turned the subject. 'How do you like England?'

'People have been very kind,' Valade said, answering for them both.

'More, I think,' put in Madame, soulfully regarding the major, 'because I have English, a little.'

'You speak it very well,' Gerald said encouragingly.

'*Ah, non,*' exclaimed the husband. 'My wife would say she is English a little.'

'Oh, she *is* English?' repeated Alderley, interest perking up. He was aware of Hilary, in company with Lucilla and the comtesse's daughter some few yards away, listening in suddenly. 'How fascinating. Were you born here, madame?'

'*Mais non.*' The lady shook her head, contriving at the same moment to utter a breathy little laugh. '*C'est à dire*, I would say from my father only comes the English.'

'Oh,' Gerald uttered, disappointed. 'Not entirely English then.'

He heard Roding snort, and suppressed a grin as he bowed, taking the trouble to salute Madame's hand and cast her a provocative look as he did so. He would pursue that little pastime on some other occasion. It might prove rewarding. For the present, he murmured his farewells, and turning, caught Hilary's eye and walked away, crossing the ballroom to move into the less opulent, and less crowded, saloon next door where servants were dispensing refreshments.

In a moment, Roding and Lucilla joined him.

'Well?' demanded Miss Froxfield, accepting a glass of lemonade proffered by a passing lackey.

'Well, nothing,' uttered her betrothed crossly, before Gerald could answer. 'Playing games to tease me, that's all he can think of doing.'

'Nothing of the sort,' Gerald said calmly, sipping at his burgundy.

'It looked to me as if he was playing games with Madame Valade,' Lucilla said frankly. Her eyes quizzed the major. 'Flirting, Gerald? A new come-out for you.'

Gerald grinned. 'Merely making a useful contact. Interrogation takes many forms, you know, Lucy.'

'Some of them more pleasurable than others, I take it.'

'Gammon,' interrupted Hilary scornfully. 'Hates doing the pretty. I can vouch for that.'

'But in pursuit of information, Hilary, I am prepared to sacrifice my preferences,' Gerald told him.

'Don't tell me. I know you. That "entirely English" comment was said just to provoke me.'

'I was merely drawing your attention to the odd prevalence of French émigrés claiming English antecedents.'

'So you think she is an *émigré*?' Lucilla put in before the incensed Roding could respond. 'Your mystery lady, I mean.'

'I don't, as a matter of fact,' Gerald said decidedly, a frown creasing his brow. 'She didn't behave in the least like an *émigré*, if these people are anything to go by.'

'She behaved like a madwoman,' Hilary declared roundly. 'It's my belief she is a nun.'

'Now why didn't I make that connection?' Gerald asked of the air in a tone of regret. 'Quite mad, nuns are. They are often to be found dashing about secret passages in strange houses, armed to the teeth. After all, where prayer fails, a pistol is bound to succeed.'

'You know, Gerald,' Lucilla put in thoughtfully, forestalling a withering rejoinder from the captain, 'there may be something in that. After all, it is not long since that a Catholic nun in this country would have had to remain in hiding. And their monasteries and convents are still not officially permitted to exist here. Though they do, in secret, I believe.'

Gerald was staring at her, an arrested expression on his face. 'Now I see why you're marrying this woman, Hilary. You can give up thinking and leave all the brain work to her.'

'She's as clothheaded as you,' Roding retorted, but he slipped an arm about the lady's waist and gave her a quick squeeze.

'But only think, Hilary,' Lucy protested, evidently too involved in her theory to waste time in scolding. 'It is all too probable that she would wish to change into lay clothing to escape recognition.'

'Yes, a pretty theory, Lucy,' Gerald said evenly, 'but for one thing. She told us that it was a disguise.'

'She told you!'

'And,' pursued Gerald, ignoring his friend's scornful interjection, 'that it was not always convenient to be dressed as a young girl.'

'And you believe her?' asked Lucilla, raising her brows.

'I believe that. Though there is something to be said for your idea of a secret convent, at least as a hiding place.' He frowned again. 'Which presupposes that she needs to hide at all. And if she is not a nun, nor a refugee, and yet is entirely English, I'm hanged if I know what she is.'

'Why should you care?' demanded Roding, exasperated. 'Obsessed, that's what you are.'

Gerald grinned. 'Yes, but I'm probably chasing moonbeams. The likelihood is that I shan't see the wench again.'

It must have been fate, Gerald decided, near an hour later, staring intently at the closed French windows on the raised alcove that led out to the terrace. Or else he was indeed obsessed. But there was a face pressed to the glass. The features were indistinct, but was that not a halo of white about it? And the dark shadow below, was that a cloak, or the habit of a nun?

Skirting the dancing, from which he had taken a breather—not from lack of energy, but to escape the inanities of the young ladies he had partnered—Gerald made his way to a side door in the saloon and opened it.

Cautiously stepping outside, he looked up towards the terrace. Yes, there was someone there. Keeping to the shadow of the house, he crept forward until he could see better without, he hoped, being seen. But the figure was evidently too intent on peering within the ballroom to pay any attention to what might be occurring outside.

It moved a trifle, stepping back and lifting an arm to rub the sleeve against the glass. Lord, but it was a nun! Just as he had suspected. He smothered a laugh. What in the world was the wench up to now? For it must be she. How many nuns were there in England who might have occasion to spy on Lady Bicknacre's ballroom? The presence of the French refugees took on greater significance.

Gerald began to ease forward, deciding just how he would accost her. Then he paused. She was shifting, moving back. Turning now, and running down the terrace.

The noise of a bolt came to Alderley's ears. Someone was coming out of the house. Either she had been seen, or they were seeking the air. Probably the latter, for the thronging ballroom was insufferably hot.

The thought passed through his mind even as he started to cross the terrace at a jogtrot, moving to head her off. He leapt down into the haha surrounding the terrace, and saw that the nun was there also and backing towards him, anxiously checking now and then above the level of the terrace. Voices floated down, but there was no sound of pursuit.

Crouching down, Gerald waited, hands at the ready. There was no way to warn her of his presence without startling her. Whatever he did, she was bound to scream. He would have to make sure of her silence.

As she came close, he took a pace forward and seized her from behind, one strong arm clamping her tight against his chest, the free hand seizing her about the mouth, stifling the cry that gurgled in her throat.

But he reckoned without his host. His only warning was a gleam of silver in the faint spill of light from the house above. Then the dagger's point came in a whirling arc towards his face.

By a miracle, he averted its path, his hold on the girl's mouth shifting fast to grasp her wrist. He forced her arm back, away, stretching it out to keep the weapon at bay.

'Desist, you little devil,' he growled in her ear. 'Let it fall!'

'Brute!' she spat, struggling, and he knew at once he had guessed aright. '*Moi, je vais vous tuer*!'

'I don't think so,' Gerald said through his teeth. 'You're not going to kill me this time. Let—it—fall.'

The command was accompanied by an increase of pressure on the wrist he held. She gasped with pain, but she did not release her grip.

'*Laisse-moi*,' she panted, shifting wildly in his hold, so that he had all to do to keep her thus imprisoned.

'Damn you, what's the matter with you?' he snapped in frustration. 'I don't want to hurt you any more. Listen, it is I. The *imbecile*. Remember?'

'*Parbleu*,' came from his still struggling victim. 'You will release me at once, *imbecile*.'

'Not until you release that dagger. Now drop it.'

A strangled sob escaped her as his thumb dug cruelly into the soft flesh of her wrist. Her fingers opened and the weapon fell from her nerveless grasp.

'That's better,' said Gerald, and let her go.

In an instant, she turned on him. The struggle had dislodged the white wimple, which was evidently too large for her, and her black hair broke free, whirling like a whiplash about her head as her hands curled into fists, coming up to beat at his chest, her little teeth bared for attack.

'*Espèce de bête*,' she snarled. '*Idiot*!'

'Enough, now! Softly, you little termagant,' he ordered, seizing her wrists to hold her off. But his own ferocity was less now that she was disarmed.

'Softly, you say?' she uttered, raging. 'Is it soft, the way you seize me from behind? *Parbleu*, my heart it is flown from my chest! Boom, boom, it goes, even now. *Imbecile.*'

'Yes, I'm sorry about that,' Gerald uttered in a rueful tone. 'It could not be helped, whichever way I made my presence known. And I guessed you would attack if I startled you.'

'You should be happy that you are not dead,' she retorted, but with a diminution of the venom and fright in her voice.

He felt her relaxation and let go of her wrists. She grasped at the right one, massaging where his grip had been and Gerald hoped he had not bruised her.

'How could I know that it is you?' She peered at him in the darkness. 'It is in truth you?'

'Of course it is I.'

'Where then is your uniform?'

'I don't wear it to balls.'

'*Eh bien*, it is your fault entirely in this case. Easily I could have killed you. Just as I might have killed another, if he had come out.'

'Ah, so you did come here to find someone,' Gerald responded eagerly. 'One of your countrymen, perhaps?'

The girl clammed up, the moon of her white face staring up at him in the darkness. Then she spoke, with a carelessness he instantly suspected.

'I do not understand you.'

'I think you understand me very well.'

He could just see the glare.

'What do you want with me? Why did you catch me?'

'You intrigue me,' he told her frankly. His gaze dropped to the black garment that covered her. 'For instance, why have you reverted to your nun's habit for this particular adventure?'

'That is easy. For a nun at night it is less dangerous than for the *jeune demoiselle*.'

Gerald eyed her. His vision was becoming accustomed to the faint light now and her features were clearer. She was trying to adjust the wimple, dragging at it and fighting with her loosened hair. The white veil had fallen to the ground and Gerald retrieved it for her.

'And how is it that you have acquired this garb of a *religieuse*?' he asked as she fitted the veil over her head.

'From the convent, where else?'

'It does not strike me that you can possibly have been in a convent.'

'*Ah, non?*' Her voice was neutral. 'And why not?'

'Because,' Gerald said matter of factly, 'convent-bred *jeune demoiselles* do not commonly know how to handle either pistols or daggers. You did not learn that in a convent.'

A giggle answered him. 'Not from the nuns, no. But there are ways to learn more than a nun would teach.'

Fresh suspicion kindled in his breast. 'Oh, are there? You are not quite alone in these adventures of yours, I take it.' He thought a wary look came into her face, but it was difficult to be sure. 'Come, I am concerned merely for your safety, you know. I am not prying for my own amusement.'

'Then leave me to guard myself, and do not ask me questions any more,' she snapped, and crouched down suddenly, searching about for her dagger.

'No, you don't.'

Gerald dropped down to join her just as her hand came up, clutching the handle. He grabbed her wrist and prised the weapon from her fingers, ignoring her other hand that clawed at his to try to retain the trophy. As he pocketed it, her open palm reached out and slapped his cheek.

'*Bête!*'

Gerald caught her hand as she pulled it back to deliver another blow. Next instant he had her immobilised, her hands behind her back, her chest crushed to his, the white veil slipping once again.

'Do that again,' he said softly, 'and I'll make you sorry you ever came to England.'

'And me,' came the guttural response, 'I will certainly murder you the very next time I am compelled to see your face.'

Sheer exasperation made Gerald release her as he broke into reluctant laughter. 'There's no controlling you, is there?' He held up his hands. 'Come, cry a truce.'

There was a pause. Then the lady smiled and her radiance, even in the darkness, warmed Gerald unexpectedly.

'I said you were *sympathique*,' she told him.

'As a matter of fact, I'm not at all *sympathique*. I'm a soldier, you see.' He bowed. 'Major Gerald Alderley, mademoiselle, quite at your service.'

'Gérard,' she said, giving the French version with a soft "g" and not quite managing the "l". 'That is a very English name.'

'I am a very English man,' Gerald said.

'And you mean this? Truly?'

'Entirely.'

'*Idiot*. I do not ask if you are entirely English, but if you say truly when you say you are at my service.'

'Oh, that,' Gerald said cautiously. 'Well, that depends.' He sat on the low wall of the haha and invited her to do the same. 'You see, it's difficult to do a service for someone when you don't know who they are, or what they're up to. Tell me. Who were you looking for tonight? One of the *émigrés*? There were several in there.'

'Assuredly there are many escaping from France at this time.'

Was there a careful note in her voice? Gerald gave no sign, keeping his own tone light.

'Like you?'

'But I am not French. I have told you. I am—'

'Like me, entirely English. Yes, I think we have thoroughly thrashed that one out.'

'Who were they?' she asked abruptly.

'Who, the *émigrés*?'

'Do I speak of the English, *imbecile*? Certainly the *émigrés*.'

Gerald tutted. 'Don't lose your temper again. Let me see now.' He scratched his chin as if he thought about it, but covertly kept a careful study of what he could see of her face. 'There were the Comte and Comtesse de St Erme. A Madame Valade and her husband. And two other ladies. I forget. Ah, Thierry and Poussaint, if my memory serves me.'

She had given nothing away. Now what? There was an interest, or why ask him who they were. He added, 'Also others, but I don't recall them.'

'*Eh bien*.' She shrugged. 'Me also I do not recall them.'

'Indeed?' said Gerald, surprised. 'None of them means anything to you at all? How odd. I was ready to wager that your name would have marched with one of them.'

'*Comment*?' she demanded with some heat. 'You think I am like that Valade? No, a thousand times.'

At last. But Gerald kept to a casual note. 'Did I say so? When last heard from you were claiming some good English name. Brown or Jones, I dare say.'

A laugh escaped her. 'Certainly those are names of the most undistinguished, and I would scorn to have them.'

'What name would you like, then?'

Her shadowed features turned in his direction. 'I am not a fool. You wish another name? *Eh bien*. Lee-o-no-ra.'

'I thank you,' Gerald said drily. 'And I suppose I shall be obliged to endure another nonsensical tale about your husband.'

'What husband?'

'Precisely.'

The lady sighed and spread her hands. Here we go, thought Gerald.

'You see, it is that my papa, he is without sympathy,' said the lady sadly.

'Indeed?' Gerald said politely.

'Yes, like you,' she snapped, with a venomous glance, her role evidently forgotten for the moment.

'Do please continue,' Gerald begged, deceptively docile. 'I am fascinated.'

She bit her lip, and then turning her face away, emitted another sigh. 'My papa he does not wish me to marry the man I choose, and thus he places me in the convent that the nuns may lock me up and I cannot escape.'

'As we see.'

'Yes, but they did do so.'

'But you managed to escape nevertheless,' Gerald said calmly, 'disguising yourself as a nun. And who is the man you are not allowed to marry? Valade, perhaps?'

'*Dieu du ciel*,' exclaimed the girl, jumping up. 'That—that—why do you speak of him?'

'Because I feel you ought to know,' Gerald said calmly, but rising and watching her closely, 'that all your trouble may be in vain. He is already married.'

'Married?'

'I did mention *Madame* Valade, did I not?'

At that, a growl of startling ferocity escaped her lips. 'She? *Sa femme*? That is the game then? That she could dare to take my place, that *salope*. This is altogether insupportable. *Eh bien*, we shall see.' She focused on Gerald's face. 'And for you, *monsieur le major*, it will be well if you do not make me a shock like this again.'

Turning, she climbed over the low haha wall. Gerald reached out a hand to stop her.

'Wait! At least tell me where I can find you.'

'So that you may interest yourself in my affairs even more?'

'Then I will go with you,' he offered.

'No! Let me alone!'

'It is not safe!'

'That is entirely my affair, and not your affair in the least,' she told him haughtily. '*En tout cas*, I have waiting for me a cavalier.'

'Oh, have you?' grunted Gerald, surprising in himself a surge of some odd emotion at these words. 'Damnation!'

Confused, he released her, and in an instant she had darted away and was running down the garden.

Gerald watched her vanish into the darkness, unusually incensed. Hang the wench! Roding was right. He was mad. Lord knew why he had any interest in an impertinent girl who would certainly have spit him with that dagger! He reached into his pocket and brought it out, examining it in the increasing light as he slowly made his way back up the terrace. A pretty piece. Gold-handled, too. Small, but eminently serviceable. For whom had its sharp point been intended?

Valade? Or perhaps his wife now that the girl had word of their marriage. What a heat that news had wrought. Had she expected to wed Valade herself? Had the fellow broken a vow of betrothal, or abandoned her? He must find out more.

Forgetting the dark thoughts of his last brush with the girl, he dropped the dagger back in his pocket, quickened his pace, and went back into the house to look for his hostess.

He was halfway across the ballroom, where the dancing had ceased for the musicians to take a well-earned rest, when Roding pounced on him.

'Where the devil have you been?'

'Consorting with a nun in the gardens.'

Hilary stared. 'You don't mean to say she's here?'

'Was,' Gerald corrected. 'She's gone. This time she tried to kill me with a dagger.'

'What?'

'Neat little toy. I'll show it to you later.' He glanced about and saw his quarry holding court at one end of the vast mirrored chamber. 'At this present, I must appropriate Lady Bicknacre.'

'You're going?' asked his friend, and the note of relief was marked.

'No, my poor guardian,' Gerald mocked. 'I'm following a scent.'

Lady Bicknacre, resplendent in purple satin, and basking in her triumphantly full rooms—for it was obvious that her patronage of the refugees had set a quickly to be followed fashion—was all sorrow and sympathy when Gerald spoke of them. He had adroitly captured her and led her away from her other guests on the pretext of feigning an interest in her charitable attitude to the newly arrived French.

Her motherly features creased into anxious wrinkles. 'Poor things. Can you imagine how dreadful it must be for them? Most of them arrive here almost penniless.'

'Gather their bankers are still able to transfer funds,' remarked Hilary, who had tagged along, apparently determined not to leave Gerald to make even more of a fool of himself. He had already spoken his mind on the folly of allowing a clearly dangerous female to escape a second time.

'But for how long?' Lady Bicknacre asked apprehensively. 'Their lawyers are working tirelessly, but they report that the situation is daily worsening.'

'Some, of course,' put in Gerald, 'have been unable to recover anything. Like the Valades, I imagine.'

'Oh, that tragic pair,' uttered her ladyship in saddened tones.

'Yes, a very sad story,' agreed the major.

'Still, the comtesse has them well in hand. She has even found them accommodation in the house where she is putting up herself. In Paddington. They are tending to congregate, our poor French friends.' She shook her head. 'Pitiful.'

'Very much so,' Gerald said, matching her tone, and at once forced the discussion back to his own point of interest by adding, 'I was particularly struck by those poor Valades. Do you know much of his background?'

'Only that he is, or was, related to the Vicomte de Valade. It seems he does not inherit the title.'

'Well for him,' remarked Captain Roding.

'He could have little comfort there, indeed. But it is not entirely without hope, for perhaps they may find some succour with Charvill. Personally, however, I doubt if—'

'Charvill?' interrupted Gerald without ceremony, all his senses at once on the alert. 'You cannot mean General Charvill?'

'That old martinet?' exclaimed Roding. 'He was our first commander, and a more stiff-necked—'

'Exactly so,' concurred Lady Bicknacre. 'Which is why I feel sure he will utterly repulse the girl, even if she is his granddaughter.'

'What, Madame Valade?' demanded Gerald. 'His *grand*daughter?'

'Yes, his son's daughter.'

'What son?' asked Roding.

'Precisely,' agreed Gerald. 'I thought it was his great-nephew, young Brewis Charvill, who is his heir.'

'Oh yes, yes. But this was long ago. Nicholas is dead. At least I imagine so, if what Madame Valade claims is true. Not that it would make any difference if he was alive still.'

'Why not?' Gerald asked straightly.

'Because,' said Lady Bicknacre in the confidential manner of all matrons when passing on a tidbit of scandal, 'Nicholas married against his father's wishes and ran away. General Lord Charvill disinherited him for his pains. I cannot think he will welcome a French *émigré* for his granddaughter.'

CHAPTER THREE

Captain Hilary Roding listened with only half an ear to the long-winded report being given by Sergeant Trodger, his idle gaze wandering over the congested traffic of Piccadilly and the many pedestrians weaving a hazardous path through it.

Just as he had told Gerald would be the case, there was nothing of interest to hear, especially as he had met the girl in London only last night. But that did not stop Trodger, who had ridden up from Kent for the purpose, from detailing every little inspection and sortie that his men had made in their allotted task of watching Remenham House.

He might have supposed the fellow would be eager to be rid of the tale, for that he might have longer to enjoy the amenities of the Triumphal Chariot where the meeting had been appointed. The inn was a military haunt. All along the wooden benches before it sat a profusion of soldiery, a collection of barbers in attendance, busily employed in replaiting and powdering their hair ready for a military review scheduled for this afternoon.

Trodger might not need his hair dressed, but the flagon of ale that each soldier quaffed would be welcome—once his captain had departed, thought Roding cynically. The day was warm even under an overcast sky and Hilary, uncomfortable, shifted his weight. He was about to cut the sergeant short, when his eye fell on a gentleman walking along Piccadilly, his manner uncertain, his eyes shifting as if he sought something out.

That was the Frenchie, Valade, surely. What was the fellow doing in this part of the town? Had not Lady Bicknacre said he was living at Paddington?

The Frenchman, booted and neat in buckskin breeches and a plain frockcoat, a flat-brimmed hat on his head, paused a moment at an intersection with one of the roads leading north, apparently seeking a street sign.

Doesn't know where he is, thought the captain. Looking for something, or someone, probably. Visiting? Dressed for it, certainly. An unwelcome idea came to him. Would Gerald wish his friend to follow the man?

He had hardly registered the decision that he had best do so, albeit with some reluctance, when his trained senses alerted him to an extraordinary circumstance. The Frenchman was already being followed.

A young lad—Roding took him for a footman, or a groom by the neat black garb—was halted some paces away from Valade, his hat in his hand as he made pretence of fanning himself. But his eyes were on the Frenchman, and as Valade moved up the other road a little way, the lad shifted alertly, and swiftly closed the distance to the intersection. There he paused again, half turning his back and pretending to look for someone among the soldiers on the benches.

'Sir?'

Hilary threw a brief glance at Trodger, and quickly returned his intent gaze to the Frenchman, who had halted once more, and stood as if thinking deeply.

'I've finished me report, sir,' Trodger said aggrievedly.

'Good, good—and not before time,' muttered Roding, glancing round again.

'Well, shan't I come to the major's house up Stratton Street, sir?'

'I'll give the major your report, Trodger.'

'But me orders, sir? Are we to—'

'Gad, but that's her,' interrupted Roding suddenly.

The Frenchman had moved back into Piccadilly from Down Street, at which the lad following him had immediately sauntered away a yard or two. But some little distance behind him, someone had come out from the shadow of the building and, seeing the Frenchman reappear, darted back again as quickly. His attention drawn, the captain was easily able to make out the pretty features under the feathered hat, and the same dark riding habit the fugitive had worn on that first occasion at Remenham House.

Don't say the wretch was also following Valade. Perhaps Gerald was not as clothheaded as he had thought.

'Beg pardon, sir?' asked the sergeant, evidently mystified.

'Be quiet, man,' snapped Hilary, watching the Frenchman go by with the lad after him. Then the girl was heading past the inn and Roding marched down to confront her.

'Whither away, mademoiselle?' he said grimly, ungently grasping her arm above the elbow.

A pair of startled blue eyes looked up into his. '*Comment?* What do you wish?'

'What the devil do you think you're up to now, I'd like to know?'

Her eyes flashed. 'It is in no way your affair, monsieur, and you will unhand me at once.'

'No, I won't.' The captain grasped her more firmly. 'I'm taking you to Gerald, my girl.'

The girl glanced up the road and turned back, annoyance in her face. 'Oh, *peste*, you make me late!' She glared up at Roding. 'I do not know your Gérard. And I do not know you. Please to release me.'

'I'm not going to release you, so it's no use complaining. You'll be telling me Gerald did not catch you snooping at the Bicknacres, I suppose. And as for not knowing me, you abominable little liar, you're perfectly aware that we met at Remenham House.'

'Remenham House,' exclaimed Trodger, who had been watching this interchange open-mouthed. 'Is she the Frenchie we've been watching for then, sir?'

The lady's furious features turned on this new target. 'I am not French in the least, *bête*.'

'Woof!' uttered the sergeant, jumping back. 'A spitfire, ain't she, sir?'

Roding ignored this. 'Are you going to come quietly, mademoiselle?' he demanded with grim determination. 'Or do I arrest you and have these soldiers march you off to gaol?'

A sweep of his arm indicated the array of military strength on the benches, every eye of which was trained on the little scene being enacted before them.

The lady looked them over in silence, and then pouting lips trembled, dark eyelashes fluttered, and in a broken voice, she pleaded, 'Honoured *messieurs*, you will not allow this—this pig, to be thus cruel? He cannot arrest me. I have done n-nothing.'

The pathetic sob which accompanied the last word had a signal effect on two of the company at least. Glancing at each other, they rose from their seats and ventured to address the captain.

'Um—begging your pardon, sir, but—um— what was you meaning to arrest the young lady for?'

'Trespassing, theft, and suspicion of spying,' announced Roding fluently.

'Woof!' uttered Trodger, gazing at the lady in some awe.

'Caught in the act by myself and Major Gerald Alderley only last week.'

The mention of Alderley's name, as Roding had confidently expected, caused the soldiers' eyes to veer across to the young lady again, this time with a good deal less sympathy, and much more uncertainty. There was a murmur or two among the watchers on the bench, but no one ventured to intervene again.

Grimly Hilary smiled to himself at the effect of Gerald's name. In military circles, highly exaggerated tales of Major Alderley's derring-do were bruited from lip to lip and passed on to raw recruits to strengthen morale.

The young lady saw the change, and almost snorted. 'Very well, arrest me. But if you mean to take me to this Gérard, I shall know what to say to him.'

'Sir!' called Trodger, as the captain began to lead the young lady off. 'Shall we abandon the guard, then, sir?'

'Certainly not.'

'But if she's going to gaol—'

'Just keep watch, like you've been told,' Roding said severely, turning to glare at his sergeant. 'The major will tell you when to stop.'

'Your major will tell you nothing at all,' put in the young lady acidly, 'because certainly I am going to kill him.'

'You ain't never!'

'Back to your post, Trodger,' ordered the harassed captain. 'As for you—'

'Do not address me. You are without sense and not *sympathique* in the least. And when I have finished killing your major, I shall also kill you.'

The listening soldiers began to snigger behind their hands. His face warm, Captain Roding glared them into silence, and firmly marched his captive off down Piccadilly, heading for Stratton Street where the town house of the Alderley family was situated.

'You're the most troublesome wretch I've ever encountered,' he told her bitterly. 'What Gerald wants with you has me beat.'

He received a glare from his captive. 'You are rude, and *stupide*, and altogether a person with whom I do not wish to speak. So now I will say nothing more to you, and you will please to say nothing more to me, for I do not reply.'

It was thus in stony silence that the pair traversed the short distance to Stratton Street, where Roding knocked on the major's door and entered a pleasant wood-panelled hall, with his prisoner firmly in tow.

'Your master in?' he demanded of the astonished footman, removing his cockaded hat and handing it over.

'In the bookroom, sir,' answered the man, his eyes round as they took in the furious beauty at the visitor's side.

'Good. I'll announce myself.'

The footman did not object, but it was plain he felt he was neglecting his duty, for he emitted an admonitory cough, causing the captain to pause in his way to the library across the hall.

'What is it?'

'Er—shouldn't I tell—I mean, the young lady, sir—'

'You can leave the young lady to me.'

'What young lady?' demanded a voice from the back of the hall. 'Don't tell me you've found her!'

'Ah, Gérard,' uttered the girl in a gratified tone as Major Alderley walked through into the light. 'You will please to tell this—this *idiot* to release me.'

'Of course he will release you,' Gerald said at once, concealing his delighted satisfaction at this unexpected piece of good fortune. 'I'm only surprised you have not released yourself. No pistols, no daggers today?'

'Would you have me show a pistol with so many soldiers? I am not a fool. And you have stolen my dagger.'

'Had the advantage of her this time,' Roding put in before Gerald could respond. He let go of the girl's arm. 'Caught her sneaking after that Valade fellow. Happened to be at the Chariot, you know, with Trodger, and it's review day.'

'Ah, the matter begins to come clear,' Gerald said. 'The place was full of barbers and military men.'

'Exactly so. And she—'

'She!' interrupted the young lady crossly.

'Yes, very rude,' agreed the major. 'Hilary, you must stop referring to mademoiselle as "she". But we cannot discuss this here.' He bowed and indicated the open door at the back of the hall. 'Mademoiselle.'

Gerald was relieved to find the girl did not attempt to run away, but meekly allowed him to usher her into the spacious and comfortable library which was his habitual haunt when at home. This lapse was possibly due to her apparent determination to make full protest of Hilary's conduct.

'All these soldiers,' she complained, adding with a sweep of one arm at the major's dress, 'all of them in red as you. And this *idiot*, he has threatened to arrest me and make them take me to prison. What would you? I cannot fight them all.'

'No, of course you could not,' Gerald soothed. 'Monstrously unfair of you, Hilary.'

'Unfair!' echoed his junior.

'And this is not all,' went on the lady, evidently determined to disclose all her wrongs. 'When I thought to make them *sympathique* for me, with a little tear, you understand, and some tricks *feminine* of this kind—'

'Feminine tricks, too?' cut in Gerald admiringly, controlling a quivering lip. 'Very useful, of course.'

'Useful certainly. But he tells them that I am a spy. One cannot expect that soldiers can be *sympathique* to one they believe may be a French spy. That is not reasonable.'

'A very low stratagem, Hilary,' Gerald said, turning on his captain with mock severity. 'How could you? No wonder mademoiselle is angry with you.'

'*What?*'

Roding's glare tried Gerald's control severely, but he pursued his theme unheeding. 'I am extremely displeased. It is no fault of your own that you are not at this moment standing there with your head blown off.'

Mademoiselle, who had been nodding in agreement at Roding during the first part of this speech, abruptly turned to face Gerald again.

'*Parbleu*,' she uttered indignantly. 'You *imbecile*. You make of me once more a game? *Eh bien*, I have told your friend that I will kill you, and if you will give me my dagger this minute, I shall do so at once.'

'But what have I done?' protested Gerald innocently. 'I'm on your side.'

'You are not on my side at all, and it will be better that, instead of saying such things to him, you would say them to yourself.'

Gerald opened his eyes at her. 'You mean I should give myself a dressing-down? Very well.' He strode to the fireplace behind the leather-topped desk and addressed his own reflection in the mirror, wagging an admonitory finger in his own face. 'Gerald Alderley, I don't know what you deserve. It will serve you out if I give her dagger back to mademoiselle, so that she can plunge it right into your chest.'

To his intense satisfaction, mademoiselle burst into laughter. 'I have a very good mind to do so, *imbecile*.'

Gerald turned and came back to her. 'That's better. Come now, I am very glad to see you again so soon, mademoiselle whatever-your-name-is. We have a great deal to discuss, you and I.'

A wary look came over her face, and Roding intervened. 'You won't get a thing out of her. Not if I read her aright.'

'Perhaps you don't, Hilary,' Gerald said mildly, smiling at the young lady and indicating one of the wide window seats. 'Sit down, won't you?' He crossed back to Roding and said low-voiced. 'A word, if you please, my friend.'

They moved to the door, while the lady shrugged, and then seated herself, glancing from the window into the street below, and then turning again to watch them in their huddle at the other side of the library.

'What is it?' asked Roding. 'What do you mean to do with her?'

'Just keep her talking, that's all,' Gerald said quickly. 'Long enough for you to see Frith for me.'

'Your groom? What for?'

'Get him to wait outside. Sooner or later she's going to run away again, and I want Frith to follow her and find out where she's living.'

Roding gave him a look of respect. 'For once, you're talking like a sensible man. I'll do it. Seems you were right about Valade. She was definitely following him. Mark you, she wasn't the only one. There was a young lad ahead of her. Footman or some such.'

'Indeed? Interesting.'

'Ain't it? Want me to give you some time with her? Not that I think she'll tell you anything.'

'Yes, she will. But probably not the truth.'

Roding gave a bark of derisive laughter and left the room. Gerald crossed back to the window.

'Would you care for some refreshment? A glass of wine, perhaps?'

'Nothing, *merci*, I do not remain,' she answered, although she did not rise. Under the plumed hat, her eye kindled. 'And I do not know why you are so polite, when you have been bad to me last night, and have taken my dagger.'

'You were quite as bad to me as I was to you,' Gerald protested mildly, sitting down beside her. 'As for your dagger—'

She held out her hand palm up, as if she expected him to give her the weapon. As she did so, the ruffles to the jacket of her riding habit fell away, exposing livid blue bruises about her wrist, ugly in the light of day from the window at their back.

'Lord in heaven, did I do that?' exclaimed Gerald remorsefully. He took her hand in his, raising it closer, and gently touched the maltreated skin. She hissed in a breath and his eyes met hers. 'It must be painful. I'm sorry. Forgive me.'

Her lips parted, but she did not speak. Only sat, staring at him, a puzzled look in her face. It was a moment or two before Gerald realised that he could feel the fluttering of her pulse beneath the light touch he had on her wrist, and that her fingers were trembling in his.

'I didn't mean to hurt you so badly,' he said, still meeting her eyes, unaware that his hold about her hand had tightened a little.

'R-*rien*. It—it is nothing,' she said, although with a tremor in her voice.

'On the contrary,' Gerald argued, frowning. 'But if you must fight so furiously, I don't see how I can promise not to do it again.'

At that, a flush drenched her cheeks and she snatched her hand away. 'I will fight to the death, if it needs.'

A faint smile crossed Gerald's lips. 'I am sure you will. My death, probably.'

'This, *monsieur le major*, is entirely your own affair,' said the lady, haughty again. 'Do not mix yourself in mine, and perhaps you will not die.'

'Yes, but I'm afraid I am far too interested to stop mixing myself in your affairs,' Gerald said ruefully. 'I'm determined to find out all about you, mademoiselle. If I am to die in the attempt, then so be it.'

'*Dieu du ciel*,' burst from mademoiselle as she jumped up. 'Do you not understand that I can trust no one—*no one?*'

'That is a pity,' Gerald said, rising to face her. 'Perhaps I could indeed rescue you if only you would confide in me.'

The girl shook her head violently, setting the feathers on her hat bobbing. 'It is not possible.'

'That we shall see. Why were you following Valade?'

She shrugged and turned away, moving as if to seek escape among the bookshelves all about one corner of the room. 'I do not know of whom you speak. As to following, there was no one.'

'Don't be a little fool,' Gerald snapped irritably.

'It is you who is the fool,' she threw at him, whipping round again. 'I have said that I will tell you nothing of this *soi-disant* Valade.'

Gerald seized on this. '*Soi-disant?* Then he is not Valade?'

'How can I know?' she countered crossly. 'I do not know him.'

'I am not the imbecile you take me for,' Gerald said with dangerous calm. 'If you will not tell me about Valade, so be it. What of madame, his wife?'

'You know more of her than me,' the girl said with a look of scorn. 'His wife? Pah!'

'You're saying she is not his wife?'

'I am saying nothing.'

Gerald eyed her. She knew the truth of it all right. 'Word has it that she is English on her father's side.'

'The word of whom?' came scoffingly from the pretty lips.

'Her own,' Gerald replied.

'*Exactement.*'

'Damnation!' Gerald burst out, crossing towards her. 'Will you stop hedging? I'm hanged if I go on with this ridiculous cat and mouse game. Give me your name, girl!'

'Again?' Mademoiselle rolled her eyes. '*Eh bien*, Eugénie. Or I should say—'

'Eugenia,' cut in Gerald grimly. 'I thank you. I daresay that is one of the names of the nuns in your convent.'

'The nuns?' she said, gazing at him innocently. 'Certainly, if I was a nun, I know of many good names.' She counted off on her fingers. 'There is Bernadette, Marie-Thérèse, Marie-Joséphine, Marie-Claire, Henriette—'

Exasperated, Gerald seized her by the shoulders. 'I don't want a list of all the nuns resident in your wretched convent. I am aware that you ran away from there, but—'

'Certainly I ran away,' she said, meeting his gaze with defiance in her own. 'And if you like, I will tell you why.'

For the space of half a minute, Gerald continued to scowl in silent frustration. But the sheer tenacity of the girl defeated him. He laughed suddenly, and released her.

'You had better kill me, mademoiselle, because otherwise I shall end by strangling you.'

'*Comment*? You wish to murder me?'

'No, I wish to beat you,' he retorted. 'In fact, I've never met anyone who goaded me to so much violence.'

The girl nodded understandingly. 'Yes, that is what the nuns they said of me.'

'You surprise me.' Relaxing back, Gerald folded his arms. 'Very well, then. Tell me why you ran away from the convent.'

'So would you run away,' she uttered impulsively. 'I do not mind to pray, no. Even, I do not mind to study this Latin so abominable. But this is not sufficient. In a convent, you understand, one is like a servant, even if one is a lady.'

'How shocking.'

'Yes, but I do not like to scrub the floor and peel the vegetables and feed the pig. So it is that I do not do these things. But I must, they say, and try to make me with the punishments.'

'Poor little devil,' said Gerald, genuinely sorry for her.

A radiant smile astonished him. 'As to that, I am a devil, say the nuns. Because for the punishments *je m'en moque.*'

'You didn't care. Yes, I can readily believe it.'

'In one little minute,' she said, snapping her fingers, 'it is over and *voilà tout.*'

'Forgive me, but if that is the case, I don't quite see why you should run away.'

'Ah, that was an affair altogether different,' she explained and fluttered her long lashes at him. The by now familiar dramatic sigh came. 'There was a priest, the father confessor, you understand. He tried to make love to me. Oh, it was very bad.' She spread her hands. 'What would you? The nuns they would not believe me, and so it was not possible for me to stay. I was compelled to run away.'

'All the way to England?'

She opened wide eyes. 'But it is entirely natural that I choose my own country.'

Footsteps sounded just outside, and Captain Roding walked in. The major hailed him with a show of relief.

'Hilary, thank God! Have you a pistol about you? Or better yet, your sword.' He moved to his friend and grasped his hand in a gesture as deliberately dramatic as the storytelling of mademoiselle. 'If you care for me at all, shoot me. Or run me through. I'd rather die than hear any more fairytales.'

'*Dieu du ciel,*' came from the lady in a furious tone, before the astonished Roding could respond. 'This is insupportable. There is no need of your friend to kill you, *imbecile*, because I shall do so this minute.'

Leaning down, she raised the hem of the petticoat of her habit to reveal a neat little pair of boots on her feet. Gerald saw her extract something and leapt aside, calling a warning to Hilary.

There was just time for the girl to raise her arm to chest height and draw it back before Roding seized her. The slim knife was wrested from her grasp, and she was flung backwards, towards the bookcases. She threw out a hand to stop herself from cannoning into them and, losing balance, tripped over her own petticoats and fell to the carpeted floor, her hat falling off as she did so.

'Oh, Lord,' muttered Gerald, going instantly to her aid.

Furiously, she dashed his hands away. '*Bête*. I will arise myself.'

Ignoring this, the major slipped his hands about her waist and lifted her to her feet.

'What the devil do you think you're doing?' protested Hilary angrily. 'You should rather be arresting the girl and throwing her into gaol for attempted murder.'

'For God's sake, don't accuse her of murder,' begged Gerald, retrieving the lady's hat and handing it to her, 'or she'll be challenging me to a duel again.'

'You,' announced the lady, throwing an explosive glare at the captain, 'are a person entirely without sense. Certainly I would not murder *mon-*

sieur le major, even that he has made a threat to beat me.'

'I like that,' Gerald protested. 'After all the threats you've made, that is hardly fair.'

'I'm hanged if I can make out either of you,' complained Hilary. 'Mad as hatters!'

'It is you who is mad,' mademoiselle told him crossly. 'Gérard is not mad, only of a disposition entirely interfering.'

'And you are of a disposition entirely untruthful,' retorted Gerald. 'Have you any more pretty toys like that knife about you?'

'The girl's a regular arsenal,' Hilary snapped, giving up into his senior's hand the nasty little weapon he had snatched.

'It is necessary that one is at all times ready to protect oneself,' explained the young lady flatly. 'So Leonardo has taught me.'

'Leonardo?' An abrupt sensation of severe irritation attacked Gerald.

'Who the devil is Leonardo?' demanded Roding impatiently, asking the question that had leapt into the major's mind.

'Oh, *peste*,' she cried out in distressed tones. 'You make me talk, you make me talk. *Diable*.'

Then she jammed her hat on her head all anyhow and ran from the room.

Hilary started after her, but Gerald stopped him.

'Let her go. Did you warn Frith?'

'Yes. He's waiting.'

'Good. When he's found out where she's staying, I'll have him keep an eye on Valade's residence in Paddington, I think.' Then memory hit and he stared at his friend. 'And just who is Leonardo?'

'How in God's name should I know?' demanded Roding irascibly.

'He can't be Valade, that's certain,' mused Gerald, unheeding. 'She obviously likes Leonardo. Which means after all that she did not expect to marry Valade. But in that case, why the raging jealousy about Madame having taken her place. Unless —' Something clicked in his mind and he stared at his friend without seeing him. 'Lord in heaven, could it be so?'

'Don't look at me,' exploded Hilary. 'I don't know what the devil you're talking about.'

Gerald ignored this. 'She knows them. Both of them. And if the woman is not a rival, she must be —yes, that must be it.' He became aware of his friend's face before him. 'What do you think?'

'What do I think?' repeated Captain Roding. 'I think you've gone stark, staring crazy. Why can't you let it be?'

Gerald grinned at him. 'What, and miss getting myself murdered?'

'She said she wouldn't murder you.'

'Don't you believe it. She'd have thrown this thing if you hadn't stopped her. My thanks, by the by.'

The captain shook his head. 'I just don't understand you, Gerald. If you know her for the vicious, scheming wretch that she is, why in God's name —?'

'She's not a vicious, scheming wretch,' Gerald said calmly. 'She's an evil-tempered little termagant, yes, but there's no malice aforethought. And she's pluck to the backbone.'

Hilary stared at him. 'You're either mad, or in love.'

'*What?*' gasped Alderley in shock. 'In love? I? Don't be ridiculous.'

'Then you're mad,' Roding said flatly, and suddenly grinned. 'But I've known that for years.'

Gerald laughed and clapped him on the back. 'Lucky I have you to keep me from Bedlam, then.'

'Don't count on it. You'll end there one day, mark my words.' Then Hilary became serious again. 'Well, I can see you won't let it alone, so what do you propose to do about the wench?'

'I'll die before I let it alone,' Gerald vowed. 'As for what to do, I wonder if young Charvill would be worth a visit. And I think I must pursue my acquaintance with the fulsome Madame Valade.'

Mrs Chalkney, a long-time friend of the late Mrs Alderley, had been delighted to oblige that lady's son. 'Get you invited to a party where the French *émigrés* will be present? Nothing easier, dear boy. I am having them to my own soirée on Monday.'

'Excellent,' Gerald had approved.

'I did not send you a card because in the normal way of things you rarely attend such affairs.'

'Ah, but I have a special reason for doing so this time.'

Mrs Chalkney lifted her brows. 'Indeed?'

Gerald grinned. 'Yes, dear Nan, a flirtation. But don't run away with the idea that I'm hanging out for a wife at last, because I'm not.'

'Gracious heaven, Gerald! If your dear mama could not drag you to the altar, I am hardly likely to succeed.'

'In any event,' Gerald told her, with a grin, 'I can't marry this one. She's already spoken for.'

He endured the inevitable scold with patience, saluted Mrs Chalkney's faded cheek, and went off to endure the necessary delay with what patience he could muster. What more was to be done? Frith's investigations had proved fruitful, and the man was now keeping an eye on Valade. Gerald hoped he had covered all options and had resisted the temptation to pay mademoiselle a visit. In any case, there was no doing anything on a Sunday and Brewis Charvill, his main quarry, had gone out of town unexpectedly. An action which gave Gerald furiously to think. Had Valade been to see him? Possibly even yesterday when he was followed by some young lad—and the girl, of course. It was all highly intriguing.

On Monday Charvill had still not returned, and the major duly presented himself at Mrs Chalkney's house in Grosvenor Square, thanking his stars that his friend Roding would not be there to spoil sport.

Madame Valade was looking heartily bored, he noted, as his searching eyes found out the couple. He could scarcely blame her. Valade, who was standing by her chair, glancing around the packed pink-papered saloon with a heavy frown on his face, was a thickset man of coarse, reddened feature, with a discontented air. Or was that perhaps because his business in Piccadilly the other day had gone awry? Perhaps Brewis Charvill had not welcomed him with open arms.

Gerald noted the lady's eyes brighten as she caught sight of him making his way through the throng towards her. Now how in the world was he to get rid of the husband?

His luck was in. Just as he reached them, the Comte de St Erme drew Valade a little apart and began to converse with him in rapid French. Valade accorded the major's greeting a brief nod and gave his attention back to St Erme.

Gerald took Madame's hand and kissed the fingers with a little more warmth than punctilio demanded. 'Madame, I trust I see you well?'

'*Merci.*' She inclined her head, looking up at him through her lashes, and passing a tongue lightly over her lips.

Gerald smiled and crooked his elbow. 'A little promenade, madame?'

Madame Valade rose from the chintz-covered chair with alacrity and a little rustle of her silken petticoats. The close-fitting round gown, if a little old-fashioned with its very narrow waist and wide skirts, was becoming on a full figure, and the low décolletage, unencumbered by any form of covering, exposed a good deal of bosom. The lady murmured briefly to her husband, and then tucked her hand into Alderley's arm.

'We will converse in your own tongue,' he said in French as he led her away. 'And I trust you will pardon my inadequacies.'

Madame gave one of those breathy laughs. 'They cannot be worse than mine in English, monsieur.'

While he trod a deliberate path through the pink saloon towards the door, Gerald encouraged a flow of harmless chatter about the people Madame had met and the parties she had attended. But once he had steered the lady down the hall and along a passage to a window seat at the end, he abandoned the subject of society.

'And now,' he said, drawing Madame to the seat, and contriving to sit close enough that his anatomy touched hers at several points, 'let us talk about you, madame.'

'About me?' The lady's lashes fluttered and her fan came up. 'You would know more of me?'

'I would know everything about you,' Gerald told her, his tone at once provocative and inviting.

The major might not indulge in this sort of flirtation in the ordinary way, but he had seen enough among his army colleagues to know just how to go about it.

She responded at once, rapping him on the knuckles with her fan. 'I hope I do not understand you.'

You mean you hope you do, thought Gerald cynically. But he seized the chance to entrap her fingers, fan and all, and look deeply into her eyes. They were a dull grey, but the dark frizzed hair that framed her face was attractive.

'To begin with,' he said, 'allow me a very tiny intimacy. Your name.'

'Ah, that is easy,' she began, laughing.

'No, let me guess,' he interrupted. 'Let me see if our minds are attuned.'

The lashes fluttered demurely. 'You would read my mind?'

Gerald was pretty certain he already had, but he did not say so. This was unscrupulous, he admitted, because he had no intention of following through on the seductive promise in his conduct. But if not himself, there would be another soon enough. Madame Valade was that kind of woman.

'I would read your body,' he whispered, and lifted her fingers to his lips. Then he released her hand, and sat back a little, appearing to concentrate his thoughts on her face. She waited expectantly.

'Let's see now. Would it be Thérèse?'

She shook her head. 'Quite wrong, monsieur.'

'Alas. Then perhaps it is Prudence?'

'Oh la la! That is not me at all.'

'No, perhaps not,' Gerald agreed with a smile. 'Léonore, then?' She shook her head animatedly, enjoying his attention. 'Then it must certainly be Eugénie.'

'But, no,' She dimpled. 'You cannot read my mind at all, monsieur.'

'I'm afraid you are right. Very well, I give up. You will have to tell me.'

'I could have done so at the first and saved you the pain,' she told him merrily. 'It is Yol—' She broke off abruptly, her face collapsing into an expression of acute consternation.

Gerald was instantly on the alert. 'Something wrong, madame?'

Her fan came up swiftly, hiding the lower part of her face. She fluttered it with a trembling hand, averting her eyes from his, and he could hear her uneven breath behind it.

'It—it is—nothing,' she uttered jerkily. 'I thought—I thought I saw my—my husband.'

Gerald cast a swift look up the corridor, but there was no one there, not even a shadow. His frowning gaze came back to her. She was making it up. It was an excuse, dredged up on the spur of the moment to cover a slip. What had she so nearly said? She had almost spoken a name—and quickly withdrawn it. He remembered also, all at once, the very first words he had heard her speak: "I was not born to this." Lord, he was right! But softly now. Let him be sure.

'Have no fear,' he uttered soothingly, reaching out to pat her free hand. 'I will make certain that we are unobserved.'

He made a pretence of rising and making a sortie to the corner to see if anyone was there. She seemed to have recovered herself as he returned, but rose as if she would go back to the saloon.

'Ah, no,' Gerald uttered at once, lowering his voice and infusing it with all the promise he could command. 'Not yet, madame. You will leave me utterly distraught.'

Madame Valade reseated herself, and Gerald set himself to flatter her into relaxation again. He succeeded so well that by the time he asked for her name once more, she fluttered her lashes as coquettishly as ever.

'You will not guess again?'

'No, no, I am quite out of ideas. And you promised to tell me. Quick, now. I can no longer bear to address you by that formal *madame*.'

'Then you shall no longer do so. I am called Melusine.'

Gerald let out a sigh both relieved and satisfied and repeated the name.

'Melusine. How perfectly charming.'

He sat looking her over in silence for a moment or two, his thoughts revolving around the name and the way it fitted so exquisitely on quite another set of features. Presently he caught her puzzled glance, and recollected himself, turning on the charm again.

'Now, madame, tell me all about your life in France. Did you grow up at the Valade estates? You were born a Valade, I take it, even though your father is English.'

'Yes,' she agreed, but her manner was a degree less warm.

Gerald at once lowered his voice to that intimate level again, and leaned towards her. 'Come, I told you I wish to know everything about you. That is my way, my dear. I cannot be intimate—' stressing the word with a deep look '—with one I feel to be a stranger.'

The breathy laugh came, and Madame Valade abandoned her fan. 'You would have a history of my life? Very well. I was born of one Suzanne Valade and an Englishman, Nicholas Charvill.'

She pronounced it with a French inflexion, but Gerald understood her to mean the English name he knew.

'You are related to General Lord Charvill?'

'*Monsieur le baron*, he is my *grand-père*,' she confirmed.

As she went on, the story began to sound more and more like a recitation. 'I lived with the Valades for some years. But then, because my papa had no money, you understand, he sent me to a convent.'

'A convent?' echoed Gerald with interest.

'Yes, for there were too many females for the vicomte to make me a dowry. It was never intended that I should marry Monsieur Valade, but after the tragedy—' her eyes darkening in genuine distress '—and that he was the only survivor, he came to me in the convent and married me, and brought me to England.'

So pat, thought Gerald. A neat tale, giving little away. He would have to probe further. He allowed his voice to drip with sympathy.

'Ah, the tragedy. Poor little one.'

Her hand shook as he took it in his, and she uttered involuntarily, 'Oh, it was so horrible! They came like animals, with long knives that they use to cut grass, and heavy clubs. They set about everyone —everyone. They did not care—servant or master, it meant nothing. People running, screaming, hiding...' She shuddered, throwing her hands over her face.

Gerald's thoughts raced as he reached out supporting hands and murmured meaningless phrases to soothe. The shock and distress were genuine. She described it so vividly. Like a nightmare memory that returned again and again to haunt her. *But she was not there.* She had just this moment past told him that Monsieur Valade came to her after the tragedy, to the convent, from where he married her and brought her to England. She had, poor inexperienced fool, given herself away. Melusine—the real Melusine—would never have made such a stupid mistake.

In a moment or two, Madame Valade recovered her sangfroid. She appeared not to have realised the implications of her outburst, but clung a little to Gerald's hands which had taken hers in a comforting clasp.

'How happy for you that Valade came to take you away from France,' he said encouragingly, adding with one of those intimate looks, 'Happy for me, too.'

She simpered, and withdrew one hand so that she might smack his fingers playfully. 'You are outrageous.'

'I know,' he said, smiling. 'Tell me about the convent? Were you happy there? They were kind to you, the nuns?'

'Oh, but yes. So kind, so good to me always.'

With difficulty, Gerald bit back a laugh. 'You must have been an exceedingly good pupil.'

'It is so in a convent, you see,' she explained airily. 'The nuns, they teach prayer and obedience.'

Oh, do they? No kitchen service? No feeding of pigs? It was evident that this woman knew nothing of nuns, if a certain young lady's artless reminiscences were anything to go by.

'And your schooling?' he pursued.

Madame shrugged. 'To read and write, of course, and to sew.'

No Latin? And no guns or daggers, naturally. 'How dull it must have been for you, poor little one.' Gerald knew the caress in his voice was a trifle ironic.

She did not learn the kind of looks she had been bestowing upon him at a convent. Nor, he would wager, had the heroic Monsieur Valade, who had rescued her from that life and brought her to England, taught her in that short time all that Gerald was certain she knew of men. A shy virgin bride would not press her thigh sinuously against his, nor consent indeed to this clandestine little comedy he had been playing.

He did not know what her game was, although he had a shrewd suspicion that she had been co-opted into it by her supposed husband, the *soi-disant* Valade. Gerald did not know who she was, but he knew who she was not. She was not Madame Melusine Valade.

CHAPTER FOUR

Two days later, it was quite another Melusine who confronted a young lad on a sunny morning, at variance with her bleak mood.

'Say then, Jacques, you have followed him?' she demanded of the black-garbed footman.

Jack Kimble nodded eagerly. 'Aye, miss, like a shadow. I done just what you asked.'

Melusine was quite aware of the effect she had on the young lad. She was sorry for his liking her too much for his own good, but her need was too desperate to cavil at turning it to useful account. She had need of a devoted cavalier and Jack had proved eminently valuable.

'That is good,' she said with satisfaction, 'for I was compelled on Saturday to abandon the chase.'

Kimble's eyes widened. 'Was you following, too, miss?'

'Certainly I was following. Only that I was prevented by one of those soldiers that caught me in the big house.'

'Militia, miss,' Kimble corrected her. 'They weren't no soldiers.'

'They wear a uniform, do they not? They march and fight with swords and shoot with guns, no?'

'Well, yes, miss.'

'Then they are soldiers. And me, I know very much of soldiers. One must be on guard. Now do not make me any more arguments, but tell me at once where that pig is gone.'

Jack blinked. 'Pig, miss?'

'The one who calls himself Valade, *idiot*,' snapped Melusine impatiently.

'Oh, the Frenchie. On Saturday he went to that there Mr Charvill's house. In Hamilton Place that is, like I told you before, miss.'

'Yes, that is Mr Brewis Charvill, as you have found out for me.' She struck her hands together. '*Parbleu*, that pig, he will ruin all. Did he see him, this Monsieur Charvill?'

'I don't rightly know, miss,' confessed Kimble. 'At least I couldn't say for sure. He went in there, and he was in there for a good half hour. But I never seen Mr Charvill, and when the Frenchie come out, I followed him again, like you told me. But he only went home again to Paddington.'

Melusine swung away and moved to stare dully out of the window of the little chapel vestry onto the mews outside. At this time of day the priest would be at his apartments in Brewer Street, a short walk away from Golden Square which the building overlooked. The house had in fact been converted into a convent, but the fact could not be advertised, not even in the Catholic enclave that existed in this part of town. The nuns wore their habit, and said all their offices, and went about their tasks unobtrusively, relieving the poor and needy and tending the sick. They troubled no one, and as long as they did not noise themselves abroad and make a nuisance of themselves in this Protestant country, no one troubled them.

The vestry was perhaps the only room in the place, except her allotted curtained off portion of the dormitory chamber that served for her cell— and she could not scandalise the nuns by having a man in there, be he never so much a servant— where Melusine could be sure of privacy. It was situated off a little hallway that led also to the kitchens and the back door to the outside. It was convenient for Father Saint-Simon, who could enter this way and prepare in the little room before going up the narrow stair to the chapel above where the nuns waited.

There was little more here than a sideboard, a chest for the vestments, and a simple wooden chair. But it was generally unused, and so was a suitable spot for these secret meetings, when Melusine plotted and delivered her instructions to Jack Kimble. He was officially in the nun's employ, but Melusine had commandeered his services immediately on the discovery that he had conceived a passion for her. Leonardo had told her it would happen, and warned her to make use of it. It troubled her conscience a little, but Melusine had learned well of Leonardo and she trusted his word

Besides, no one could expect that a *jeune demoiselle*, in a foreign land, might carry out quite alone the difficult task with which she was faced. Not even, it seemed, this interfering *monsieur le major*. Although she had refused to answer his impertinent questions. He was every bit as much a pig as this Emile.

The image of Major Alderley came into her mind. She was obliged to concede that his features were pleasing, his strength and vitality attractive; and there was no denying how well this uniform of a militia suited his figure, which was lean and powerful both. The picture in her mind altered and she saw again the way Gerald had looked with consternation upon the bruises he had inflicted on her wrist. Something softened in Melusine's chest. No, this was not reasonable. A pig, yes, a little. But not so much a pig as *that* man.

A smile trembled at the corners of her mouth as she recalled Gerald's ridiculous upbraiding of his own reflection in the mirror. Decidedly this was *imbecile*. But Melusine was a little inclined to like this side of the major. Although she did not understand why he persisted in this pursuit of her affairs. A pity, *en effet*, that she dare not truly desire him to rescue her. An unhappy little sigh escaped her. He was a man *tout à fait capable*, this Gerald. In truth, she would quite like to have him rescue her.

Melusine gave herself a little mental shake. But, no. Of what was she thinking? She must rescue herself. Conquer the difficult situation in which she found herself. Through no fault of her own. But through the fault of that pig, who dared to call himself Valade and masquerade in society under her birthright. Sometimes it seemed that she would never recover it. And if this *soi-disant* Valade had already gone to Monsieur Charvill—

'Very well,' she said to Jack without turning round, 'but now is Wednesday. What does he do these three days?'

She had come daily to the vestry, hoping to meet the lad and hear his report. But on Sunday he had been obliged to attend to certain matters for the nuns. And on Monday and Tuesday she had failed to find him here. What had been happening all this time?

'Do you tell me he has not again left his apartment?'

'Only to go to some party or other Monday night,' Kimble said. 'But I ain't been idle, miss, I swear it.'

Melusine heard a note of triumph in his voice and turned, a questioning look in her face. 'You have something more to tell me?'

Jack grinned. 'Yes, miss.' He reddened a little, and shuffled his feet. 'I thought as how it couldn't do no harm, and as it turns out, it done me a bit of good.'

'Yes, but what is it, Jacques?' demanded the lady.

'Well, I thought as how someone in the house in Paddington might see me hanging about outside like. So Monday, when I see one of the maids come out with a basket, for to go fetch summat for that other Frenchie—the female as I told you about, miss, as is forever coming and going with the nobs.'

'Madame la Comtesse,' put in Melusine, for she had learned much by pumping *le père* Saint-Simon, who was acquainted with all the French exiles. The Father did not know of course about her connection with the Valades. He thought her only an orphan in search of her English relatives.

'Well, this maid,' went on Kimble eagerly, 'and me, we gets to talking, see, and that's how I knew he were off to this party. Anyways, we gets friendly and chats each day, and yesterday I mentions about that Mr Charvill, and the maid ups and says that Frenchie and his missus is going out of town to visit him.'

'*Comment?* But already he has made this visit—in town.'

'Just what I thought, miss. So I asks the maid a few questions like, and it seems it ain't Mister Charvill they're going to visit again, but General Charvill.' He stopped suddenly, dismay creeping into his face. 'What's wrong, miss? Ain't I done right?'

Melusine's mind was reeling, but she reached out and seized his wrist. 'No, no, Jacques, you have done very right. But, when? When do they go?'

'Today, miss. That's why I come to tell you.'

'*Dieu du ciel!* But this is *catastrophe.*'

Kimble gaped at her and Melusine struggled to pull herself out of the shock.

'What can I do, miss?'

'Nothing at all,' cried Melusine. 'I do not know if even I can do anything now. Oh, *peste*, he will ruin all. If he succeeds there, I do not know how I can prove myself.'

'Melusine!' came sharply from the doorway.

She turned quickly. The nun on the threshold was of middle age and heavily built, her back uneven from toil and her hands roughened. Martha had the square look of solid English citizenry, which was not deceiving. She came originally of country stock, and had been virtually in sole charge of Melusine almost from the hour of her birth—a thankless task, as Melusine had heard her bemoan countless times, with the rider that she had carried it out with a conspicuous lack of success.

Melusine sighed with frustration. Why must her old nurse discover her precisely at this moment?

'What are you at now, may I ask?' Martha glared at the footman. 'Kimble, you shouldn't be here. Not alone with her, that's sure.'

'No, sister, I know that, but—'

'You needn't tell me. Go away now, there's a good lad. Must be plenty of work for you to do.'

'But, sister, I—'

'Get along!'

Melusine gave Jack a smile as he cast a worried look at her, and nodded dismissal. She turned to Martha as the lad exited by the back door, but her nurse forestalled anything she might have said.

'Now then, my girl, why the long face?'

Melusine had no hesitation in placing her trouble before her old nurse, for it was Martha who had made her aware of her true history. She owed the nun a great deal, including her command of English, for no one else thought to ensure she could speak her mother tongue.

'Oh, Marthe,' she groaned, using in her accustomed way the French version of her nurse's name, 'that pig is going to *monsieur le baron.*'

'Mercy me,' gasped the nun. 'The general himself?'

'How shall I get my inheritance if the general will believe that pig?'

'Do wish you wouldn't keep on calling him a pig,' Martha begged. 'Not at all ladylike.'

'Of what use to be ladylike when I cannot be a lady?'

'None of that. You're a lady all right and tight, and nothing anyone does can take that away from you.'

'Yes, but if it is only we that know, it is of no use at all to me.' She flounced back to stare out of the window again.

'Well, if that's what the good Lord wants, then you'll just have to accept it.'

'But me, I am not very good with accepting,' Melusine said bitterly over her shoulder.

'Oh, dearie me, I wish I'd never told you anything about it,' lamented the nun, moving to the only chair the vestry possessed and sinking down into it. 'All this gadding about. And don't tell me what you've been up to, dashing off to Remenham House with that Kimble lad, and Lord knows what besides, because I don't want to know. I'd only have to do something about it, and that I can't. What our dear mother would say back home I dread to think.'

Melusine turned, an irrepressible giggle escaping her lips as she thought of the Mother Abbess in the convent at Blaye. 'She would say, *espèce de diable*, this Melusine.'

'And she'd be right,' Martha said severely. 'A devil is just what you are. It's that father of yours you take after, no question.'

Melusine shrugged. 'I do not wish to be like him, but it is entirely reasonable that it should be so.'

'Aye, more's the pity. But perhaps he was right not to tell you the truth.'

'How can you say so?' protested Melusine.

'Well, only look what's come of it. You won't settle and I'm going mad.' She shook her head. 'I should never have told you.'

'But, Marthe, you do not imagine that I would have taken the veil like you, even if you have not told me. And to wish not is useless, because you have told me from when I was a little girl.'

'True enough,' nodded Martha sadly. 'Thought it was downright wicked to keep you ignorant of your proper background. How was I to know what would happen? He always said if he couldn't get you a dowry, you could take the veil.'

'He said!' Melusine uttered scornfully. 'What a fate he finds for me. Rather would I have gone with Leonardo—and he wished me to do so.'

'*Melusine*,' shrieked the nun. 'That's wicked, that is. You don't know what you're saying, and I hope you never will.'

'Well, but Leonardo he was excessively useful to me, you know,' Melusine said airily. 'Many things he taught me. Things that you and the nuns would not think about for—'

She stopped, biting back the words "for a young girl". If Martha knew all, she would certainly die of shock.

'You were supposed to be nursing him,' Martha grumbled, 'and helping him convalesce. And Mother trusted him. Italians. That's Italians for you.'

'Pah! One little kiss, *voilá tout*.'

Martha got up with a swish of her black habit. 'That little kiss cost him his sanctuary, my girl, and don't you forget it.'

Melusine did not forget. She had agonized over it for weeks. Moreoever, it had cost her a whipping and several days' imprisonment in her cell on bread and water. But her tears had been for Leonardo's expulsion, and the loss of his companionship. He had changed her life dramatically, and she had missed him dreadfully.

'Let me tell you,' went on the nun severely, 'it would have been better for you if you had taken the veil.'

'You think it would have been better for me to stay as a nun and be killed like the Valades?' said Melusine, brutally frank. 'Or perhaps to marry the *soi-disant* cousin that Emile portrays?'

That silenced Martha, for the Mother Abbess had sent her off with Melusine to England not only for the sake of the girl herself, but to save at least one of her nuns from the growing wrath of the populace of France. Many a black veil hid a high-born dame, and the religious habit was no protection.

But Melusine's own words had thrown an idea into her head. 'Cousin? But I am a fool. Monsieur Charvill, he is also my cousin. If Emile can see him, then so also can I.'

'What are you about now, child?' demanded Martha apprehensively.

'You know what I am about,' exclaimed Melusine impatiently. 'To go to these Charvill, it was not in my plot. I wish nothing at all from them. And by *monsieur le baron*, of a disposition entirely unforgiving, I do not desire to be recognised in the least. Now I require it, only that I may stop this pig from ruining all. *Alors*, one must steel oneself.'

Gerald Alderley stepped out of a house he had been visiting in Hamilton Place and the door closed behind him. He stood on the top step for a moment, lost in deep thought. As he hesitated, unable to make up his mind what to do for the best, a heavy rumbling on the cobbles penetrated his absorption.

He looked up to see an ancient coach making its ponderous way down the street. A grimy, battered object, which had no place in the fashionable quarter of town. It had evidently seen better days before being relegated to the ministrations of a hackney coachman, one who evidently served the less affluent inhabitants of London.

Gerald watched its approach with vague interest, which quickened when he saw that it was drawing up outside the very house out of which he had just stepped. The door opened. A black-garbed young lad leapt out and let down the steps. Immediately a feathered hat emerged, under which a familiar countenance was visible.

Of all the amazing coincidences. Though Gerald must suppose it was inevitable she should eventually come here. But to choose this of all moments. Or had she, like himself, been held up until the fellow returned to town? He waited, his ready humour anticipating her likely reaction.

Melusine—the real Melusine—evidently did not see him immediately, for her attention was on her descent from the high vehicle. She accomplished it with the aid of the young fellow's hand, and stepped down into the road, glancing up at the house as she did so. Gerald saw her eyes change as she recognised him.

'Oh, *peste.*'

'How do you do?' Gerald said pleasantly, stepping from the pillared portico and coming down the shallow stairway.

'What do you do here?' demanded the young lady, moving to meet him. 'Again you seek to interfere in my affairs?'

'I did warn you I had every intention of doing so,' said Gerald. 'And I am delighted to see that you are ready to admit that the Charvills—or rather the Valades—are indeed your affair.'

A multitude of changes flitted across Melusine's features as she stood there for a space, unusually silent. Gerald guessed she was biting her tongue on an explosive retort as she eyed him. No doubt she was wondering what he had done in Charvill's house and what he intended now. That she was provoked by his interference was obvious.

Aware of the footman hovering, and the hackney coachman's curious eyes looking down from his box, Gerald leaned a little towards her and spoke in a lowered tone.

'Come, mademoiselle, it is of no use to conceal anything from me, you know. Which are you— Valade or Charvill? Or, no, let me guess. Both, perhaps?'

At that, her eyes darkened with fury. 'I have told you that I am entirely English.'

'Charvill, then,' Gerald concluded, unperturbed.

'This is altogether insupportable!'

She dug a hand into the recesses of the petticoat of her riding habit and a moment later Gerald found himself once again confronting the barrel of her overlarge and tarnished pistol. There was a concerted gasp of shock from both the black-garbed lad and the coachman.

'Don't, miss,' uttered the boy.

'Don't concern yourself,' Gerald said calmly. 'She won't.'

He took a pace forward, seizing the gun with one hand, while the other locked her arm so that he could forcibly wrest the weapon from her. The struggle was brief, and Gerald stepped aside, the pistol in his possession, while the girl Melusine stood trembling and glaring. She turned on the lad with her, who was visibly relieved.

'Jacques! This—this *bête* he attacks me, and you stand there and you do nothing.'

'But he's a major of militia, miss.'

Gerald noted the mixture of respect and apprehension in the glance he received from the boy. 'You see, unlike you, mademoiselle, your cavalier here would not wish to be arrested.'

'You will not arrest him, because I will shoot you first,' snapped Melusine.

'But I have the pistol,' Gerald pointed out. He looked the boy over with interest. 'I suppose he isn't this Leonardo you spoke of?'

'Certainly he is not Leonardo. He is Jacques. *En tout cas*, Leonardo is also a soldier.'

'Oh, is he?' Gerald said grimly.

'Give me my pistol!'

Gerald shook his head, slipping the pistol into his pocket. 'I can't do that. Besides, you cannot visit people armed with a pistol in London, you know. It is not at all *comme il faut*.' He bowed slightly, and indicated the house behind them with a wave of his hand. 'But don't let me stop you from going to see Charvill. That is why you came here, isn't it?'

'*Alors*, now we know who is the spy, Monsieur Gérard.'

'And now we know also who is the *prétendant*, Mademoiselle Charvill.'

Her eyes narrowed. 'Ah, yes? To what do I pretend?'

'That,' Gerald said regretfully, 'I have not yet been able to fathom.'

'And you will not,' came triumphantly from the cherry lips. 'So now you will please to go away and leave me to my business.'

'But I am not stopping you from carrying on your business. Why don't you go in? Charvill is there. I've just seen him.'

'*You* have seen him? *Exactement*. And me, I wish to know why you have seen him. What is it that you wish from me? You would like to arrest me for spying? Very well, arrest me. I do not care, but only that you will *leave my affairs to me*.'

She ended on a note of sheer frustration, clenched fists beating the air. Gerald sighed. 'You're right. It is perfectly intrusive of me, and I quite see that you must be sick to death of running into such an interfering busybody all the time.' He regarded her thoughtfully. 'I'll make you an offer.'

'What offer?' she asked, suspicion rife in her voice.

'If you are not going to visit Charvill today, I'll escort you back to the convent in Golden Square.'

Shock spread across her lovely features. Then she uttered a strangled, '*Espèce de bête!*' and burst into tears.

'Oh my God,' uttered Gerald in some dismay. 'Not in the open street.' He turned to the goggling footman and thrust him towards the coach. 'Open the door, fool!'

Then he had Melusine by the shoulders and was hustling her into the hackney. With a curt command to her cavalier to get up on the box and give the direction to the interested coachman, he jumped in beside the girl and shut them both into privacy.

Turning to Melusine, he grabbed both her wrists and held her away from him, as if afraid that she might go for him.

'*Laisse-moi,*' she threw at him, her brief attack of sobs already ended, although the trace of tears on her cheeks bore witness to its sincerity. 'Let go!'

'Do you take me for a fool?' Gerald demanded. 'Don't concern yourself. It is a precaution merely. I have to see if you carry any more weapons.'

'How can I have more? You have taken my pistol. You have taken my dagger. You have taken even my knife. Do you think a *jeune demoiselle* may possess more weapons than this?'

'Most young ladies would not be in possession of any weapons,' Gerald said tartly. 'You, Mademoiselle Charvill, are as unlike most of your sex as you can be. I'm taking no chances.'

She tried to shake his hands off her wrists, but Gerald held them fast and tutted at her.

'*Bête,*' she flung at him. 'You do not dare look in my clothes.'

'Oh, don't I? What do you have under all those petticoats, a holster?'

'But yes, and they are empty.'

'They? How many are there?'

'Oh, *peste.*' She struggled. 'You have said you do not wish to hurt me.'

'I also said, if you remember, that I could not promise not to do so. Now keep still. You will only make me hurt you the more.'

'But I have told you I have not another dagger, even a little one.'

'A dagger, is it then?'

The girl froze. 'What do you mean?'

Gerald grinned. 'In fact you admitted only that you had no more weapons. But you have, haven't you?' He tutted again. 'You have a knack of saying just the wrong thing.'

'To *you*,' she said angrily. 'Because you are a *bête*, and a pig, and *imbecile*.'

'I am whatever you like,' he agreed pleasantly, 'but nothing is going to stop me from searching for this dagger. And meanwhile, we'll just have these no doubt potentially lethal little claws of yours out of harm's way.'

So saying, he pulled her forward, slipping her arms about his back. The strong fingers of one hand secured both her wrists there, and Melusine found herself chest to chest with him as he threw off his hat, and began to pat at her petticoat, searching for tell-tale protrusions.

Melusine was unable to repulse him—even had she tried. The thought did not occur to her, for all thought had flown out of her head. She could not say a word, much less move. All the fury had left her, swamped by an inexplicable flood of warmth. Her cheeks seemed to burn, her veins ran riot, and her heart was beating so fast that she was sure he must feel it through his scarlet coat. His face, as he looked down where his hand sought for a weapon concealed in her petticoat, was so close that she could see only the line of his firm jaw, the drag of his powdered hair that drew it into the military pigtail, and the black ribbon that adorned it.

Then the incredible happened. The major's hand stilled. Slowly, he drew back his head and looked into her face. His eyes swept down and Melusine felt the quiver at her lips where he gazed. His glance came up again and met hers. Melusine saw fire in his eyes and a streak of heat rushed through her to match it. And then she could see nothing at all for his lips founds hers.

The kiss was powerfully moving. Drowning, her brain dizzy, Melusine clung to the source of the flooding warmth, her hands, no longer forcibly held, moving without will about the firm back. Her feathered hat fell from her head and down her back, and she felt fingers writhing in the mass of her hair and caressing the flesh of her neck beneath so that she shivered uncontrollably. A strong arm pulled her closer, and the lips that mouthed her own in tender touches sent her senses reeling. They pressed more insistently, forcing her lips open.

A moistened velvet touch found her tongue. A shaft of searing heat plunged downward. Shocked, Melusine shot out of that blanketing warmth of sensation. *Dieu du ciel!* Gerald was kissing her!

She struggled to be free, and the arms that held her loosened, the lips leaving hers.

It was a moment or two before Gerald, opening his eyes on the girl's astounded expression, recollected himself sufficiently to pull out of the extraordinary impact she'd had on him. He stared at her stupidly, forgetting to guard against the tactics he had come to expect from her. Until he felt a sharpness digging into his coat at the point of his heart.

He glanced down between the still narrow distance that lay between Melusine and himself, and discovered her hand there, a very small dagger within it. His glance swept up again and found her staring at him with much of her usual defiance, if a touch less of her customary assurance.

'Ah, there is the little menace itself,' he drawled, recovering some of his own sangfroid.

'Yes, th-there it is,' she uttered, stumbling a little over the words. 'And n-never would you have f-found it. It has instead found you.'

'So I see. It was not quite the search I intended,' he said with a touch of self-mockery as he released her, 'but success comes in all sorts of unexpected ways.'

'Success?' Her eyes narrowed. 'You kissed me that you might make me find it for you instead?'

'I had no such intention. I certainly didn't mean to kiss you.'

'*Parbleu*, you deserve I should stick this dagger in you this minute.'

Gerald raised his brows. 'For kissing you, or for not meaning to do so?'

'*Imbecile*,' exclaimed Melusine impatiently. 'You should not kiss me at all, and undoubtedly I should kill you.'

'Undoubtedly,' Gerald agreed. He held her eyes. 'Why don't you?'

Melusine frowned at him, grasping the dagger more firmly. 'You wish to die?'

'Not in the least. But I shan't try to stop you. You have threatened to kill me for nothing, I know not how many times. Now I have done something for which you might be pardoned if you did kill me. So here is your chance, Mademoiselle Charvill.'

He held his hands out of the way, surrendering his chest for her assault. Her eyes flashed and she withdrew the dagger, pulling away from him.

'But it is *idiot*. Certainly I cannot kill you if you tell me to do so.'

'Only in hot blood, eh?' grinned Gerald.

'*Exactement.*'

Gerald held out his hand, and she meekly gave the dagger up to him. He did not pocket it, but sat hefting it lightly from hand to hand, watching the girl thoughtfully.

'I might have killed you,' she snapped, 'if only you did not say anything. For my blood you made it very hot indeed.'

'Did I so?' Gerald said, amused. 'I assure you it was mutual.'

Which effectually silenced her. She blushed prettily, and in a moment regained command of her tongue.

'Why did you kiss me?'

'I don't know,' Gerald admitted.

'There you have soldiers. For nothing they kiss.'

'Oh, do they?' Gerald said, sudden wrath kindling. 'I suppose I need not ask to which other soldier you refer.'

'That is not your affair. *En tout cas*, we are not talking of that kiss, but of this one.'

'Must we talk of it? I'm trying to forget it.'

Melusine glared. 'I find you excessively rude. Why should you wish to forget it? Unless it is that you did not enjoy it.'

'I didn't say I did not enjoy it,' Gerald protested.

She smiled. '*Eh bien*, does that mean that you will do it again?'

'Not if I can help it,' Gerald uttered, alarmed.

'Ah.' Melusine sighed in a satisfied way. 'So it is that you could not help it. That can be very useful, that.'

'You little fiend,' exclaimed Gerald wrathfully. 'If you imagine you're going to use one ungentlemanly act to manipulate me, you very much mistake the matter.'

'Yes, but when I think about this, I do not think I can do so,' she said candidly. 'For that, I must conceal that I also have enjoyed the kiss.'

'It's too late for that,' Gerald told her evenly. 'But the fact remains that you should not have enjoyed it, you were quite right to threaten to kill me, and I—God help me!—should not have kissed you at all.'

'Then why,' demanded Melusine, 'did you do it?'

Gerald closed his eyes. 'Here we go again.'

She giggled suddenly. 'Gérard, you are a great fool.'

'Indeed, I'm beginning to think so,' he said ruefully. 'But I'm hanged if I know why you find it so amusing.'

'But it is *stupide*. Each time that we meet I try to kill you. Each time also we quarrel, and even if you are laughing very much, you become angry. And still you interest yourself in my affairs. And when I ask you why it is you do so, you have no answer.'

'Now you come to mention it, it is stupid,' Gerald said, struck. 'Hilary was right. He will have it that I've taken leave of my senses.'

'That is silly. Certainly you have a reason.' She eyed him. 'It does not seem to me that you can be an emissary for that pig.'

'You mean Valade? Certainly not.'

A little sigh escaped her. 'I did not think so.'

Gerald reached out and took her hand, enclosing it between both his own. 'Can't you trust me a little?'

His touch sent shivers running through her, but Melusine did not withdraw her hand. 'I do not know. I am used, you understand, to guard my secret. And Leonardo told me never to trust any man.'

'Leonardo again,' Gerald muttered and, to her disappointment, dropped her hand. 'Who in the name of heaven is this Leonardo? And why did he kiss you?'

'He was an Italian soldier, and he wanted to kiss me,' Melusine said, goaded. 'He wanted me also to run away with him, and I wish very much that I had done so.'

'What, a common soldier?'

'He was not a common soldier. He was an officer, and a person of very great sense, and altogether a desirable parti.'

'He doesn't sound like a desirable *parti*. How did you meet him?'

'He was wounded and came to the convent for sanctuary,' Melusine told him, stung by his criticism into revealing more than she had intended.

'If he needed sanctuary, it raises grave doubts about his activities.'

'Well, but he was a deserter, you see. That is very bad, certainly, and for this he was extremely sorry. It was a duel, you understand, and that is not permitted.'

'A pretty tale. Almost worthy of your own fertile imagination. He sounds to me like a soldier of fortune.'

'Yes, that is what he said,' agreed Melusine, pleased to find him of so ready an understanding.

'Lord,' Gerald uttered, his inexplicable annoyance evaporating. 'You don't even know what it means, do you?'

Melusine frowned. '*Comment?* What do you say?'

Gerald looked down into her face, and found himself touched by the uncertainty he saw there. Who was he to tread on her dreams? She had hero-worshipped an unscrupulous adventurer, who had not hesitated to impose on her youth and her ignorance. But she had loved the man. Loved his memory still, for all he knew. The thought caused him an odd kind of pang—of pity, naturally. It would be downright cruel to disillusion her.

'Don't let us quarrel over your Leonardo,' he said, summoning a faint smile. 'But tell me this instead. What were you doing at Remenham House? I can't puzzle that bit out.'

Melusine's eyes flashed. 'That is not your affair. *En tout cas*, no one has asked you to puzzle out anything at all. Least of all myself.'

'Yes, but I'm hanged if I see what your game is.'

'I have no game.'

'Your plan, then. Why are you doing all this?'

To his surprise, Melusine relaxed back, emitting a laugh that sounded perfectly genuine.

'But that is easy. It is so that I may marry an Englishman. Why else?'

Gerald stared at her blankly. 'Marry an Englishman! Which Englishman?'

Melusine shrugged. 'That I do not yet know. I shall have to discover one suitable.'

Taken aback, Gerald let out a short laugh. 'Don't be so absurd.'

'It is you who is absurd,' countered Melusine, the spark returning to her eye. 'You will not believe any of my very clever lies. Now when I tell you exactly the truth, you will also not believe me.'

'Because I have never heard anything so ridiculous,' Gerald announced. 'You escape from your own convent, at great personal danger. You come to England, and hide in a secret convent in London. You break into a gentleman's residence—'

'I did not break in.'

'Don't interrupt me! You break into a gentleman's residence, I say, and hold up two members of His Majesty's peacekeeping forces with a pistol. You creep around in a nun's habit, peering into a private ballroom. You skulk in shadows, following an *émigré*. You come to visit a completely different gentleman at his home. And you tell me that the reason you are doing all this is so that you can marry an Englishman!'

Melusine giggled. 'When you say it like this, certainly it appears absurd. As absurd as that you take this interest in my affairs. But it is the truth.'

'Then who is this Englishman?' demanded Gerald on a sceptical note. 'Some ineligible that your parents would not tolerate, I suppose.'

'Ah.' There was satisfaction in Melusine's voice. 'That was one of my own clever stories.'

Gerald frowned in an effort of memory, and then laughed as he recalled one of the lies she had invented for his benefit. 'So it was.'

'And it is very stupid of you to think of such a thing, because in this case, why should I seek out my family?'

Triumph rose in Gerald's breast, but he took care to conceal it. That was an admission all right.

'You are not the only one to seek them out,' he said.

'Do you think I do not know? If this pig has not done so, there would be no need for me to do it. I do not wish to seek them out, *en effet*.'

'Will you go back there?' asked Gerald. 'To see Charvill.'

She sighed. 'I must, for that the pig has already gone to *monsieur le baron*.'

'You mean Valade? Don't be downhearted. Charvill does not believe the general will accept them.'

She seemed to recollect herself suddenly. '*Parbleu*, how you make me talk!'

'Your secret is safe with me, I promise you,' Gerald said reassuringly.

The coach was slowing down, and he realised that they had arrived in Golden Square. He looked about for his hat, and put it on. Then, seeing Melusine's feathered beaver had fallen to the floor, picked that up for her.

She held out her hand for it, but Gerald smiled. 'Allow me.' He fitted the hat onto her head, and was aware as he did so of her eyes watching his face. He looked down and met them.

'*Merci*,' Melusine said, and smiled.

Gerald's breath caught. But before he could say anything, the vehicle rolled to a halt. He tore his gaze away, aware of the quickening of his heartbeat. Hastily, he reached for the door. As he turned the handle, it moved, and the door was taken from his hand and pulled outward by the young footman.

'Ah, yes,' Gerald said, jumping down from the coach and waiting for the fellow to let down the steps for Melusine, 'I had forgotten about you.' He held out his hand to help the girl descend. 'I suppose this is the cavalier you had with you when you —er—attended the ball the other night?'

'Jacques is very useful to me,' Melusine confirmed, bestowing that same radiant smile on the young man, whose features were instantly suffused with scarlet. She turned back to Gerald, holding out her hand. 'And now, *monsieur le major*—'

'I will see you to the door,' Gerald said, looking with interest at the building that his observant groom had told him housed a small collection of nuns. He glanced up at the coachman. 'Wait for me.'

Melusine shrugged, and crossed to the plain door beside which hung a bell. The lad had just barely jangled it, when hurrying footsteps could be heard inside. It opened and a nun's head popped out.

'I thought it must be you,' cried the woman. 'Come inside at once, child. I've been on the watch for you.'

'But why, Marthe,' asked Melusine, as she walked into the house.

Seeing the footman about to follow her in, Gerald clamped a hand onto his shoulder.

'I want a word with you, my lad. Await me in the coach.'

Without stopping for a response, Gerald pushed past him and entered the convent just in time to hear Melusine protesting.

'I have told you I will take Jacques. There was no need to be afraid for me.'

'It's not that,' the nun said urgently, 'but I've remembered something important.'

'Truly?' Melusine said excitedly. 'Speak, then.'

But the nun's eyes had caught Gerald behind and she took instant umbrage. 'Who's this, then?

Not soldiers again. Oh, what have you been about now?'

'There is no need to be concerned. Mademoiselle has had no harm of me,' Gerald said soothingly and bowed. 'I am Major Gerald Alderley of the West Kent Militia.'

'Oh, you are, are you?' said the nun, evidently not mollified, but she was forestalled.

'Why have you come in here?' demanded Melusine, turning on him. 'This is not a place for a man. You will go out at once, if you please.'

She fairly pushed at Gerald, who grinned and gave in, moving back to the still open door. He stepped out but, rather to his surprise, found Melusine following him. She pulled the door so that it was not quite to, and held out her hand, palm up.

Gerald looked at it, then at her face. 'Is that a gesture of friendship?'

She stamped her foot. 'It is nothing at all of the kind. Give me my pistol and my dagger.'

Gerald hissed in a doubtful breath. 'I don't know that I dare.'

'But you must. How will I protect myself if you do not?'

'If you will only confide in me, I will be happy to protect you,' Gerald said cheerfully.

'You cannot be always with me. How can you protect me? Moreover, it is stealing that you have done, and therefore—'

'Don't tell me you expect me to arrest myself again.'

Melusine giggled. '*Imbecile.*' Then she came closer and put her hand on his chest so that it rested on the braid that decorated his scarlet coat. 'Gérard—'

'What now?' he asked, rife with suspicion. 'Cajolery? This is not your style.'

Melusine hit lightly at his chest. 'Do not be foolish. You see, it is that I begin to like you, even that you are of this disposition extremely interfering. But I do not know you at all, in truth, and I do not understand why you do this.'

'Because I like you, of course,' Gerald said promptly. 'But I don't trust you an inch. What are you after?'

'But my pistol and dagger, *imbecile,*' she exclaimed impatiently, moving sharply back.

'I doubt very much whether they are yours at all. In fact, it would not surprise me to discover that they were both Leonardo's.'

'But he gives them to me.'

'Willingly?'

'*Parbleu*, what a person you think me.'

'I think you—' He broke off abruptly, astonished at what he had been about to say. A little darling? Lord in heaven, he *had* taken leave of his senses. Her voice recalled him.

'Quick, Gérard. Before Marthe will become impatient and come out. She will die if she knows I have a gun.'

'Very well, Melusine, you win,' Gerald said unguardedly, and dug his hand into his pocket.

Her mouth at half-cock, Melusine stood there staring at him. She received into her slack grasp the pistol and dagger, only half aware of taking them.

His expression altered. 'What is the matter?'

'Is there nothing you do not know?' she asked faintly.

He cocked an eyebrow. 'Why, what have I said?'

'You said to me my name.'

His features relaxed again and he grinned. 'I told you I would find out all about you, Melusine.' His finger came out and Melusine felt it stroke her cheek. A shiver slid down inside her. 'It's a pretty name. As pretty as its owner.' Then he bowed, raising his hat in salute and, crossing to the coach, spoke briefly to its driver and leapt into it without looking back.

Recovering herself, Melusine tucked the weapons out of sight, down into the deep holsters hidden under the petticoat of her riding habit, and went back into the house where Martha awaited her in some impatience.

'Who is that man? What has he to do with you? No, don't tell me. I don't want to know.' She grasped the girl's arm. 'Anyhow, never mind that now. Melusine, I've remembered something that may help you. You'll have to go back to Remenham House.'

CHAPTER FIVE

'Now then, young Jack,' Gerald said, turning to the lad, who was sitting in the place lately vacated by his self-appointed mistress, but in a state of far less relaxation.

He was perched on the very edge of the leather seat of the coach, his three-cornered hat twisting nervously in his hands, and from time to time he passed a tongue over dry lips. Gerald had been confident that the boy would not dream of disobeying an order thrown at him by a major of militia, but he guessed Jack might be wondering if he was about to be haled off to prison.

In fact, Gerald had given order to the coachman to drive out of Golden Square and then stop around the corner. He had no wish to drag the footman out of his way, once he had got his questions answered.

'No need to shake in your boots,' Gerald said soothingly. 'I'm not going to arrest you, young Jack —yet. It was Jack, wasn't it?'

'Aye, s-sir. K-kimble, sir,' stammered the lad.

'Very well, Kimble. You need only answer me truthfully and you have nothing to fear.'

Kimble nodded. 'Aye, sir.'

'That's better. How long has Miss Charvill been in England?'

'Not long, sir. Little more'n a week.'

'I presume you were not with her in France?'

Kimble stared. 'Who me, sir? Lor' no, sir. I only seen her when she come with that Sister Martha. Thought she was a nun at first.' He sighed. 'Like a vision she were.' He flushed. 'I—I mean, she were —'

'Pretty as a picture?' suggested Gerald.

'More nor that. Looked like them statues of the Holy Mother I see about the place.' His colour deepened. Seeming to feel that this statement called for explanation, he added, 'I been working for the sisters six month, see. Folks don't like 'em. Nuns, I mean. But they been good to me, they have, sir. Down on me luck, I was, and they took me in.'

'What sort of "down on your luck"?' asked Alderley.

The lad looked alarmed. 'I ain't done nothing wrong, I swear it. Lost me place, that's all.' He grimaced. 'Me and the butler didn't see eye to eye.'

Gerald suppressed a grin. Kimble was clearly a plain-spoken fellow. And he did not lack courage. His initial nervousness had already abated, and it took some valour to allow himself to become embroiled in Melusine's crazy schemes. Even given that he was hopelessly enamoured of the wench, a fact which was obvious to the meanest intelligence. Gerald's judgement was borne out a moment later.

'Tell me what you know of Miss Charvill?' he ordered severely.

Jack Kimble stiffened, looking at his interrogator with wary anger in his face. He glanced out of the window, looked back at the major and grasped the handle of the door.

'Don't even think of it,' warned Gerald, in the voice generally reserved for his men.

The lad hesitated. 'You ain't got nothing on me.'

'On the contrary. You have been seen loitering with suspicious intent in several places—Paddington, for instance—and I have no doubt at all that you were party to a break-in last week at Remenham House in Kent.'

Kimble's widening gaze told its own tale, but still he kept his fingers on the handle of the door. 'You can't prove nothing.'

'Do you care to test that theory?' Gerald suggested easily.

Not much to his surprise, Jack Kimble shook his head. No doubt he knew enough of his world to recognise that he stood little chance against the word of a major of militia. Looking sullen, he released the handle and sat back.

'Very wise,' commented Gerald. 'Now let's have it. Miss Charvill.'

'You can arrest me,' answered Kimble belligerently, 'but you can't make me say nothing about her. Wild horses wouldn't drag it out of me, even I knew anything, which I don't.'

Amusement flickered in Gerald's breast. 'My dear boy, your loyalty is misplaced. I mean Miss Charvill no harm. On the contrary.'

'How do I know that?' demanded Jack.

'I should have thought it was obvious. By rights I ought to have arrested her days ago. But I have not done so, and will not. I have discovered something of her background. I know who she is, and I know that she has been cheated somehow by the people calling themselves Valade.'

Kimble chewed his lip, but his hostility was visibly lessening. 'Seems to me like you know just about as much as me.'

He had abandoned the "sir", Gerald noted, realising that the footman's respect for him had dropped sharply.

'Possibly,' he said. 'But then again, possibly not. I have not found the secret way into the house, for instance.'

Jack gasped. 'You know about that?'

'It was the only possible deduction. Now tell me, if you can, something about the man who calls himself Valade.'

'The Frenchie? I only knows as how Miss says he will ruin everything. She calls him a pig, and she says he ain't Valade. But I swear she ain't told me nothing more, sir.'

Authority had won again, Gerald thought with satisfaction. But it looked as if the boy was not going to be of much use. He tried again.

'Do you at least know how he came to be in a position to cheat Miss Charvill, and to pass off his wife in her place?'

'In her place?' There was no mistaking the boy's ignorance of this part of the tale. 'You mean that his missus is pretending to be my mistress? Lord-a-mercy!'

'Precisely. And I have no doubt at all that there is a great deal of money in the case. Which, if we are not all of us very careful indeed, will be stolen from Miss Charvill.'

Jack Kimble took a deep breath. 'I knowed he were a wrong 'un, but that.' He clenched his fists and grew red in the face. 'Well, sir, if I've to choose betwixt him and you, I'll take you, no question.'

'I thank you,' Gerald said drily. 'Would that your mistress were as trusting.'

'Aye, but she don't reckon to militiamen. Thinks they're the same as soldiers. Seems as she don't trust soldiers easy.'

'That was hardly the impression I got,' Gerald murmured, remembering Melusine's attitude to Leonardo.

'Sir?' enquired the lad.

'Nothing. Listen, Jack. If you can tell me nothing I don't already know, so be it. Only promise me this. If Miss Charvill should take it into her head to dash off on some foolish errand, go with her by all means. In fact, I order you to do so. But send me word. Do you understand?'

'Aye, sir. But—but how?'

'Can you write?' Gerald asked, digging into one of his capacious pockets and bringing out a leather ring purse.

'Only me name,' Kimble said apologetically.

'Very well, never mind.' He opened the purse and extracted a couple of guineas. 'I'll send one of my men to see you here this very evening.' He added, as alarm spread over the lad's face, 'Don't concern yourself. He won't be in uniform. He'll appoint a meeting place with you and be ready at any time to bring a message to me.' Handing over the guineas, he added, 'For you.'

An expression of livid fury contorted the young man's face and he thrust the coins back at the major. 'I don't want no gold! Not for serving my mistress.'

Gerald raised his brows. 'I can see why you lost your place, young Kimble. Pity you aren't under my command. We'd soon cool that temper of yours.' He paused for the effect of his words to sink in, and then added, 'Don't be so ready to show hackle. The guineas are not for serving your mistress. They are for serving me. Are you satisfied?'

Grudgingly, Jack Kimble took back the coins. Had he but known it, his outburst had done him no harm in the major's eyes. He might not condone it, but the feelings that had prompted it augured well for Melusine's safety.

Having accomplished his intent, Gerald let the lad go and had himself driven back to Stratton Street. He had barely settled at his desk in his library, when he was disturbed by two morning callers. Captain Hilary Roding and his inamorata, Miss Lucilla Froxfield.

'Nothing would do for her but to come here,' grumbled Hilary, wiping his heated brow with a pocket handkerchief dragged from his immaculate white uniform breeches.

'Naturally I had to come,' confirmed the lively blonde, her eyes twinkling up at Alderley. 'Gerald, what have you been about? Dorothée tells me that you were flirting outrageously with Madame Valade on Monday night.'

'And who, may I ask, is Dorothée?' asked Gerald.

'Don't try to turn it off,' ordered Miss Froxfield. 'You know perfectly well that she is the daughter of the Comtesse de St Erme.'

'It's no use blaming me, Gerald,' uttered Roding, shrugging helplessly as his senior turned questioning eyes on him. 'I told her you couldn't have been flirting, but she wouldn't believe me.'

'Do you take me for a fool, Hilary?' demanded his betrothed. 'I know just what he was doing. For heaven's sake, give him some Madeira or something, Gerald! Anything to calm him down.'

Alderley grinned as his incensed friend refuted the suggestion that he was in need of a pacifier, and moved to the tray which his butler had just a short time past brought into the room and laid on the desk.

'Something for you, Lucy?' he asked, interrupting a heated argument that had obviously been in progress for some little time before their arrival.

'I'll take wine,' the lady said briefly, turning back instantly to Hilary. 'It is of no use to try to stop me. I know very well Gerald has been fishing for information about that girl, and I am determined to find out what he knows.'

'Why the devil should you be interested, I should like to know?' rejoined Roding.

'Because I'm a female,' declared Lucilla unanswerably. With a swirl of her floral chintz petticoats, she placed herself in the capacious window seat, accepted the glass Gerald handed to her, and smiled mischievously up at him. 'Now then, Gerald, out with it.'

He took his seat next to her, waving the fulminating captain towards the tray. 'Help yourself, Hilary.'

'I've a good mind to leave the pair of you to it and take myself off,' threatened his junior, marching across the room and snatching up a decanter.

'Don't be silly. You cannot possibly leave me here alone with Gerald. Only think how compromising.'

'Lord, yes,' agreed Gerald, in mock horror. 'Don't put me at the necessity of marrying the abominable little wretch.'

'You traitor, Gerald,' laughed Lucilla, her yellow curls bouncing under a huge straw bonnet all over flowers. 'For that I shall certainly not leave until you have told me every tiny detail.'

'I don't know that there is so much to tell.'

'Aha, you have found something out. I knew it.'

'Gammon!' burst from the captain, who had just tossed off a glass of Madeira. 'How could you possibly know it?'

'I know it,' Lucilla told him frostily, 'because Dorothée told me that Madame Valade went off with Gerald positively purring in her ear—which is a thing he never does—and came back with him looking like the cat after cream. Gerald, I mean, not Madame Valade. She looked, Dorothée said, just as she always looks. Like a trollop in heat.'

'*Lucilla*,' gasped Hilary, his cheeks reddening with wrath.

'Well she does,' insisted Miss Froxfield impenitently, and turned to Gerald. 'Doesn't she, Gerald?'

Gerald held up his hands. 'Don't involve me in your lover's tiff.'

Lucilla let out a peal of laughter. 'Lover's tiff indeed.' She threw a melting look at Roding. 'Poor Hilary. I'm behaving shockingly, I know. Never mind. There is only Gerald to see me, after all.'

'That has put "only Gerald" very firmly in his place,' mourned Gerald. 'I wonder why the females of my acquaintance have absolutely no respect whatsoever for male authority?'

'Ha!' came from Hilary. 'Seen her again, have you? Well, if she's been giving you as much saucy impudence as I've had to contend with, I can only say I'm glad of it.'

'Then you will not be disappointed. I have been insulted, and cursed at, and threatened with both pistol and dagger. I am apparently a beast, a pig and an imbecile, too, if memory serves me.'

Lucilla burst into laughter and clapped her hands. 'Oh, famous. How I wish I might meet this delightful mystery lady of yours.'

'She is no longer a mystery,' Gerald said.

'What?' Roding snapped, coming quickly to tower above the window seat. 'You've found her out?'

'Tell us at once,' urged Miss Froxfield.

'Give me an opportunity to open my mouth, and I will.'

'Sit down, Hilary,' ordered Lucilla, and to Gerald's amusement, her betrothed did so, perching on the desk close by and staring fixedly at the major.

'Her name is Melusine Charvill,' Gerald began.

'Charvill?' uttered Roding frowningly. 'You mean—'

'Hilary!' Lucy turned excited eyes back to Alderley. 'Go on, Gerald.'

'Miss Melusine Charvill,' he repeated, 'is a convent-bred genteel girl, who is in all probability the granddaughter of General Lord Charvill.'

'*What*? But—'

'Precisely, Hilary. That was supposed to be Madame Valade. Only she is not Madame Valade at all. Who she is I have not discovered, but she is masquerading as Melusine, and for all I know, is not even married to the man who calls himself Valade.'

'But what a perfectly famous adventure. And so your Melusine is busy trying to prove that she is the real one.' Lucilla frowned. 'But what in the world was she doing at Remenham House?'

'Your quickness is astounding, Lucy,' Gerald told her admiringly. 'It is precisely that point over which Melusine and I fell out.' Reminiscence made him smile. 'Because she, naturally enough, does not consider that it is in any way my affair.'

'What about this Leonardo fellow?' Hilary asked, still frowning heavily.

Gerald was conscious of that sliver of irritation again at mention of the name. 'That,' he said stonily, 'is yet another point over which we fell out.'

Lucilla eyed him with one of those particularly feminine looks it was difficult for a mere male to interpret.

'But who was he, Gerald?'

'A damned *condottiere*,' exploded Gerald, forgetting his company.

'Good God!' uttered Roding.

'What in the world is that?' demanded Miss Froxfield.

'Italian adventurer,' explained her fiance briefly. 'Soldier of fortune. You know the sort of thing. Lives by his wits and gambling. Likely as not outside the law, too.'

Lucilla gaped. 'But how did she meet such a person in a convent?'

'He was wounded and came there for sanctuary,' Gerald explained, adding almost through his teeth. 'Thanks to him, Hilary and I nearly had our heads blown off. I might forgive him that, for he obviously taught her a good deal that she has found useful. But what else he saw fit to teach her I do not care to stipulate.'

Lucy was silent for a space, once again wearing that inscrutable expression. Faintly bothered by what it might mean, Gerald rose from his seat and crossed to the tray to pour himself a glass of wine. He turned just in time to see Lucilla exchange an amused look with Hilary. Just what in the world was that about? Before he could hazard a guess, Lucy looked back at him.

'What are you going to do now, Gerald?'

He sipped his wine and shrugged. 'There is little I can do at present. I've made an ally of her champion.'

Hilary's brows shot up. 'Champion?'

'The lad you saw following her. Jack Kimble. He's a footman who works for the nuns and has taken up the cudgels on her behalf.' He glanced at the captain. 'By the by, get Trodger to send up one of our best men, will you? Someone discreet. I want him immediately, so you can send Frith with my phaeton if you like. And I want him out of uniform.'

Roding blinked. 'What the devil for?'

'Messenger,' Gerald explained. 'I don't want that girl running her head into any more danger.'

'As if you could stop her.'

'Probably not. But, whether she likes it or not, I aim to be on hand to get her out of it.'

'Quite right, Gerald,' approved Lucilla.

'She won't like it,' prophesied the captain gloomily. 'And nor do I. You'll end up dead, that's what.'

'Nonsense. I'll have to wait here, of course, which means you, Hilary—'

'Will have to do tomorrow's patrol. Yes, very well. Better check on Remenham House, I suppose.'

'Yes, do. I've seen Brewis Charvill, by the by.'

'Eh? Why did you not say so, man?' demanded Hilary crossly.

'I am saying so,' protested Gerald mildly.

'Dunderhead. Get on with it, then. I suppose you came right out and asked him about his family?'

'Nothing of the sort. I was extremely subtle—in fact, as devious as Melusine. I told him Valade had tried to borrow money off me and asked if he could vouch for the fellow. It seems Valade visited him that day to present his credentials, and Charvill posted straight off to inform his great-uncle. Which is why I wasn't able to see him until today. He gave Valade the go-ahead and they've gone off to visit him.'

'Well? Well? What did the fellow have to add to this rigmarole?'

'He confirmed that Nicholas Charvill—presumably Melusine's father—had been disinherited for marrying Suzanne Valade.'

'Ah, so that's where Valade comes in,' nodded Lucy.

'Precisely. Madame Valade—for want of any other name to call her by—told me that she, in her character of Melusine, was the daughter of Suzanne Valade and Nicholas Charvill.'

'But that would make her half French,' Hilary pointed out.

'Whereas Melusine insists she is entirely English,' agreed Gerald. 'Therefore she cannot be the daughter of Suzanne Valade. *Voilà tout*, as Melusine herself would say.'

'Oh, this is becoming nonsensical,' exclaimed Lucilla.

'Of course it is,' corroborated Hilary. 'Must be another of her lies.'

'Or she imagines that being half English is the same as being completely English,' suggested Lucilla.

'*Parbleu*,' said Gerald. 'I borrow the expression from Melusine. She may be an infuriating little devil, but she is far from stupid. Moreover, she claims that this whole enterprise of hers is purely for the purpose of marrying an Englishman.'

'That's fortunate,' murmured Lucilla.

Gerald frowned. 'What?'

'Nothing,' snapped Roding, with an odd look at his bride to be that Gerald could not interpret. 'Does Charvill know that this Melusine of yours is here?'

The question distracted Gerald. 'You mean that there is a rival Melusine to the one he has heard about? He does not. At least, I frustrated her design in calling upon him this morning. I can't but feel it's an undesirable complication to drag in the Charvills at this point. Time enough to do so when she has her affairs settled—if she can settle them.'

'And if she can't?' asked Lucy.

'We'll cross that bridge if and when we come to it.'

'What if she goes back to Charvill?' demanded Roding.

'Why do you think I want a man ready to run to me with every move she makes?' countered Gerald. 'She may well try to go back. She says she will have to, though she does not wish to. Which is also puzzling.' Gerald frowned. 'I only wish I might have won her confidence.'

Lucilla sat up. 'She won't confide in you? Now, why?'

'Because that scoundrel Leonardo drummed it into her head that no man was to be trusted,' Gerald announced viciously.

'The more I hear about this Leonardo,' Lucy said severely, 'the more I want to meet your Melusine. I daresay you have the whole thing wrong, Gerald. Men usually do.'

'It's immaterial, in any event,' Roding put in. 'What we have to find out is whether or not the wretched female is in fact Lord Charvill's granddaughter. What had Brewis Charvill to say to that, Gerald?'

'He had nothing to say to it. It does not matter to him either way. But what he did say is that he thinks the Valades will receive very short shrift from his great-uncle the general.'

Everett, General Lord Charvill, master of a barony stretching over a wide estate that encroached on the hundreds of Witham, Thurstable and Dengy, stood before his own fireplace, glaring at his visitors from under bushy white brows from a head held necessarily low above a back painfully bent by rheumatism. He was a thin old man, a wreck in a ruined body, but nothing would induce him to stand in any other way than as stiffly erect as possible like the soldier he had always been, even though he was obliged to lean on his silver-handled cane to do so.

That he received guests of the name of Valade at all would have surprised anyone who knew his history. But he had been forewarned by his great-nephew. His first reaction had been explosive as the hurts of the past rose up to taunt him. Lord Charvill's sense of justice would not, however, allow him to repudiate his granddaughter, if indeed this female proved to be the infant lost to the family so many years ago.

To be confronted with the girl's damned Frenchman of a husband was another matter altogether. Particularly when it was obvious the fellow was one of these pitiful wretches weak enough to allow themselves to be ousted from their inheritances and thus obliged to come seeking succour of their neighbours. The general had little doubt he was going to be asked to provide for the fellow as well as for his legitimate descendant.

Five minutes ago, his butler had entered the green saloon, an austere apartment, with dark forest-green wallpaper flocked with a swirling design, and heavy mahogany furniture. The news that his granddaughter desired an audience Lord Charvill had greeted with merely a grunt, which turned into a roar as his gorge rose when he heard that she was accompanied by her husband.

The visitors, when they entered, looked thoroughly intimidated and Everett concealed a grim smile. Just so had his subordinates shown their apprehension. It suited him to dampen the spirits of any who sought to impose upon him, as these relics of the loathed family of Valade seemed like to do.

Charvill did nothing to ease their path and it was left to the man to open negotiations, which he did by producing a set of folded papers, slowly approaching the general, and holding them out at arms' length.

'The credentials, *milor*,' he ventured.

Without a word, the general reached out and took them, but his glance searched the girl's face. Under this unnerving scrutiny, a slow flush mounted to the woman's cheeks. She fidgeted and looked away. Everett's gaze dropped to the papers in his hand.

He passed but a cursory glance over the formal certificate that identified the Frenchman before him as one André Valade, distant cousin to the Vicomte Valade. The marriage lines that confirmed a union between the said André Valade and Mademoiselle Melusine Charvill touched the old scars and he gave vent to a muttered expletive. But the letter, written in his son's own hand, and addressed to the Mother Abbess of the Convent of the Sisters of Wisdom near Blaye in the district of Santonge, dated a little over five years previously, exercised a powerful effect upon him.

Recognising the handwriting, he glanced swiftly at the signature, and uttering an explosive curse, cast the paper from him. That it provided proof of the girl's identity was one thing. Charvill's command of French was enough to tell him that, for its entire content was devoted to commending Nicholas Charvill's fourteen year old daughter into the care of the Abbess. But the mere recognition of his son's signature was enough to stoke the fires of his long-held rage. Proof that the scoundrel had risen from the dead—for he was dead to his father!

He glared at the female whose appearance in England had revived those painful memories—churning unbearably since Brewis Charvill had brought him the news and put him in the worst of tempers—and the fury spilled out.

'Tchah! So you're the whelp's girl, are you? Suppose you've nothing but that villainous French in your tongue.'

'I have English a little,' the girl offered, her voice shaking as she essayed a smile and sank into a curtsy.

English a little! 'You ought to have English only.'

Her lashes fluttered. 'But this is not to my blame, *grand-père*.'

A burning at his chest, the general ground his teeth. 'Don't dare address me by such a title.'

The girl bit her lip and backed a little, while her husband shifted to stand at her side.

'Monsieur, my wife intended not to anger you,' he said in a tone of apology.

'Then let her keep her Frenchified titles to herself. She may address me as "Grandfather" if she chooses, since I'm obliged to accept her in that capacity. But I don't wish to hear that abomination on her lips again.'

'Please forgive, *milor'*, but my wife, and even I myself, have yet very much trouble with English.'

Charvill eyed the girl with resentment. 'Well, she'd better learn fast if she wants any truck with me. I won't tolerate any foreign tongue in this house, least of all that confounded French.'

The fellow seized on this. 'Then it is that you will have pity? Here we have come, we poor, for aid. Pardon! I wish to say, for your granddaughter, we seek succour.'

'I dare say you do,' said the general, grim satisfaction overtaking his anger as his prophesy proved accurate.

'It is not for myself, you understand,' pursued the man, in an unctuous tone that sickened the general, 'but for this poor one. Lost from all protection, all her family dead—as are mine.'

Shock ripped through Charvill's chest. 'What, is Nicholas dead?'

He saw the two of them exchange glances and an instinct of danger rose up. What was the fellow about? Was he being imposed upon? He watched as the man Valade turned back, spreading his hands in the French way.

'General, we do not know. The last that is known of Monsieur Charvill is when he departed the Valade estate.'

Departed? 'Tchah! I suppose the vicomte threw him out?'

Watching the fellow's face, Everett felt his suspicion growing. Was the man debating whether or no to tell the truth? A grimace played about Valade's mouth and the general waited, maintaining his own rigid pose.

'It is, you understand, that Monsieur Charvill did not—how do you say in English?—having an eye to an eye—'

'Didn't see eye to eye with the Vicomte Valade? That I can well believe.'

'It was so,' said Valade, becoming a trifle more fluent. 'And that Suzanne, the sister of my cousin the vicomte, must choose between Monsieur Charvill and her brother. For a pity, she has chosen to remain, and it has been her death.'

'Slaughtered with the rest, was she?'

Despite his hatred of the woman who had caused so much grief, the general found he could not rejoice as he wanted to. Brewis had told him the Valade family had been victim to wholesale murder, and a twinge of compassion had wrung even his deliberately hardened heart. Well, let him be honest. Had this not been the case, he must have refused even to see his Frenchified granddaughter.

'Monsieur Charvill,' pursued Valade, 'has left the chateau, and since we have heard from him nothing at all, but for the letters to his daughter from Italy.'

'But two letters,' put in the woman. 'And if he is dead I know not.'

A question leapt into Everett's head and he recalled the letter to the Abbess. 'Was this when Nicholas commended you to this Abbess?'

'But, yes. Papa has sent me to be *religieuse*.'

Fury rippled again. 'That rascally knave sent you to become a French nun?'

Looking positively terrified, the girl nodded dumbly.

'Dolt! Muttonheaded oaf! Why the deuce couldn't he have sent you home?'

Valade cut in at that. 'Monsieur Charvill thought perhaps that his daughter would find not a welcome.'

'Tchah! Better a doubtful welcome here than a confounded French convent. The fellow is little better than a lunatic. How the deuce did I ever manage to father such a brainless nincompoop? A nun, for God's sake! A confounded Catholic nun. A granddaughter of mine!'

The idiocy of this notion stuck in his craw and he could think of nothing else for a moment.

'Pardon, *milor*,' said Valade, 'but Monsieur Charvill, he was not at fault. Not entirely.'

'I find that difficult to believe,' snapped the general, jerking to and fro as his agitation mounted.

'As I have said, it was a quarrel between the vicomte and Monsieur Charvill. The vicomte has, he say, enough *femmes* in his hands. He will not provide for the daughter. He is the one who has said that she must go to the convent. Monsieur Charvill, he has not the means to choose different.'

'Hadn't the wit, you mean.'

'Also madame his wife—'

Charvill's gorge rose. He'd borne mention of the woman's name. But that title he would not endure.

'Don't dare call her that to my face.'

Both Valade and the granddaughter gazed at him blankly. Then Valade—was the man as big a fool as Nicholas?—tried again.

'Suzanne, if I may say, had also not the choice. One would say she could try to—to prevent that her daughter will go to the convent. But the vicomte has said that his sister may remain, but that the daughter must go. Even the love of a mother does not sway him.'

Abruptly, the niggling doubt that had been plaguing Lord Charvill came sweeping to the surface. Mother? Suzanne Valade, her mother?

With deliberation, he spoke. 'Do you tell me that my disreputable son had the infernal insolence to pass you off as that whoring Frenchwoman's daughter?'

His answer was in their faces. His anger gave way to grim humour and he thrust towards them, leaning heavily on his cane.

'Typical. Hadn't the stomach to admit the truth, had he? I'll lay any money he labelled you with some foul French name as well. What was the name on those marriage lines you showed me?'

'M—Melusine,' stammered the woman, her countenance yet registering shock.

'I knew it.' The snaking suspicion rolled through his mind again. 'And you come to me, thinking yourself half French, and expect me to take you in. What is it you're after? Money, I suppose. Don't you know I disinherited the rogue?'

'This we knew, milor',' said Valade. 'Also that it was that you did not wish the French connection.'

'And your precious vicomte didn't wish for the English one,' said Charvill, acid in his voice. 'They eloped. But he didn't marry her. Not then. Too damned chickenhearted to confess to me he'd run off with the woman. If I'd known, there would have been a different story.' Bitterness rose up as he looked at the female. 'And you, my girl, if you'd been born at all, would have been just what you think you are. Half French.'

The woman shrugged helpless shoulders, looking to her husband. 'André? *Que dit-il?*'

'My wife does not understand,' said the fellow, frowning deeply.

'Of course she don't understand,' snapped Charvill irascibly. 'Been led up the garden path by that confounded rapscallion. Your mother, for what it's worth to you—for there's nothing for you here, by God!—was the woman I chose for Nicholas. An Englishwoman. Good-looking girl.' He looked the girl up and down. 'You don't favour her, bar the black hair. Don't favour your father much, either, if it comes to that.'

It had not before occurred to him, but this realisation fuelled the general's growing conviction that he was being imposed upon in some way. How would it serve Nicholas to keep the truth from his daughter? A tiny thread of disquiet troubled him.

'But this Englishwoman,' asked the man Valade, his puzzlement plain to see, 'who was she?'

The question irritated Charvill. 'What are you, a nincompoop? She was Nicholas's wife, of course. His first wife. Married the other and ran off after Mary died.' His eyes found the girl again, and he added rancorously, 'Giving birth to you. Couldn't face me with what he'd done, the miserable blackguard.'

The crack in the iron front widened a little, and the general was obliged to clamp his jaws tight against the rise of a pain too well remembered.

'Might have forgiven him,' he muttered under his breath, 'if he hadn't taken the babe.'

At this, the fellow Valade burst into unwise speech.

'*Sapristi*. Then Melusine is in truth your granddaughter. Yes, yes, you do not like the French, and so this English lady here, she is altogether your flesh. It is that you cannot refuse her sanctuary.'

The girl held out her hands. 'Ah, *grand-père*.'

Fire enveloped Charvill's mind and he brought up his cane, pointed like a musket. 'Keep your distance! You dare to tell me I cannot refuse?' He glared at the girl. 'Do you think I could endure to hear you prattling your abominable French in my ear day by day? Enough to drive me straight into my grave. I'll give you *grand-père*!'

'But *milor'*—'

'Pardon!'

No longer master of his actions, the general lurched forward, waving his cane. 'Get out! Out, I say! Think I want another miserable cowardly good-for-nothing wastrel on my hands? Begone! Out of my house!'

He drove them to the door, grimly satisfied when the girl's nerve broke.

'*Ah, bah*, it is enough,' she cried, and turning, ran out of the room.

Valade stood his ground, holding the doorjamb, and facing up to the general. Charvill's fury was burning out. He stopped, panting hard, slamming his cane to the floor to make use of its much-needed support.

'Well?' he uttered between heavy breaths. 'Still—here? Wasting your—time. Get nothing out of me. Try your luck with Jarvis Remenham—if you will.'

A sudden frown sprang to the fellow's face. 'You said—who?'

'Remenham. Maternal relations. Kentish family. Find them at Remenham House—if you can.' A gleam of rare humour slid into Charvill's chest. 'For my money, you'll not get much out of old Jarvis either. He's dead.'

CHAPTER SIX

Creeping along the dark narrow passage, with lantern held well ahead to keep her step steady on the uneven stones—and to warn her of the advent of rats—Melusine kept her long petticoats fastidiously clear of the dirt with an efficient hand, a habit she had learned in the convent.

'*Parbleu*, I hope that I do not have many more times to come in this way to the house,' she muttered fretfully.

'What, miss?' asked Jack Kimble from behind her.

'This journey I do not like,' she said more loudly. 'And if it was not for that *imbecile* of a Gérard, who has put his soldiers to watch for me, it would not need that I make it.'

'Even if they militiamen weren't there, miss,' cautioned her cavalier, 'you couldn't go marching into the house open like. That there gatekeeper would've called them out again.'

'Ah yes. He will be sorry when he knows who I am,' decided Melusine with satisfaction.

There was some justification for her annoyance, for negotiation of the secret passage demanded either a stout heart, or a desperate one. The original passage, Martha had told her, had led only from an upstairs room to one downstairs. But the Remenhams in the days of Charles the First, with the need for an escape route from Cromwell's increasingly victorious forces, had cut a trapdoor through its floor into the cellars below, and thence hewn the long rough passageway that led underground right outside the boundary of the estate. The entrance was concealed between two huge boulders within a clump of trees, and was now so overgrown that no one who did not know of its existence could ever hope to find it.

Even Melusine, armed with special knowledge, and the enthusiastic assistance of Jack Kimble's strong arm, had taken almost half a day to locate the place. She had known that Remenham House would be deserted, for Martha—released, as she had carefully explained to her charge, by her vows to God from servitude and obedience to Nicholas Charvill, a mere mortal—had begun a correspondence with a friend of her youth, Mrs Joan Ibstock, née Pottiswick. That good woman, although astonished to hear of Martha's conversion to Catholicism and embracing of a religious sisterhood, responded with the news of Jarvis Remenham's death.

Martha had been careful to make no mention of Melusine, and did not reply to Mrs Ibstock's enquiry about the fate of the little babe. When she confessed all this to her charge, telling the now grown up babe that there was no hope in the world of establishing any claim, she very soon discovered her mistake. Rebellious and resentful, Melusine decided there and then that she would do exactly that, come what may. Once in England, she made all haste to visit Remenham House.

On that first occasion, the delay in locating the entrance to the secret passage meant that she had to wait until morning to make her search. She had been obliged to spend the night in that fateful bedchamber, the faithful Kimble—who had foraged at a nearby inn, bringing back a large pie and a jug of porter for his mistress—guarding the door outside. In the early hours of the morning, unable to bear the suspense any longer, Melusine had ventured to explore the mansion, the lantern she had brought in hand, commenting to herself all the time on the state of the place and the difficulties of her task, and having no idea of the consequences she was bringing on herself thereby.

To her intense disappointment, she discovered that all papers had been removed from desks and cupboards. Not the most stringent search, conducted all morning, turned up one solitary sheet. There was nothing to replace the all important letter from her father. But she found an unknown lady's discarded garments, and selected some of those that she tried on, sending Kimble off down the secret passage to load them onto the horse she had borrowed—unbeknownst to its owner—from Father Saint-Simon. Kimble had bedded the animal down at the local inn. And then she had been disturbed by the eruption into the room of Major Gerald Alderley and his companion, Captain Hilary Roding.

On this second excursion, forewarned, she would use no light and keep as quiet as a mouse, she vowed, and thus refrain from attracting the attention of the militia at the gates. Arrived at the secret door, she grasped the lever that opened it and placed the lantern on the floor.

'This we will leave. I do not wish that the soldiers there will see it shine.'

A panel slid open and she stepped into the relative light of the little dressing-room, Kimble close behind her. Coming from the gloom of the passage, even the corridors seemed sufficiently illuminated for them to see their way. And the bedchamber, for which Melusine instantly headed, was almost bright.

'That is good. There is light enough from the sun,' she said, relieved.

'What are you after this time, miss?' asked Jack.

'A thing Marthe told me of,' Melusine answered, her attention on the garments that were still lying higgledy-piggledy, just as she had left them. She saw her discarded nun's habit still on the floor and scooped it up. Martha had not been pleased to find her spare one borrowed for that expedition when the major had found her outside the ballroom. Besides, it did not fit her well, which was why the loose wimple had slipped. She would take this one back with her. One never knew when it would be necessary to resume her disguise.

'Jacques,' she said, turning to the lad, and holding the habit out, 'take this for me and leave it in the passage where we have left the lantern. I do not know if I will have to escape quickly once more.'

'Aye, miss,' Kimble agreed, taking the garments, 'but where will I find you?'

'I do not know. I must go perhaps in all the rooms. Not up here, I think. I shall start at the bottom. Oh, wait!' She seized Jack's arm as he was about to go out of the room. 'Go you through the passage and find the other door. Martha said to me that it must come to the *bibliothèque*.'

'The what, miss?' asked Kimble, frowning.

'I do not know the word in English. The place for reading.'

'You mean the bookroom, miss. Will I meet you there?'

'Yes, yes, I shall await you. Now go.' She thrust him out of the room and made for the stairs.

The library was on the ground floor, Melusine recalled from the previous visit, for she had searched through a desk in a room filled with book-shelves of leather-bound volumes. But she was not sure just how to reach it. It had been brighter than the rest, for dawn light had come in through high unshuttered casements above the bookshelves.

Melusine glanced at the walls as she sped down the four flights of stairs, and noted with relief that some paintings remained. Here and there, a rectan-gular patch, darker than the rest, showed that some had been removed. Well, one must hope, that was all.

In the flagged entrance hallway at the bottom, where extra light came in from a window above the double doors, it was easy enough to distinguish a family group, and a landscape which clearly in-cluded Remenham House in the distance. But, moving through into the first of the large main rooms that led one into another around the house, with here and there an antechamber between, it was obvious that the task was not going to be easy.

If only one might open the shutters and let in the light. This gloom was impossible.

Moving to the shuttered window, Melusine dragged the heavy drapes back. Yes, this was a little better. *Parbleu*, but must she do this all through the house? Evidently she must, for not only could she not properly see the paintings and portraits that hung on the walls, but she was in imminent danger of bumping into the sheet-shrouded furniture.

She had just passed into a little antechamber beyond when she suddenly heard a faint knocking.

Her heart thudded. *Dieu du ciel*, what was it? She turned slowly, listening for the direction of the sound. It came again. It seemed to emanate from the back of the house. She looked about and discovered a door partially hidden by shadow.

Melusine crossed to open it, and immediately the knocking intensified in volume. The room behind was another small antechamber, presumably linking the back rooms. Swiftly following the sound of knocking, she crossed right and passed through a door near the windows—and found herself in the bookroom. Suddenly remembering Kimble, her heart thudded with excitement. Had he found the secret door?

Running to the centre, she tried to judge where the knocking came from. There was a huge desk of heavily carved ebony at one end, and at the centre, a couple of straight-backed chairs stood before a great fireplace at the outer wall, flanked by two bookshelves with casement windows above. Over the mantel, set into an ornately carved panel with fluted columns at each end, was a portrait of a man on horseback. Every other wall comprised book-cases, except where the doors appeared. The entire place was a masterpiece of wooden carving, a design of interleaving carried throughout.

Melusine turned and turned, unable to imagine just where the secret door could be. Upstairs, in the little dressing-room, the panel was opened by means of tugging a small candlesconce in the wall. Here, it might be anything at all. And nothing to tell her where to begin.

'Jacques?' she called out, forgetting the need for silence.

'Here, miss,' came faintly from somewhere close at hand.

'Can you not open it?' she cried.

'I dropped the lantern,' Jack's muffled voice told her. 'Can't see a thing.'

'Oh, *peste*,' exclaimed Melusine, and louder, 'Where are you? Call, that I may find you.'

She moved quickly to the nearest bookcase, and listened intently to the sound of Jack's voice. She could not judge its direction, and began to move swiftly along the bookshelves, her hand running behind her across the spines of the calf-bound volumes.

She had traversed perhaps three bookshelves, passed across the door that must lead to the hall, turned the corner, and was just about to reach the fireplace when she abruptly became aware that something under her fingers had felt wrong. Moving back to the corner again, she ran a hand back over the leather-bound books—which, she realised, were not books at all.

Her fingers passed over a cunningly wrought surface of wood, with just the correct amount of protrusion, the precise colours of dyed leather, and cleverly gilded surfaces and neatly painted lettering. But the whole set of some three or four shelves were of wood.

Melusine tapped on it. At once there came an answering knock. She had found him! Excitement welled.

'Wait, Jacques! I will find the way to open this.'

It took several frustrating moments, working at the protrusions of the carving down the side of the bookshelves, tugging at leaves, pushing at flowers. But at length, there was a click, and with a swish, the panel of painted books swung outward from the wall.

An astonished Jack Kimble was revealed in the aperture. Melusine started back, blinking.

'*Parbleu*, but I find that this is excessively clever, this passage.'

Jack stepped out, and pushed the door to. It clicked and the bookshelf was once more intact. They stood back together and stared at it.

'You could not tell it,' said Melusine, 'unless you were as close as we.'

A sudden clatter of booted feet sounded in the hall beyond. Jack looked towards the door. At the back of her mind, Melusine noted an odd look in the boy's face, but there was no time to explore it. Swiftly she ran her hands over the carvings, trying to find the lever to the secret panel again. She was too late. The door to the library burst open.

'Ha!' uttered Captain Roding triumphantly. 'Got you!'

'You!' Stunned, Melusine moved quickly away from the tell-tale bookshelf. 'But how do you come here?'

'Down on a routine patrol, unluckily for you,' he answered grimly. 'I was just looking the place over when I heard you calling out.'

'Oh, *peste*,' exclaimed Melusine crossly. 'It is all the fault of that lantern.'

'I'm that sorry, miss,' Kimble said glumly.

'It does not matter, Jacques.' She glared at Hilary. 'If it is that your men there are going to arrest us, then why do they not do so?'

'Left to myself, I'd let them,' he replied grimly. But he looked back into the hall and spoke to the sergeant who could just be seen behind him. 'All right, Trodger. I'll take over here. Get the men back to their posts.'

'Sir!' came from Trodger, and the booted feet clattered off and out of the front door.

'Now then,' said the captain sternly, 'I'm not going to ask you what you're doing here. I'd only get a pack of lies in reply.'

'Then it is good that you do not ask me,' Melusine snapped, and flouncing away from him, went to sit in the large chair behind the desk at the far end of the room. She watched, puzzled, as her cavalier frowned at the newcomer, glancing from him to Melusine and back again.

The captain saw it too and nodded at the boy. 'You the fellow Gerald spoke to?'

Kimble flushed beetroot, and Melusine had a flash of insight.

'Jacques!'

She got no further, for Kimble came towards her, speaking fast and low. 'It were that there major, miss. I didn't betray you, I swear I didn't. Seemed like he knew so much—more than me, miss. And—and he wanted to help you.'

'So this is the way you serve me,' exclaimed Melusine, her quick temper flaring as she jumped up, slammed her hands on the desk and leaned towards him over it. 'What is it that you told him?'

'Nothing, miss, I swear. At least—'

'Don't be more of a lunatic than you can help,' broke in the captain, addressing himself to Melusine. 'If the boy had sense enough to send word to Gerald as he was told to do, then God be praised!'

'*Parbleu*,' broke from Melusine, as she turned on him instead. 'By traitors I am surrounded!'

'Stop talking utter twaddle,' ordered Roding, marching up to the desk. 'You ought to be glad someone cares enough about your wretched little neck to try and save it. And if you dare to produce any kind of weapon at all,' he added, taking a plain brass-barrelled little pistol from his own pocket and levelling it, 'I will have no compunction in blowing off your head, you madcap female. You're dealing with me now, not Gerald.'

Melusine looked resentfully at the pistol. 'I see well that I am dealing with you. Do not imagine that I cannot do so, as well as I can this Gérard.'

'Do you tell me you think you can outwit Gerald? I wish I may see it.'

Melusine did not reply. Her anger died and she eyed him. She could manage the major. Let her see if she could manage this one, perhaps turn all to suit herself?

'What do you think to do with me now?'

The captain lowered the pistol. His tone changed, becoming a little more moderate. 'I don't propose doing anything with you. The thing is, Miss Charvill—'

'He told you my name?' cut in Melusine, surprised.

'He told me everything, if you mean Gerald.'

Impatience overtook Melusine's resolve momentarily. 'Do you think it is the man in the moon that I mean? What is it that Gérard has told you?'

'That you need help.'

Melusine sat slowly down again, looking him over thoughtfully. This became very interesting. Let her see what she could make here. She watched the captain tuck the pistol back in his pocket, and perch on the edge of the big desk. Very good. He became a little less *en garde*.

'I do not know how you think you may help me,' she said slowly.

'Neither do I,' he responded, frowning, 'but for Gerald's sake, I'll do anything I can.'

Mischief overtook Melusine. She ran her gaze over him, and allowed her eyelashes to flutter down.

To her satisfaction, the captain reddened a trifle. 'No need to upset yourself. Happy to do anything in my power.'

Melusine sighed deeply. 'You see, it is that I have a plan to marry an Englishman.'

His brows rose. 'So that's true, is it?'

'Certainly it is true,' Melusine said, opening her eyes wide. 'And I am thinking now that you may be very suitable.'

'Eh?'

Almost Melusine betrayed herself at his startled look. But she must not laugh.

'You will like to marry me, yes?' she pursued. 'That will be very helpful to me.'

'Marry you!'

He shot off the desk, such horror in his face that Melusine felt a little irritated. Was she so bad a prospect?

'No good, Melusine,' said a new voice from the doorway.

Melusine jumped up, turning swiftly. 'Gérard!'

Before she could react to this new menace, the captain spun round. 'She wants me to marry her.'

'So I heard.' Gerald came into the room as he spoke, his eyes on the stormclouds rapidly gathering in Melusine's face. 'He's already spoken for, Melusine. You'll have to find someone else.'

'You, perhaps?' she flung at him furiously, stepping out from behind the desk.

He uttered a short laugh. 'Lord, no! I've a better regard for my skin, I thank you.'

'*Parbleu*, but I find you excessively rude,' she snapped, marching to meet him.

'You usually do,' he said lightly.

'Do not smile at me and try to make me not angry any more,' Melusine warned, 'for I am very angry indeed with you.'

'What, for not wanting to marry you?'

'*Imbecile*. Do you think I would marry you? Rather would I marry the pig in the convent.'

'You mean the one that you refused to feed?' demanded Gerald, seizing this promising cue and adopting a mournful note. 'But that is excessively unkind of you, Melusine. To compare me to a starving pig.'

She bit her lip, but her eyes betrayed her. 'Do not say such things, you—you *imbecile*.'

With satisfaction, Gerald noted that her voice was hopelessly unsteady and drove home his advantage.

'I will not, if you will assure me that an imbecile is a better marriage prospect than a starving pig.'

Melusine bubbled over and warmth rose in Gerald's chest.

'*Idiot*. Near as *idiot* as this *capitaine* of yours. He believed me when I asked him to marry me. You would not have believed me, I know well.'

Gerald eyed her with interest. 'Did you sigh and flutter your eyelashes?'

'Certainly I did.'

'No, I wouldn't have believed you.' He glanced at Roding. 'Don't concern yourself, Hilary. She was only trying to distract you so that she might escape.'

'Distract me? She nigh on gave me an apoplexy.'

Gerald laughed, and turned back to Melusine, who was frowning again. 'What now?'

'Now,' she answered flatly, 'you will please to tell me at once why you have come here.'

'That's easy. You're trespassing again, and I've come to arrest you,' Gerald said promptly.

'I do not believe you. *En tout cas*, I am not trespassing at all. This—' waving an imperious hand in a sweeping arc about the library '—is my house.'

So that was it. Gerald glanced at Hilary and saw the stunned look on his face. The fellow Kimble, to whom Gerald was indebted, was gaping.

'You will have to prove it, you know,' Gerald said quietly.

'Do you think I do not know? What am I doing here, do you think?'

'That's just exactly what I've been asking myself,' he returned. 'Are you going to tell me?'

'But looking for proof,' Melusine uttered impatiently. 'Have I not said so?'

'No, as it happens.' He smiled down at her. 'But that will do for a start. Now I'd like the rest of your story.'

Melusine's eyes flashed. 'You would like? And do you imagine that I will tell you?'

'Won't you?'

'No, a thousand times.'

'Damnation!'

'What the devil ails you?' demanded his friend, striding forward. 'You know pretty much everything you need to know.'

Melusine swung round and stared at him, while Gerald silently cursed.

'How much does he know?' Without waiting for a reply, she turned narrowed eyes on Gerald. 'So it is that you have made Jacques betray me.'

'No, miss,' cut in Kimble.

She glanced at him and made a dismissive gesture. 'Do not be alarmed, Jacques. I am not angry with you, but with this—this—'

'Idiot? Imbecile?' offered Gerald in a helpful tone.

Melusine choked on a laugh, and Gerald at once seized the initiative, speaking in a tone deliberately soothing.

'You have every right to be angry with me. You see, I kidnapped poor Jack and made him promise to send me word if you went careering off anywhere. He was extremely loyal to you. Indeed, he told me nothing at all. But he was at last persuaded that I mean you no harm, and that I might—just possibly, since I am both a gentleman and a major of militia—be able to be of more assistance to you than he himself. So, you see—'

'Do not say any more,' Melusine uttered, flinging away and moving to the fireplace. She turned there, clasped her hands behind her back and put up her chin. 'I see that Leonardo was right. One cannot trust any man at all.'

The lad Kimble moved swiftly to the door and walked out of the room. Disappointment flickered in Gerald's chest, and he did not hesitate to speak his mind, unable to help a reproachful note.

'I don't think he deserved that, Melusine.'

Quick remorse raced through Melusine's veins, but she hit back strongly. 'It needs not that you tell me.' Then she ran swiftly out of the library, calling out as her cavalier was almost at the front door. 'Jacques!'

He stopped, but he did not turn. Melusine ran to catch at his arm.

'Jacques, do not go!'

Jack gazed steadfastly at the floor. 'You were right, miss. I didn't ought to have sent for him.'

Melusine's heart twisted. 'Jacques, you have been very much my friend. I have had no one but for you. But it is that I have a very bad temper, you understand.'

She sighed relief to see a faint grin as he ventured to raise his head.

'I know that, miss. I don't mind it.'

'But you mind that I say I do not trust you. This is not true at all.'

Melusine put her arm through his in a friendly way and moved with him outside to stand on the porch, leaning into him in a confidential way.

'Even the nuns they say I am like a devil. But you have looked after me very well, and we will not allow this Gérard, who makes me all the time excessively angry, you understand, to make trouble between us.'

'I think he only wants to help you, miss,' offered Jack. 'He don't mean you no harm.'

Melusine withdrew her hand. 'Yes, but I do not know why he should wish to do so, and therefore I cannot permit that he interferes.'

She was about to develop this theme, when Jack's gaze became fixed, and his expression changed. 'Inside, miss!'

'But what is it?'

'Quick! We need the major.'

Before she could object, Melusine found herself hustled back into the house and dragged willy-nilly towards the library door, where Jack called softly.

'Major, sir!'

The major appeared so swiftly that Melusine was instantly suspicious. Had he been listening inside?

'What is amiss?'

'That Frenchie, sir. He's riding down the drive.'

'Valade?'

'Aye, sir.'

Shock threw Melusine's heart out of kilter and she looked instinctively towards the major. 'But—but how can he know?'

His soldier's instinct overtook Gerald and he dropped all his insouciance in a bang, becoming brisk.

'Never mind that now.' He called through the library door. 'Hilary!'

The captain appeared, alert at the note in his major's voice as Gerald had known he would be.

'What's to do?'

'Valade is here. Go out there and head him off, will you? Tell him anything you like, but don't let him in, and don't tell him Melusine is here.'

Roding left the house instantly, not even pausing to nod.

Gerald seized Melusine by the hand and drew her towards the stairs, throwing a command at Kimble as he did so. 'Keep watch, Jack! If Captain Roding fails to keep the man out of the house, run upstairs and warn me quickly. We'll be somewhere on the floor above.'

'Aye, sir,' Kimble said at once, and took up his stance at the bottom of the stairs as Gerald dragged Melusine up them.

'But, Gérard—'

'Don't start arguing,' he said in a tone that brooked no defiance. 'We'll have you right out of the way, just in case. And don't talk until we're well out of earshot.'

Rather to his surprise, she obeyed this injunction as he led her up two flights of stairs to the first floor. Moving swiftly to the end of the corridor, he pushed open a door at random and entered a large room, which looked to have been a saloon, judging from the faded gilt and crimson wall-paper, a mirror above the fireplace which was surrounded by an ornate gilded frame, now sadly tarnished, and a worn Chippendale sofa with striped upholstery and tasselled cushions.

Gerald closed the door and released Melusine, and then went to open the shutters on a window that faced the side of the house. Light flooded the uncarpeted chamber, revealing the decayed state of the place.

'Lord,' he uttered, glancing about with a disparaging eye. 'One would take it that the house had been ransacked.'

Melusine had crossed to the window that overlooked the front of the house, and was trying to peep through a crack in the shutters. Cursing under his breath, Gerald moved swiftly across and dragged her away.

'You'll make shadows.'

She allowed herself to be pulled to the centre of the room, but uttered in a low tone, full of suppressed anxiety, 'How can he know? How can he know?'

'You mean how can he know that this is your house?'

Melusine looked up at him, distress in her eyes. 'There is no one who could have told him this. No one.'

'What of your grandfather?'

Her lips parted in surprise. 'You know?'

'Come, come, Melusine. Remember that I've seen Brewis Charvill, and I'm well aware of your identity. You told me yourself you are not half French, which means the girl calling herself Madame Valade is completely misinformed, so Valade himself cannot know. But they've just been to see General Charvill.'

Fury was in her face. '*Alors*, I see how is this. He will not help them—and I told Emile so—and thus he sends them to my other *grand-père*, even that he knows he is dead. Pah! What a pig is this *générale*.'

'I thought so,' Gerald said with satisfaction. 'Jarvis Remenham was your mother's father.'

She bit her lip, frowning. 'How did you guess?'

'I guessed as soon as you said this was your house. Didn't I say that this whole business of your camping in Remenham House was the one aspect I could not puzzle out?'

'You are very clever, *monsieur Gérard*,' she conceded, although Gerald was amused by the grudging note, 'but in truth it is not yet my house. I do not know how I shall get it, but I must, you understand.'

'Why must you?' asked Gerald calmly.

Melusine opened her eyes at him. 'But for my dowry, what else? One cannot expect that an Englishman will marry any *jeune demoiselle* without a dowry. That is not reasonable.'

'Not if you want one of good family, no,' he agreed mildly. 'Unless he is himself a man of substance.'

'Even that he is, one must be practical. For that such a man does not mind about the dowry, he must be in love *en désespoir*. And even if that,' she added bitterly, 'he must be also a person of a disposition extremely mad, that he can go against the family.'

'Like your father,' Gerald put in deliberately.

Her eyes flashed. 'Exactly like my father. Only my father he is also of a disposition extremely *stupide*. And it is all for his behaviour *tout à fait imbecile*,

and that of *monsieur le baron* his father entirely unforgiving, that I am put at this need to come myself
and get a dowry that I may marry in all honour.
And an Englishman, which is my right of birth.'

She turned and swept away from him, pacing the
length of the room to the window Gerald had unshuttered. And turning again, as if the emotions she
had churned up kept her on the move, she paced
back to the mantel and there stopped, staring at her
own reflection in the tarnished mirror.

Gerald watched her perambulations in silence,
his heart wrung. So this was what it was all about.
Hurt beyond what he could imagine by the selfish-
ness and pride of her forbears, whose fateful dis-
putes had robbed her of the life she should have
led, the plucky little devil had taken matters into her
own hands. It was not only Leonardo who had instilled in her this distrust of men. Small wonder she
had learned to be self-reliant. Every man in her life
had betrayed her one way or another.

'Well then, Melusine,' he said calmly, 'it seems as
if we must get you your dowry willy-nilly.'

She turned, her eyes narrowed. 'We?'

Gerald smiled. 'Precisely. You may command
my services at any time. I told you that at the outset.'

'No.' She advanced towards him. 'I do not command your services, *mon major*. I do not command
the services of a person who will not tell me why he
offers them.'

Gerald moved to the long sofa, dusted it with
elaborate care with one of its cushions, and with a

gesture invited her to sit down. Melusine approached with caution and sat warily at one end, looking up at him expectantly. He removed his cockaded hat, putting it down between them as he sat at the other end, placing himself at an angle and, crossing his legs, leaned back at his ease, his eyes fixed on her face.

'*Eh bien?*'

'You are perfectly right, Melusine. It is quite outrageous of me to go about rescuing a damsel in distress—'

'Who does not in the least wish to be rescued,' put in Melusine.

'—without telling her why,' he finished, ignoring the interjection. 'So I shall do so.' He sighed, spread his hands quite in her own manner, and fluttered his lashes.

To his intense satisfaction, Melusine bit her lip on a tremor.

'You see,' he pursued blandly, 'I lead a life of the most intolerable boredom. And the opportunity to share in your exciting adventures was just too tempting to be put aside.'

A derisive snort greeted this passage.

'I beg your pardon?' said Gerald.

'Do not beg my pardon. I know well that you are making a game with me.'

'I swear to you, it is the exact truth,' he protested. 'You have no idea how dull the militia is compared to the Army. I had to sell out, you see, when my father died, for the estate is in my hands.'

'Estate? But are you not obliged to do this work of the *milice*?' asked Melusine, her eyes round.

Gerald grinned. 'Believe it or not, I do it for pleasure. At least I rather hoped I might spend my time chasing smugglers, which would have afforded some excitement. But sadly, at Lullingstone we are too far off the coast to be of use. It would have given me intense satisfaction to have been able to catch a French spy.'

'That is what you thought of me.'

'Yes, but in fact you've offered me far more entertainment than any French spy could have done. And that's why I'm at your service. Now do you see?'

Melusine frowned. 'I do not see at all. It seems to me very silly.'

'So did your business about marrying an Englishman seem to me,' Gerald returned. 'Until today.'

'And why are you not married,' she demanded suddenly, 'if it is that you have land?'

Gerald grimaced. 'I've never found a woman who did not drive me into a frenzy of boredom.'

'But what age are you? Do you not require an heir?' Melusine asked, her tone shocked.

'I am nine-and-twenty,' he answered. 'As for an heir, I have Alderley cousins enough.' He sat up. 'While we're on the subject of age, it may be relevant to your claim to this house. How old are you?'

'I have nineteen years, and it is quite unimportant. Marthe has told me that the house comes to my mother, Ma—ry Re—men—ham.' She pronounced the name with painstaking accuracy, Gerald noticed. 'And if not her, for she is dead, then me. For it cannot be that this Jarvis will leave the house to my father. That is not reasonable. But there is need for the proof that I am me, and that is what I look for.'

She jumped up, and moved impatiently to the door. 'Has this *capitaine* of yours not yet rid us of this Emile? What can he find to say to him?'

'Don't be impatient,' Gerald said, rising too and coming to draw her away from the door. 'Keep still, for God's sake! Hilary will send him off all right and tight, never fear.'

Melusine shook him off. 'But do you not see that he will come again? I think it is better if you, both of you, go and leave me here to find—' She broke off, looking away.

'To find what?' demanded Gerald. 'What is this proof?'

'I will not tell you.'

'Hang it, Melusine!' Losing patience, Gerald seized her by the arms. 'I've had enough of this. Haven't I shown you over and over again that I mean you no harm? What do I have to do?'

'You can go away and leave me to my affairs,' she threw at him.

'Left to yourself, my girl, you may not have any affairs. Can't you see that Valade is an extremely dangerous man?'

'Do you think I am afraid of that pig?'

Gerald gave her a little shake. 'You should be. That he's come here at all shows he'll stop at nothing. The minute he discovers Roding here, he'll know something is up. Why would militia be infesting the place? And he must by now be aware of my interest. He may not know you're in England, but if he has the smallest knowledge of your character, he must surely be expecting you. How long do you think it will take him to put two and two together?'

'*Eh bien*, then if he will try to harm me, I will kill him.'

'You may not get the chance.' He let her go. 'Now be sensible, Melusine, and let me help you.'

She tossed her head. 'Me, I do not need the help of anyone.'

'Oh, don't you?' Gerald said grimly. 'Do you think because you've managed to pull a gun on me —not to mention several daggers and a vicious little knife—that you can get away with it against a man who means business?'

'Do you think that the trigger I would not have pulled, or stuck the dagger into you, if you had not been as you are?' she countered.

Gerald's temper flared. 'You little fool! I'm a trained soldier with ten years experience at my back. I've more than twice your strength and at least ten times your cunning, when it's needed. If I'd meant it, my girl, you'd be dead meat.'

'That is what you think? Let us try!'

'Don't be idiotic!'

She was backing from him, reaching through one of the slits she had carefully manufactured in her petticoat. 'I can take care of myself, *bête*.'

Exasperated, Gerald glared at her. 'You obstinate little devil. I'm minded to take a whip and beat some sense into you.'

'Pah!' scoffed Melusine. 'I have told you, a whip it is nothing. The nuns, they were very good with a whip. You do not make me afraid like this.'

The dagger was in her hand. Gerald lost his head.

'Then mayhap this will persuade you!'

With a scrape of steel, he drew his sword from its scabbard. Melusine cast one swift glance at it, and her eyes, flashing magnificently, came back to his face. But whatever she may have said was lost as Gerald pinned her to the wall, the point of the sword at her throat.

'I'll play you at your own game,' he growled, holding the foreshortened foil in place with rigid control.

Melusine's eyes blazed into his. Then her fingers moved. Pain sliced into Gerald's hand and his sword arm jerked. The sharp point of the sword at the girl's throat bit sideways. A thin line of red appeared in the white neck.

CHAPTER SEVEN

'Oh, my God,' burst from Gerald. He jumped back, wrenching the sword away. It fell with a clatter to the floor.

He heard Melusine cry out, but his attention was all for the nick he had made in her neck. Diving towards it, he tried to press against the rivulet that was seeping from it, hampered mightily by Melusine's fingers, which were grasping at his other hand.

'For God's sake, let go my hand,' he begged. 'I must get a handkerchief.'

'But you are bleeding like a pig,' came the frantic response.

Gerald glanced down and saw her dash at a spread of blood on his own hand, only now realising that her dagger had found its mark. Lord above, had they wounded each other? But Melusine's need was paramount with Gerald and he tried to shake off her clinging fingers.

'Will you let be?'

Instead she grasped his hand tighter. '*Laisse-moi!*'

Impatience swamped him. 'You're only making things worse, you little idiot.'

'*Parbleu*, it is I who am the *idiot*?' she scolded furiously, removing one hand and digging it into her sleeve. 'Who has begun this but you?'

Gerald barely heard her. 'Melusine, if you don't let go my hand—' He broke off as she dragged a pocket handkerchief from her sleeve. 'Give me that!'

He took his finger away from her neck and made a grab at the handkerchief.

'No!' Melusine snapped as he tugged at the thing. 'Leave it, *imbecile.*'

'Damn you, I should have beaten you,' Gerald swore, holding fast to his corner of the little square of linen. 'Only you made me lose my temper, and —'

'I made you do so? Pah!'

Gerald at last succeeded in ripping the handkerchief from her grasp, and swiftly held it to her neck, oblivious to her now bloodied fingers clawing at his hand.

'What in God's name is going on?'

Glancing swiftly towards the doorway, Gerald saw his friend's disbelieving face and burst out, speaking over the top of Melusine as she made another grab for the little square of linen.

'This idiotic female—'

'This *imbecile* has made me—'

'—made me lose my temper, and I—'

'—cut him with my dagger, and he is—'

'—damn near slit her throat!'

'—bleeding like a pig!'

'Whoa, whoa!' stormed the captain, starting forward.

Next instant, Gerald felt his wrist seized in an iron grip. It was wrenched away from Melusine's clutching hands.

'Gad, what a mess!'

Gerald pulled free, and Melusine broke back, staring at him. Her neck was smeared with red and remorse flooded him.

'Oh, my God, Melusine, what have I done?'

Melusine shook her head. 'No. It is what I have done.'

'Don't start arguing again, for God's sake,' snapped Roding irritably, dragging out his own large pocket-handkerchief. 'If ever I met such a pair of lunatics!'

'Give me that, Hilary,' Gerald said at once, ignoring his remark and reaching out for the handkerchief. 'She's still bleeding.'

His friend held it out of the way. 'So are you.'

'But—'

'You'll get her all over blood again. Let me bind you up, and then you can attend to her.'

To Gerald's chagrin, Melusine regarded Hilary with approval.

'That is very sensible, *mon capitaine*. But I do not need that Gérard attend. I will be very well without him.'

'Which is exactly what started us off,' Gerald said to his friend with a grin, as he gave up his injured hand to the other's ministrations.

'What started you off, you madman,' Roding told him frankly, as he set about tying his handkerchief around the wound, 'was being born at all.'

'That wasn't my fault.'

'No, but you've made up for it since.'

Gerald laughed. 'This from a man who calls himself my friend.'

'Yes, well, I was too young to see it,' the captain said, tying a knot in his makeshift bandage. 'Too late by the time I realised to what a dunderhead I'd pledged my friendship.'

'You mean imbecile, don't you?' Gerald said, and turned his head to share the joke with Melusine.

She was no longer there.

Consternation gripped him. 'Oh, my God, she's gone!'

Wrenching his hand from his friend's slackened grasp, he darted for the door, Roding behind him.

'How the deuce did she get out without me seeing her?'

'Took advantage of the distraction, cunning little devil,' Gerald snapped, racing down the corridor.

'But you know everything now,' protested Hilary, keeping pace as Gerald took the stairs two at a time. 'Where's the sense in running away?'

'Doesn't trust me,' Gerald said briefly.

He reached the top floor and ran down the corridor to the little dressing room at the end where he had lost her before. It was empty. Gerald kicked the panelled wall in frustration.

'Damnation! Too late.'

'Wait!' Leaning forward, Hilary tapped on the panel. 'Hollow.'

Triumph leapt in Gerald's chest. 'The secret passage!'

It did not take long to find the mechanism of the candlesconce that opened the door. Gerald studied the darkness beyond the aperture.

'Think it's worth getting some sort of light and following her down there?' asked Roding. 'That is, if she's gone that way.'

Gerald considered. 'I doubt it. Though I'll wager she used this passage, and we certainly ought to investigate it.'

'What about the lad?' said the captain suddenly. 'Must be still downstairs.'

'She will have taken him with her. And it's no use thinking he'd stop her. The boy's besotted.' He thought Roding gave him an odd look, but his next question was already in his head. 'What did you tell Valade?'

'Well, when I asked him what he wanted, he told me straight out that he had been told his wife was related to Jarvis Remenham, and he had come to see whoever lived here now that Jarvis was dead.'

'So Charvill did tell him,' Gerald said, once more staring into the hole in the wall.

'Looks like it. In any event, I explained that no one lived here and that we'd been called in because of suspected intruders.' Roding's voice changed. 'That piece of information seemed to interest him very much.'

Gerald looked round. 'Did it indeed?'

'I should think he's guessed, don't you?'

'Without any doubt at all.'

'Oh, she'll be safe enough, Gerald. He doesn't know where she is, and I told him he'd have to apply to Remenham's lawyers if he wanted anything to do with this place.'

Gerald's jaw tightened. 'That's not much comfort. He must know she'll be at a convent. Where else could she go?'

'And there aren't too many of them around,' agreed Hilary on a gloomy note.

'She hasn't said so, but I presume Valade had got hold of all the useful papers,' Gerald went on. 'Which means if he goes to the lawyers, he'll get in ahead of Melusine. She has no proof—yet.' He sighed. 'No, I don't see much future in pursuing her down this passage. We'll have Trodger check it out later.'

He closed the panel and came slowly out of the little dressing-room, Roding at his heels.

'Suppose you don't know what sort of proof she was after?' he asked.

'That's what started the fracas,' Gerald admitted ruefully, nursing his injured hand as he recalled it. 'She wouldn't tell me.'

'Take care,' warned Hilary, his eyes on his improvised bandage. 'Don't want it to break out bleeding again.'

'Lord, man, it's only a scratch!' Suddenly Gerald snapped his fingers. 'Wait a minute, though. Proof? There is someone who might be willing to help. Why in heaven's name didn't I think of that before?'

'What are you talking of?'

'Never mind that now. I'll have to make a visit out of town. But first, we've got to secure the convent. I'll need you to go back to the barracks and fetch more men up to town. Not Trodger. We'll leave him here, with a couple of others.'

'Think Valade will come back here then?'

'Melusine thinks so,' Gerald said, pausing at the top of the stairs. He looked at his friend. 'What would you do in Valade's place?'

'You mean, knowing that the girl was here and liable to queer my pitch?'

'Precisely.'

'Get rid of the wench,' Roding said brutally.

Gerald's chest tightened. 'Yes, I thought you'd say that.'

'Wouldn't you?'

'In Valade's place, with so much at stake—and more perhaps than he thought, for if he goes to the lawyers he's bound to find out about this house—'

Hilary said it for him. 'You'd do the same.'

There was a silence. Abruptly, Gerald turned. 'Come on. I've to collect my sword and hat, and then we must get back to London. Fast.'

Speeding down the two flights of stairs, Gerald mentally thanked God that it was the practice of himself and Roding—in case of emergency, of which this was a prime example—to stable their horses at the posting inns all the way to London. He had got here at speed by that means. By now the horses would be rested and he might go as swiftly back again.

But on arriving in the tattered saloon where he and Melusine had hidden, a shock awaited Gerald. One swift glance about the room, and a sensation of grim foreboding swept through him.

'She knows what she's up against. She's taken my sword.'

The tapping for which Melusine had been waiting came at last. She sighed with relief. It was cramped even at the end of the passage. It was also cold, and dark, for there had been no time to light the lantern.

'Jacques?' she called.

'They've gone, miss,' came the answer, muffled through the panel door.

'Then open it quickly.'

It was a wait of several minutes while Melusine chafed. She guessed Jack was having trouble finding the right piece of carving. At last the panel swung back into the library. Melusine grasped the hilt of the sword she had been carefully holding, and came out into the light.

'*Parbleu*, but it is not comfortable in the least in there. Such a time that it takes for them to go.'

'Only a few minutes, miss. I waited for them to get right out of the grounds. They went to the gate and stopped there, gabbed with their men, and didn't even dismount. Then they rode off at speed.'

Melusine nodded. 'Gérard will think that I have gone back to London. That is good.'

'I still think you ought to have waited, miss. That there Frenchie didn't look any too friendly to me.'

'Certainly he is not a friend,' Melusine agreed, 'but he has gone, after all.'

'Begging your pardon, miss, but I think as how you ought to go back to London,' Jack ventured.

'I will do so. But first,' said Melusine with determination, 'I will find that which I came to find. Everyone has gone away again, so that I can do so all alone.'

'Alone, miss?'

'Certainly alone. Do you not remember that this *capitaine* has heard us talking? You may believe that Gérard will not let the soldiers leave from the gate. If they come here to walk around, they will hear us. So you, Jacques, must go and wait for me with the horse. Only first you must find the lantern and light it again and leave it here, near the door, for me to find.'

'But—'

'Do not argue with me, but go at once,' ordered Melusine swiftly, taking a high tone intended to subdue the independent spirit Kimble had lately shown himself to possess. She held out the foil. 'And take you this sword. Stow it in the saddle, for I will take it with me.'

Kimble frowned direfully, staring at the weapon with its gold hilt and decorative pattern down the blade. Suspicion was in his face.

'Where did you get that, miss?'

'It is the sword of *monsieur le major.*'

'How did you come by it? You didn't steal it, did you?'

'Certainly I did not steal it,' said Melusine indignantly. 'I have only borrowed it.'

'What?' squeaked Kimble. 'But the major—'

'The major can say nothing at all. Has he not himself taken my daggers and my pistol and my knife? *Alors*, he has given me back my pistol and one dagger,' she conceded conscientiously, 'which is a very good thing. And you need not fear that I shall not give back the sword when I have finished using it.'

'But what do you want it for, miss?'

'But to protect myself. Do not be a fool, Jacques. And go quickly that I may finish to search.'

She thrust him into the aperture, and pushed the hilt of the sword into his hand. Next moment, she had shut the bookshelf panel upon him.

Melusine sighed with relief at being alone at last and free to resume her search among the portraits. Leaving the library by the same door she had first used to enter it earlier that day, she crossed the two little antechambers and moved on through the rooms. She made a slow tour of the front of the house without success, and then started back along the rooms behind, dragging open the drapes each time to get just enough light to recognise what was on the walls.

As time went on, she began to think Martha had been mistaken. When she judged that she must be nearly back at the library, she began to feel somewhat dispirited. Would she ever find it?

Sighing, she opened the door to the next room, and drew back the drapes. One of the shutters was a trifle damaged, letting in added light. Melusine turned to look at the walls, and saw, immediately

opposite, set between two candelabra above a marquetry side table, a gilded mirror.

'Ah, now I may see what damage Gérard has
done to me,' she muttered, crossing to the table and
putting her hand to the sore place at her neck.

The image in the glass was not clear, for the light
was not bright enough to see properly, but the
shadows of her riding habit and the hat with its
waving plumes framed a countenance that gazed se-
renely back at her out of long-lashed blue eyes.

Melusine tilted her head to catch sight of her
neck, and froze, staring at the image. The image did
not move. Her pulses began to race.

'*Comment?* This is not a mirror!'

It was a portrait. Melusine stepped back a pace,
her gaze fixed on the vision before her. She had
thought it a mirror, because it was her. It had her
raven locks, her pouting lips. And the fact that it
was dressed in riding gear had fooled her into
thinking it was her own image.

'But it is entirely myself,' she exclaimed aloud.
Martha was quite right. Mary Remenham had
passed on her every feature to the daughter whose
advent had taken her from this world.

Melusine came close again, and reached up a finger tentatively to the face depicted there.

'*Maman?*'

'How touching,' said a sarcastic voice behind her
in French.

Melusine whirled.

At the door through which she had entered the
room stood the so-called Monsieur Valade. He was

alone, hatless and without his boots, and he held a wicked-looking French-made duelling pistol, covered in silver and gold—property no doubt, was Melusine's fleeting thought, of the late vicomte.

'You!'

'Yes, it is I, mademoiselle,' he continued in his own tongue. 'I knew I should find you still here.'

'Emile Gosse,' Melusine said flatly, in the same language.

'Valade, if you don't mind.'

'Pah! You can never be Valade. Gosse were you born, and Gosse will you remain to your death. Which, let me assure you, villain, will not be so far away.'

'That,' said Gosse, 'is a matter of opinion. Indeed, it is rather a matter of whose death is close.' He glanced at the portrait behind her. 'And that object confirms me in the belief that it is not I who will shortly meet my maker.'

Melusine edged a little away from the portrait. 'That is my mother.'

'So I infer. A pity you did not think to tell me that part of the tale at the outset.'

'I had never the intention to tell you anything, pig!'

Gosse moved forward a little. 'No, for you had your own selfish plans already made, that is now seen. You wanted to play a lone hand. *Eh bien*, you have now the opportunity. You really are extremely stupid, Melusine.'

'Don't call me by name,' she snapped. 'You have not the right.'

'Because I was a servant in the vicomte's house? Things have changed. Or had you not noticed?' He sneered. 'You have made a serious mistake, Melusine.'

She edged sideways a little more, her eyes on the pistol in his hand. 'What do you mean?'

'You should have gone to Charvill.'

'Nothing would make me do so, except to tell him how you have cheated me.'

He nodded. 'As I said, a mistake. Too late now. Neither Charvill nor his heir know anything of your presence in England.'

'But Gérard knows. He knows everything. That you are not Valade at all, and that I am Melusine Charvill, the granddaughter of *monsieur le baron*, the general.'

Gosse smiled and Melusine read triumph there. 'But Gérard—if you mean the fellow Alderley who was making eyes at Yolande—is not here. I saw him ride away with that other fellow.'

'You saw? Where were you? How did you see?'

'Your heroic *milice* are not as clever as they thought. Easy enough to look as if one rides away. I did so.'

'Then Gérard may come back,' Melusine cried involuntarily on a sudden rising hope.

'Not if I heard him aright. Shouting to his companion, even as they passed by where I hid myself, he called out that he thought to find you at the convent.'

Melusine bit her lip. Now the pig knew where to find her—for it would not take long for a Catholic to locate the convent in Golden Square—even if she escaped him here.

'And so you sneak back,' she threw at him, 'like the jackal that you are. How did you get into this house?'

He shrugged. 'I broke in. Easy enough. It is a big house and there are many rooms in which to hide.'

Her flesh crept. He must have been following her from room to room, silent in his stockinged feet. Too intent on her search, and convinced besides that she was quite alone, she had been an easy prey. She recalled that she had heard nothing that first time when Gerald and the captain had burst in upon her. *Parbleu*, but she was a fool. And now she had sent Jack away. She was alone with a deadly enemy.

As if he read her thought, he spoke it aloud. 'No one is here, Melusine, except you and I.' He laughed. 'You see now how dangerous it is to play this lone hand. You should have confided in me, and fallen in with my plan at the beginning.'

'I spit on your plan,' Melusine told him furiously. 'Rather would I die than fall in with such a plan.'

The expression on Emile Gosse's face was vicious under the smile. 'A convenient desire, Mademoiselle Charvill.'

Melusine looked from his coarse red features to the pistol, and froze inside as she recognised his intention. Gerald's voice came back to her, saying that she could not hope to outwit "a man who means business". The challenge gave her courage. *Eh bien*, they would see about this.

She must weigh her situation. She was, she guessed, close to the library. But how close? She glanced about at the shrouded furnishings for possible cover. None this end. A couple of gilt straight-backed chairs only. The fireplace was at the other end, with the sheeted shapes of two sofas either side. The *soi-disant* Valade held the centre of the room now, only an uncovered but closed card-table, its surface dusty, between him and the suite at the fireplace.

There were three exit doors. The one nearest to her, which must lead to the library. The one through which she had come and Gosse had entered behind her. A third that joined this to the chambers at the front of the house. The man could put a bullet through her before she could hope to reach any one of them. *Eh bien*, she must use her tongue against him.

'You do not use your head, Emile,' she said flatly.

'How so?' he asked, and she noted that he allowed his pistol to dangle a little from his fingers. So confident, Emile?

'You fire the gun and you make one big noise. Immediately the soldiers of the major will come from the gate. They will find me dead, yes. But they will also find you. And this is not France, you understand. You cannot do a murder and expect that you will not be punished. *En tout cas*, Gérard will very likely kill you before the hangman has the chance.'

'Why should Gérard care?' sneered Gosse.

'Because he knows you for an imposter,' Melusine flashed. She pointed suddenly at the portrait. 'Moreover, no one will believe any more that Yolande is me when they see this.'

Gosse's eyes went to the portrait, and evidently took in the uncanny resemblance, looking from it to Melusine and back again. A snarl contorted his features, and he marched up to it, laying his pistol down on the marquetry table so that his hands were free to grab the picture off the wall.

Melusine seized her chance. Turning, she flew for the nearest door. She had just managed to reach it, grabbing for the handle, when the enemy's cracked command halted her.

'Stand where you are, or I shoot!'

Like lightning, thoughts zipped through her mind. He might miss at this distance. He had not had time to aim the pistol. If she kept on, would she make it out of the door? Then what? He could come after her before she could reach the secret passage. She dare not risk it.

Keeping hold of the doorhandle, she turned slowly. The decision had been sound. Gosse had moved forward, his pistol arm out straight, his aim true, the gun cocked. The picture of Mary Remenham was still on the wall.

'Very wise,' he commented, slightly relaxing his arm. He laughed lightly. 'Do you know, Mademoiselle Charvill, you are a thought too clever for your own good.'

'What do you mean?'

'You must be got rid of, that is seen. And this damning evidence—' with a brusque gesture at the portrait '—must also be destroyed. But to draw the attention of the *milice*, no, that is not at all desirable.'

Dieu du ciel, but she was a fool. Now he would take her away from the house before killing her, and no one would find her body at all. But at least it gave her more time.

Gosse was backing towards the table. His eyes on Melusine, he uncocked the pistol, and then reached out to the portrait, grasping it by one edge. He grunted a little with effort, and she realised the gilt frame must be heavy. It dropped sideways and fell with a bang to the table. But in a moment, it was tucked under his arm and, raising the pistol again, he gestured towards the door opposite the one where Melusine stood.

'That way. Move.'

Melusine hesitated. What could she do? Reluctantly, at a second curt command, she began to step across the uncarpeted floor, her eyes never leaving the threatening pistol. Gosse took a step or two towards the centre of the room.

All of a sudden, there was movement behind him. Melusine's eyes shifted. The door leading to the front of the house was stealthily opening. Her heartbeat quickened. Who? Could it be Gerald? Quickly, she looked back at Gosse's face, and found him frowning. Her steps slowed.

In the periphery of her vision, she saw the door pulled back. A black-garbed figure crept forward, noiselessly, towards Gosse's back. Jack! *Mon dieu*, but he was unarmed. She must not show anything. The flicker of an eyelash might betray his presence. Her mouth dry, she made her feet walk on, not daring to utter a word.

As Melusine approached the door, she saw Kimble speed up. Her heart in her mouth, she heard his foot scrape on the floorboard and knew from his expression that Gosse had heard it too. She saw his finger pull back on the hammer of the gun and shrieked a warning just as Jack launched himself forward and Gosse turned and fired.

The deafening report froze time. As in a dream, Melusine saw her faithful footman struck, his head-long progress checked. His hands came up, his face broke apart. He reeled, and crashed to the floor.

CHAPTER EIGHT

For an instant in the silence that followed, shocked into immobility, Melusine stared in horror at the body lying there so still. Then a surge of rage welled up.

'*Espèce de diable*,' she screamed.

Running to Gosse, she seized the portrait from his hand and lashed out, taking him off guard, so that he staggered back and fell against the card table. Following him, and acting out of instinct rather than intent, Melusine took a firm grasp of the gilt frame with both hands, lifted it high in the air and, with a shrieking curse, brought it down hard.

There was a tearing sound as the canvas gave way, and the precious portrait ripped apart as the top of the Frenchman's head came through it. Gosse sagged under the impact, knocking over the card table, and falling to sit, half stunned, the discharged pistol flying from his slackened grasp.

Satisfied he was immobilised for the moment, Melusine fell to her knees beside Jack, dragging at his suddenly heavy body to turn it on its back.

'Oh, *mon dieu*. Jacques, Jacques!'

His face was white, but his eyes were open, if a trifle glazed. He groaned, much to Melusine's relief.

'Jacques, where are you hurt?'

But as she asked the question, she saw the wound. It was at his side below the breast, hidden by the dark colour of his close-fitting jacket. Melusine ripped at the buttons of the garment, dragging it open and away, and gasped at the massive red stain on his shirt.

She glanced at the Frenchman, and found him struggling with the portrait that was embedded around his scalp. All at once she became aware of sounds outside. Furious shouting, and the thunder of running feet.

The soldiers! They must not find her here. Nor Jacques. Better they should find the so-called Valade. They would arrest him for the French spy they had thought her at first. What better way to be rid of him?

'Jacques,' she uttered urgently. 'Quickly! You must get up. We will go to the passage and then I shall bind you. Come, *mon ami*, come!'

Ever faithful, Kimble dragged himself into a sitting position, gasping at the pain this caused him.

'*Parbleu*, the bullet is still inside you,' Melusine guessed, remembering how the Mother Abbess had diagnosed Leonardo's suffering when he had first come to the convent.

She looked round wildly, as if seeking some source of help, as the boots halted at the front door and the shouting intensified.

But there was only Gosse, still struggling with the picture, looking dazedly towards Melusine and the lad he had shot, then away towards the sounds of pursuit, and back again.

'Do not think—' he panted, 'that I am finished —with you, mademoiselle.'

'Let's...go...while we can,' Kimble managed, and dragged himself onto his knees.

Melusine got to her feet and, tucking her shoulder under his arm on the uninjured side, put her arm about him to hold his waist, and thus contrived to take most of his weight. Together they made their painful way to the door, not even checking, in the effort this cost both, on what Gosse might be doing.

Once they were on the move, Kimble seemed to find strength from somewhere. 'I'll make it, miss. Hurry...before them soldiers...get in. The panel in the bookcase...it's open.'

They passed through a little antechamber, and Melusine sighed with relief as she entered the library next door. Activity in the hall intensified. The militia were in already. They must have a key. She hurried with Jack as fast as she could to the open door to the passage. The lantern was on the ground inside, ready. She let Jack go as he passed through the opening. He went in and leaned, panting, against one wall.

Melusine came in, picked up the lantern, and heard the library door bang open just as the panel clicked closed behind her.

'Come, Jacques, *mon pauvre*,' she uttered, and reached for the lad again, hardly aware of the muted sounds of running feet and much banging and crashing beyond the secret door.

She helped Jack to sit down, and dragged the jacket off him, lifting his shirt to expose the gash that had sliced across his side. Using the shirt, she cleaned away the blood. It was not as bad a wound as she had at first thought, and the blood was only oozing now. Melusine sighed with relief and set to work by the light of the lantern.

Jack seemed glad enough to rest, his back against the wall, and closed his eyes. Melusine ripped strips off her under-petticoats and fashioned a pad, which she bandaged as tightly as she could over the wound, working swiftly, unperturbed by the gore. She had not nursed Leonardo for weeks for nothing. The nuns had no regard for the sensibilities of a "lady" and expected Melusine—for it was her allotted task—to clean and tend the soldier's wounds even when they festered.

While she worked, Melusine worried over the problem of getting Jack home. First the passage to be negotiated. Then a ride to London on horseback. Could she hold him and manage the reins? If only Gerald had not gone. No, this was *imbecile*. She had begun alone. She would end alone. *Voilà tout.*

'Up, Jacques, up,' she ordered.

Her faithful servant struggled, with her assistance, to rise. Melusine's heart ached for him, but she had to force him on.

There was barely room for one, let alone two, in the passage, and Melusine ended up backwards, supporting Jack as best she could as he stumbled along, grasping the rough walls on either side with both hands.

Melusine cursed herself for his injury. Cursed him for his devotion that had made him come back for her, only to get himself shot by the fiendish

Gosse. And where was that devil? Had the soldiers found him? She could not think he had escaped, for she had only just made it into the passage as they entered the library. Unless—would he hide from them as he had hidden from her? It was a big house, he said. Catch him, she begged silently.

All at once she realised that Kimble had halted, leaning heavily against the wall.

'Jacques?'

'No...good, miss. I can't...'

He slid slowly down and collapsed to the stone floor, fainting dead away.

'Jacques!'

Melusine dropped to her haunches beside his inert form, feeling for the wound. It was bleeding again. She tightened her bandage and sat back, biting her lip. They could not go on. Tears sprang to her eyes. What a pig she was. If Jack should die, all though her fault, she could never forgive herself.

She put a hand to the lad's cold cheek and choked on a sob. 'Jacques, do not die while I am gone.'

Grasping the lantern, and heedless now of the discomforts of the passage, Melusine flew like the wind back towards the library, the vision of Jack Kimble's white face driving her on. Reaching the panel, she was able with the aid of her lantern to find the lever at once. Her heart full of dread, she dragged on it.

As the secret door opened, the sounds within the house came at once to her ears: the tramping of feet above, and the hoarse voices echoing through the mansion. Leaving the panel wide, Melusine dashed to the library door and flung it open, racing into the hall.

'You, soldiers,' she yelled. 'To me, quickly!'

There was a brief hush, and then the shouts resumed and several pairs of feet clattered towards her from, as it seemed, several directions. A militiaman came belting down the stairs, another leapt from outside the front door, and a third, stalwart and stolid, came in through the door that led to the rooms to the front of the house. Melusine recognised the burly form of Captain Roding's sergeant.

'Ha! It's you, is it?' He threw a glance at his two juniors. 'Cover her, men. That Frenchie, that's who she is.'

Relief flooded Melusine. 'You are the one that I have met in London.'

'That's right,' agreed the militiaman, coming forward to stand before her. 'Sergeant Trodger is who I am. Now then, missie—'

'*Bon*,' said Melusine, interrupting him without ceremony, and paying no attention to the muskets that were pointing at her from two directions. 'I am glad it is you, because you can help me.'

'That depends, that does,' said Trodger guardedly. 'Now then, where did you spring from?'

'Do not concern yourself from where I come,' Melusine snapped. 'More important is that you help me instantly, as even your *capitaine* would command.'

'Capting Roding wouldn't never command me to help no Frenchie,' said the sergeant positively.

'*Parbleu*, you waste time. Certainly your major—'

'Ah, now that's just it, missie. According to what I've heard, you oughtn't to be here. Major said you'd gorn.'

'Yes, but I have not gone,' Melusine said impatiently.

'That's just it. Why ain't you gorn? Seems to me I had ought to arrest you.'

'You may arrest me later. Now it is—'

'What are you doing still here, missie, that's what I'd like to know?' demanded the man Trodger, sticking to his guns.

'Oh, *peste*. What matters it? My servant, he is wounded—and by a Frenchman, if you wish to make an arrest.' She frowned suddenly. 'And why have you not arrested him? Do not tell me you have allowed him to escape you.'

Trodger eyed her with suspicion. 'What Frenchman would that be, missie? We ain't let no one escape.'

'But if you have not seen him, then he has certainly escaped.' Disappointment flooded her. Gosse had hidden himself successfully then. 'That is the man who tries to kill me, but he wounded instead my servant. Did you not hear the shot?'

'I ain't saying as I didn't hear no shot,' Trodger said carefully, peering at her out of eyes narrowed with interest, 'but what I do say is, it's mighty peculiar you saying as how there's a Frenchman in the case, when it's as plain as the nose on your face that you're a Frenchwoman yourself. And you know all about that shot.'

Melusine threw her hands in the air. 'But you are *idiot*. I tell you, if you do not help me this instant, you will find that your major he will very likely shoot you.'

'Woof!'

The sergeant appeared nonplussed, and Melusine pressed her advantage. 'While you are making me this interrogation, my poor Jacques bleeds to death.'

'Who's bleeding to death?' demanded Trodger.

'But I have told you. My servant. He is in the secret passage.'

'Secret passage, is it?' The sergeant seemed to brighten at this. 'Well, we'll just go on up and have a look at this here passage, missie, shall we?'

'Have I not been saying so?' snapped Melusine, exasperated. '*En tout cas*, it is not up at all, but down.'

Trodger had started towards the stairs, signing to his men to get behind the lady. But at this, he halted, turning his frowning gaze back on her.

'Now see here, missie. The major himself told me that this secret passage started upstairs. And if you've any notion—'

'Yes, it is upstairs,' Melusine agreed, crossing to the library door. 'But so also it is downstairs. There are two ways to go in, you understand. But you must come this way now. *Vite*, I pray you. Jacques is very bad, and I am afraid he may die.'

Upon which, she darted through the library door, galvanising both the sergeant and his two militiamen into action. She heard them diving after her, and noted their starting eyes as they spied the opened panel. She did not wait, but grabbed up the lantern and slid into the passage, calling to them to hurry.

Her heart in her mouth, hoping against hope, Melusine made her way back to where she had left the boy. Jack was lying so still, for a moment she panicked.

'Jacques, are you dead? Jacques, do you hear me?'

Melusine put her cheek to his lips, and felt the faint warmth of his breath. Relief flooded her.

'*Grace à dieu*, he breathes still.'

Looking round, she found the little coterie of soldiers crowded into the passage behind them. 'Why do you stand there? Take him up, and bring him out at once.'

But she reckoned without the fellow Trodger.

'If you'll have the goodness, missie, to move yourself out of the way,' he said aggrievedly, 'and let us at him, we might have a chance of doing just that.'

She was obliged to acknowledge the justice of this complaint, and moved further into the passage to allow the men access. But her temper almost flared again when the sergeant spoke.

'Now then, my lad, you're under arrest you are. But I suppose as I'll have to wait until you can hear me to tell you again. Now then.'

Melusine had to bite her lip to stop herself from interfering as, under Trodger's direction, the two militiamen gave up their muskets into his keeping and lifted Jack. With some difficulty, they managed to negotiate the passage with their burden and carry him out into the library.

'Lay him down on a sofa,' Melusine said, coming out behind them and moving towards the ante-chamber.

'You keep a-hold of him,' Trodger ordered his men.

'*Parbleu*, do you think he will run away? He has a bullet inside him, and it must be taken out.'

'If he has a bullet inside of him,' said the sergeant stolidly, 'there ain't no one can take it out better nor me. Many's the bullets I've dug out of fellows in my time.'

'But you are not a surgeon,' protested Melusine.

'I'm a soldier, missie. Been in the wars with both the major and Capting Roding, I have,' Trodger informed her loftily. 'I knows how to do better nor any surgeon.'

'Then do it,' Melusine said with impatience. 'But lay him down.'

'Ah, but I'm thinking as how this here house ain't the best spot for an operation of that kind, missie,' explained the sergeant, and Melusine noted that his men exchanged anguished glances. Trodger laid down their muskets and turned on them. 'That's right, you bone idle do-nothings. You can come back for these, for you'll carry him to the gatehouse, that's what you'll do.'

Melusine jumped. 'The gatehouse? But why must you move him at all?'

'Listen, missie. If you can't see as how there ain't nothing in this barrack of a place to help me do the job, I can. Water I need. Clean water. A handy knife, and a good tot of something sharp to clean out the wound. Blue Ruin will do the job nicely. Ah, and put him under if he wakes up. Now I ain't saying as how that there Pottiswick—'

'How you talk,' interrupted Melusine impatiently. She pushed at the closer of the two soldiers bearing the precious burden. 'Go then. At once. If it is that you need these things, then of course we will go there.'

'Get going, then,' Trodger told his men.

Next moment, he had Melusine by the arm. 'Now then, missie. You'll come along of me, for you're under arrest, too.'

'Pah! Your major will say something to this. But you need not fear,' she added, shaking him off. 'Do not imagine that I will leave poor Jacques. I will go with you.'

'Can't say as I'm sorry to hear you say that, missie,' confessed the sergeant, on a relieved note, as he locked the front door of the mansion and pocketed the key. 'Couldn't reconcile it with my dooty to leave you here—'

A thought made Melusine stop dead, turning to him. 'You did not find Gosse, that is seen, but—'

'Gosse? Gosse? Who's this here Gosse then?'

'He is the Frenchman of whom I told you. You did not find him, but did you find his pistol? In the room beyond the bookroom there—a big room where a table had fallen. And a broken picture that was torn when I hit him with it.'

'Woof!' Sergeant Trodger's eyes fairly popped out of his head, and he seized his prisoner's arm again. 'Seems to me, missie, as you're as dangerous a female as I'm like to see. Pistols and pictures? Now it fair goes agin' me nature to act rough with a lady, but you'll come along of me at once. I got to have you under guard in the gatehouse, I can see that.'

Melusine gave it up. There was nothing to be got out of the man. 'Certainly you may have me under guard. I do not care in the least. Only that you will hurry and help Jacques.'

In the cosy little parlour that Pottiswick rarely used, Melusine paced restlessly to and fro. She had removed her hat and utterly disarranged her already unruly black locks by running agitated fingers through them. Outside the door stood one of the soldiers. The other was helping Trodger with his operation upstairs.

In truth, she had been quite glad to lose the argument about remaining while the bullet was dug out of Jack's side. She was not squeamish—although the sight of the sergeant's ominous preparations had severely tried her fortitude—but Kimble's white face plagued her conscience. She allowed herself to be ejected, therefore, and retired to the parlour after cleansing the blood from her hands and her own slight wound in the kitchen.

With the immediate necessities in train, Melusine fell to brooding on her situation, which she found insupportable. With Jack so badly injured, how would she get him home? How get herself home, now that Trodger had arrested her. What of Gosse, whom those soldiers had allowed to escape? Hiding —or perhaps gone. Then there was also the horse. *Peste*, but everything had become difficult. And all to find that picture of Mary Remenham.

The thought of the picture but added to her despondency. The sergeant had not seen it for he understood nothing of what she told him. What had happened to it? She had broken it, certainly. And severely hurt that pig, which was a very good thing. But it was her proof. Had Gosse taken it as he escaped? What could she do? Gosse now knew that she was the daughter of Mary Remenham. If he wished, he could even take this inheritance from her.

For the first time, Melusine heartily regretted her rejection of the major's services. She cursed herself for a fool. Was not Gerald altogether on her side? He was, even though he played games like an *imbecile*, a person *tout à fait sympathique* as she had discovered at the outset. And what did she do? Not only did she cut his hand in her rage, but she refused to let him help her, and then she ran away from him. Of a certainty, she also was *imbecile*. Or mad, just as the captain had said so many times. For was not Gerald a gentleman? An Englishman, whose services any female—excluding her own self so *idiote*—would be very happy to have.

Her eyes filled as she thought of him, the image of his laughing countenance coming into her mind, to be swiftly followed by a vision of the blood running from his cut hand. A hollow feeling opened up inside her, and she felt her heartbeat quicken.

She would write to Gerald. He would come swiftly to her aid, she knew it. For she needed him. How she needed him!

Next moment, she had wrenched open the door, and was confronting her guard. 'You! Tell this fool who is the keeper here to come to me at once.'

'Miss?' gaped the soldier.

'The old man who lives here, *idiot*.'

'Pottiswick, you mean, miss?'

'Yes, yes. Go quickly and call him.'

'But I can't leave you, miss.'

'Pah! Do you think I will run away? Do not be so foolish, and go and fetch him this instant.'

Thus adjured, but mindful of Trodger's orders, the militiaman went down the hall backwards, his eyes fixed on the prisoner. At the door to the kitchen, he called out, 'Pottiswick!'

The old man came out, shoving his chin in the air and glaring. 'Now what?'

The guard jerked his head up the corridor. 'She wants you.'

Melusine caught the fellow eyeing her with resentment and beckoned as she called out to him. 'You! Have you pen and paper?'

'Pen and paper now, is it?' grumbled the old man as he shuffled down the hall. 'Ain't enough as my bed is took, my sheets all bloodied, and my gin took for to waste on that fellow's wound. Ain't enough as I've got militiamen quartered on me this se'en-night, lazing about all day, eating me out of house and home and drinking my liquor into the bargain. Nor as I've to put up with a French spy in my parlour—'

'*Peste*, how you talk,' interrupted Melusine impatiently, barely taking in his complaints. 'Pen and paper, do you have them?'

'Danged if I have,' came the truculent response. 'What was you wanting it for, may I ask?'

'You may not ask, for it is none of your affair,' Melusine snapped. 'But I will tell you this, *mon vieux*. The day comes when you shall regret how you have spoken to me.'

Pottiswick sucked at his teeth through the gaps. 'Don't rightly know how you make that out, you being a French spy and a prisoner and all.'

'I will tell you how I make that out,' Melusine said fiercely. 'Me, I am Mademoiselle Charvill, the granddaughter of Monsieur Jar-vis Re-men-ham.'

'You ain't never,' gasped Pottiswick. 'Danged if I ever hear the like! A Frenchie is what you are, and there ain't no granddaughter Charvill no more. Not these twenty year.'

'That is what you think? *Eh bien*. You have a daughter, no? Madame Ibstock, I think.'

The lodgekeeper's jaw fell open. 'Who telled you that?'

'Do not ask me impertinent questions, but only go you and fetch this daughter here to me. At once.'

The old man simply stared at her. 'Danged if I ever hear the like,' he repeated blankly.

'*Parbleu*, you are deaf perhaps? It is seen that you are very old, certainly.'

Colour suffused the man's face. 'Deaf? Deaf? I'll have you know, miss—'

'Do not have me know anything,' interrupted Melusine crossly, and digging into her habit, produced the fateful dagger that had cut Gerald's hand. 'To the contrary, I will have you to know something. You will do as I say, or—'

'Hoy!' called Trodger from down the hall. 'You put that thing away now, missie. We don't want no trouble, do we?'

At sight of him, everything went out of Melusine's head but the thought of Jack Kimble. She started forward.

'Jacques? You have done it? He is alive?'

'Oh, he's alive, all right,' confirmed the sergeant, putting the petrified Pottiswick—stockstill and staring in horror at the dagger—firmly out of his way and taking his place before Melusine. 'Sleeping like a baby, he is. He'll do.'

Melusine sank against the wall of the corridor, closing her eyes. '*Merci, dieu.*'

'Now then, missie,' began the sergeant severely, 'just you hand over that dagger. Nice goings on. Ladies with weapon's on 'em.' He took the thing from Melusine's listless grasp and went on, 'Now then, what's all this here argy-bargy with Pottiswick?'

Melusine opened her eyes and straightened up. She had hardly noticed the loss of her dagger, so strong had been the waves of relief that attacked her on hearing that Jack had returned from death's door. But this was important.

'*Bon*. You will make him get his daughter, if you please. She is called Madame Ibstock, you understand.'

'Is she now? And what would you be wanting of her, may I ask?'

'Because she knows something that may make this fool understand that I am the mistress of—' She broke off. There was no sense in creating further difficulties for herself by arguing with the sergeant over her identity. An admirable alternative presented itself and she sighed, spreading her hands. 'You see, it is that I am a female, and you all are men. It is not at all *comme il faut*.'

Trodger frowned, and chewed his lip. 'Something in that, missie. But I'm thinking as how I'd best report to the major over this here shooting.'

'Yes, do so,' rejoined Melusine enthusiastically. '*En effet*, it is for this that I was enquiring of this man if he has pen and paper. I will write to your major, and you will send the letter very quickly. Also, you must send someone to fetch my horse— at least, it is not mine but I have borrowed it to come here—because it will be dark very soon and —'

'Woof! Hold it, hold it,' begged the sergeant. 'One thing at a time, missie.' He turned to the lodgekeeper behind him, whose shocked fear had given place to a direful frown. 'Here you, Pottiswick. Get pen and paper for the missie. Then go and fetch this daughter of yourn. Don't stand gawping, man. And you'd better have her fetch in some food for the missie, an' all. Get on, do.'

He gave the gaping Pottiswick a shove, passing him on to his junior, who was waiting patiently by the kitchen door. The militiaman at once thrust the old man between the shoulder blades, pushing him into the kitchen.

Melusine soon found herself seated at a table, with a dirty piece of paper in front of her, and a badly mended pen between her fingers. The ink, contained in a grimy bottle unearthed in the outhouse, was old, and made blotches as soon as it touched the paper. But it would serve.

Mon cher major, Melusine began. And then scratched it out and wrote instead, "Gérard". She sat in deep thought for a moment or two, and then nodding briskly, dipped the pen in the ink again and began to write.

"Jacques is wounded and we are arrested by this imbecile of a sergeant. The *soi-disant* Valade escapes and takes my proof, which I have broken on his head. Hurry to me, I entreat you. Never did I need a rescue so much. It is at the lodge that we stay. I pray you, Gérard, do not fail me. *Á bientot*—Melusine."

To her relief, Trodger sent one of his men posthaste to London with this missive, while the other went to fetch the horse, having been given precise directions on how to negotiate the passage so that he might find it at the other end. The old man Pottiswick, still grumbling, much to Melusine's disgust, had gone on his errand to his daughter's house some two miles distant. And the sergeant, having carried out all Melusine's instructions as if they had come out of his own head, went up to check on his patient, apparently at last convinced that his prisoner would not attempt to run away.

Nothing could have been farther from Melusine's mind. She had come to the end of her resources. It had been a trying day. She was tired, hungry—and thus somewhat impatient for the food Mrs Ibstock might bring—and downcast.

She sat in a chair in the parlour and regarded the darkening sky through the small casement window. It seemed to her at this moment that there was nothing left for her to do. Gosse, if he had any sense, would immediately seek out the Remenham lawyers. Once he had managed to stake his claim, she would have all to do to prove her identity and win it back. If only *monsieur le baron* had said nothing, or perhaps instead accepted the couple as the Valades and agreed to help them. Not that there had ever been any hope of that. She had told Emile. She had warned him.

Her mind wandered back to that fateful day. Was it a week ago? No, perhaps more. Time was moving so fast, she could no longer count the days since Gosse had come to her with his preposterous suggestion at the *Coq d'Or*, where they were staying and where he had robbed her and left her and Martha to their fate.

'Mademoiselle,' he had greeted her, entering the little private parlour where, Martha being at prayer in their room, she sat alone, reading over and over the letter Mother Abbess had given her and revolving plans in her head.

She had looked up from her seat at the small round table in the centre of the parlour which, together with the wooden armchairs beside the small fireplace, and a sideboard next the single casement, was all the furniture the place afforded. Melusine, used to the stark surroundings of the convent at Blaye, had no complaint to make. Her desires were not for riches. Only identity, and a chance to be someone other than a nun.

Not so Gosse. But at this point he was still subservient, still outwardly humble, in spite of the blackhearted villainy that was even then burgeoning in his breast.

'Mademoiselle, there is a way to win to freedom and prosperity.'

To be sure there was a way. For freedom at least. Why did he imagine she was making this journey to England? She feigned interest.

'But what way, Emile?'

'Your family, mademoiselle, the family of your father.'

'You mean *monsieur le baron*, the General Charvill, my grandfather?'

Melusine laid aside on the table the letter she had been studying and turned so that the frame of her nun's wimple no longer obscured her view.

'*Pardon*, mademoiselle, but perhaps your father went to England, after all, and—'

'My father went to Italy,' interrupted Melusine, her heart tightening with the familiar sensation of loss. 'Never would he have gone to England. And if you mean that he may have reconciled himself with his own father, you waste your breath.'

'That was not what I had in mind.'

'*Eh bien*, what then?'

Emile sidled closer. 'To what do you go, mademoiselle? The life of a nun in a convent, in a country where nuns are unwelcome. Where even to be a Catholic, they say, is to be looked upon with scorn and disgust.'

Melusine shrugged. She had no intention whatsoever of spending her life in a convent, but that was not his affair.

'It is the life I know.'

'But you must want more. You should have more.'

'I am going to England,' Melusine stated flatly, 'because there is no safety at the convent at Blaye. And for that I am connected with the Valades, after what you have told us has happened to them, the Mother Abbess will not consent that I remain in France. *Voilà tout.*'

The Mother Abbess—and indeed all the nuns, some of higher birth more fearful than others— were aghast at the horrors that had befallen the family Valade. Gosse had come to Blaye, so he had said, feeling it his duty as the vicomte's erstwhile secretary to deliver the fateful tidings, bringing with him one of the servant girls, Yolande, who had also escaped the fury of the mob. Her evident terror and distress reinforced the tale he told.

He had drawn a horrid picture of the fate that awaited mademoiselle when once the populace discovered her relationship to the Valade family. Too close, he reasoned, for safety. He had offered to escort the young lady to England where she might seek refuge with her relations there, and proposed that the maid Yolande might serve Miss Charvill.

The Mother Abbess, while thankful, could not be brought to consent to allow the girl out of her charge alone with unknown servants, and Martha was delegated to accompany her erstwhile nurseling to the homeland she had thought never to see again.

'You do not want to be a nun,' he said now, and Melusine noted with a prick at her senses the irritation in his tone.

She had not felt comfortable in his presence from the first, and with Leonardo's precepts in mind, was loath to trust him. She did not therefore reveal to him that he had guaged her with accuracy. She fluttered her eyelashes, and adopted the soulful tone that served her well at times.

'It is what my father intended. I must obey.'

To her astonishment, Gosse's servile attitude vanished abruptly. Grasping one of chairs about the little table, he drew it forward and sat astride it, in a fashion as insolent as it was unexpected.

'You wish a life of obedience? So be it, Mademoiselle Charvill.'

Melusine's instant annoyance must have shown in her face.

'Do not look at me so,' he snapped. 'I may have been only a secretary, but times are changing. I am not of the *canaille*, but a *bourgeois*. There is no future for me here. I wish to rise in the world, mademoiselle, and you are going to help me.'

Amazed, Melusine stared at him. Caution forced her to speak calmly.

'I fear you mistake, Emile. I have said that I am but a nun now.'

'You need not be a nun,' he said, leaning towards her. 'You have the means to take up your rightful place.'

Melusine's eyes narrowed and she drew back. He could not know about the Remenham connection, could he? No one knew but her father and Martha.

'What do you mean?'

'You have papers of identity, for the Mother Abbess told me so.'

Melusine frowned, placing her hand on the letter lying on the table. Then she cursed herself for his eyes went to the letter and came back to her face.

'And so?' she asked.

'And so also have I.' He reached into an inner pocket of his coat and brought out a packet of papers. Out of these he selected a faded parchment and restored the rest to safety. He then unfolded his choice and held it before her face. 'This, as you see, is an identity for your cousin, André Valade. I do not choose the vicomte, for that would be foolish. His heir is dead, yes, and his name and title available to me. But it would be too risky. The vicomte must be well known to those high-born who have gone to England. Besides, I do not want a price on my head.'

Melusine was beginning to fill with dread and a burgeoning of anger as the meaning behind his words began to penetrate. But she veiled her feelings.

'I do not understand you.'

'Listen. I can be a gentleman. I have been around them for long enough. Who is to say that I am not André Valade, an obscure relation of the late vicomte.'

Melusine remembered a thin man of sour aspect, living—like her father and his wife Suzanne—off the vicomte's bounty. He must be more or less of an age with this man. Rage flooded her at his intent, but she controlled it.

'You will take the place of André?'

'Exactly so. And you, Mademoiselle Melusine, will support this claim.'

'From a convent? Even if I wished to do it, I could not.'

Emile reached out both hands and grasped her shoulders. 'But you will not be in a convent. You will be with me. You will be—my wife.'

For a moment Melusine stared at him as she took in the full horror of his scheme. Then fury claimed her and she could no longer pretend. Wrenching his hands from her shoulders, she thrust them away and leapt up from the chair.

'Your *wife*?'

'My wife,' he repeated, rising also, his smile mocking her. 'Is it such a terrible prospect? I will take care of you—as long as you obey me. I will make your grandfather extend to you his protection, and his support.'

'It is money you mean, no?' Melusine asked with scorn. 'You are mad, if you think he will give you a sou. You do not know him. And you think I would marry you?'

'Why not? I am unworthy, eh? Because I am a servant.'

'Because you are a pig!' retorted Melusine hotly.

'Nevertheless, you will marry me,' he snarled. 'I have the means to compel you.'

'Compel me? You do not know me, monsieur.'

'And you do not know me. Do not underestimate my power. I have been the vicomte's secretary, remember.'

Shock suspended Melusine's breath and she gasped. 'You have rifled his papers.'

'He had no further need of them,' Gosse said and his laugh sounded heartless to Melusine. 'Whereas my need was very great indeed. Do not mistake me. I have proofs of many things that can endanger you. Believe me, it will be better by far that you should consent to marry me.'

'I do not marry a man who makes me a threat like this,' she flashed. 'A man who is false, who steals papers, who has a plot to take another's name, who lies to the Mother Abbess and to me, and above all this—' her voice near to breaking '—one *who is French.*'

Gosse blinked. 'French? But what else?'

'I do not like Frenchmen,' Melusine snapped. 'Least of all, one who takes advantage of another's misfortune. You disgust me.'

Emile's eyes blazed. 'I disgust you, eh? Very well, then. You may enjoy your pride, your arrogance— in a coffin.'

'*Comment*? How will it serve you to kill me?'

'I do not need to kill you. I have only to denounce you as a member of the family Valade.'

Melusine gasped. But what a monster was this Emile. He would condemn her to the vengeance of the mob all for refusing to marry him. But she did not believe he would do that. It hardly served his interests.

'And then you will be obliged to remain in France,' she pointed out. 'You cannot be André Valade if you tell them I am one of this family.'

For a moment he looked daunted. Then he rallied, smiling a little. 'Come, mademoiselle. You have not considered the advantages.'

Melusine bit her lip on a sharp retort. That would not help her. The man was dangerous. She prevaricated.

'*Alors*, what advantages?'

'But think,' he said earnestly, moving a little closer. 'As Madame Valade, you will be an *émigré*, not a nun. That is what they call these aristocratic refugees, the English. As such, you may command the sympathies of the gentry. I hear they are very much affected by the tragedies of their neighbours in France. You will join a world of fashion, a world of wealth, a life of ease.'

'A life of ease?' repeated Melusine. 'When one is penniless, one does not expect a life of ease.'

'Ah, but why remain penniless? After all, your grandfather Charvill—'

'Again with the grandfather? *Mon ami*, if you imagine that this grandfather will welcome a daughter of Nicholas Charvill, whom he has never forgiven that he married a Frenchwoman, then you have an imagination entirely wrong.'

'But it was not your fault,' protested Gosse, shocked.

'That is true,' Melusine conceded. 'Nevertheless, he will neither help me, nor will I seek his help.'

'But if I am with you, as André Valade, as your husband, an *émigré*—'

'Pah!' Melusine spat. 'Never. This is a plot entirely abominable, and I scorn to be part of it.'

'Then you will die at the hands of the *canaille*.'

'Better than to live at the hands of a villainous blackmailer,' Melusine threw at him.

'*Sapristi*,' he shouted angrily. 'Obstinate fool!'

She saw Gosse raise a hand, and dug into her nun's habit for the knife she had not thought to need. Too late. Emile's fist crashed into her temple and stars exploded in her vision.

When she came to, she was lying with her head in Martha's lap, and a livid bruise was forming at the point of a raging headache.

'The man's gone,' her old nurse told her, when she had recovered a little. 'Taken the girl with him.'

'Yolande, my maid?'

'You don't need a maid,' Martha said stoutly. 'Not where we're going.'

'Where are we going?'

'Back to Blaye, my girl. Can't travel alone, a pair of nuns.'

'Back?' Melusine put a hand to her aching temple. 'No, I do not go back. Never. You may go back, Marthe. But me, I am going to England.'

'Don't talk soft,' begged Martha. 'You can't go to England. Leastways, not on your own. How will we get there, I'd like to know? We've no money. The rogue took everything we had.'

Melusine cursed Emile roundly, but raised a defiant head. 'Then we will beg. We are nuns. At least, you are one, and I am disguised like one. We will beg our bread and our shelter, and our passage on a boat. But to England we will go.'

Not all the arguments Martha advanced, and they were many and varied, had the power to move Melusine. Although Martha did not know it, she had her pistol and her daggers, and her knife. More importantly, she had her wits. Vitally, she had the letter that proved her identity as a Charvill: the one her father had written to the Abbess when he sent her to the convent.

Only she hadn't. When her shock and the headache subsided, and she remembered that she had been reading the letter when Gosse had accosted her, she looked for it in vain. It had gone with the rest.

She had not thought anything could equal her despair at that moment. Almost had Martha won out. But Melusine had overcome the weakness, calling the loss but a temporary setback. She had braved all obstacles to pursue her dream. Arrived in England, she had sought out Gosse, to keep an eye on his activities and thus keep one step ahead of him, meanwhile hoping that she might find herself another means of proof at Remenham House.

Melusine came back to the present to discover that tears were rolling down her cheeks. She had found that proof. And now the fiend Gosse had taken even that away from her. This time she was indeed beaten.

The tears flowed faster. Melusine dashed them away, but they kept on coming. *Peste*, where was her handkerchief? She remembered then that it had been lost in the struggle with Gerald. At the thought of the major, her tears redoubled and she was obliged to rip off a piece from the remnants of her already maltreated under-petticoats with which to blow her nose and soak the damp from her cheeks.

If only Gerald would come. Even that he was an interfering person, if he walked through that door this moment, she would fling herself at him and weep all over his chest.

Bête, she told herself fiercely. *Imbecile. Idiote.* What need had she of Gerald, or anyone? Yet, if he was here, would he not make some foolish game with her and make her laugh? Instead of behaving in this fashion so *stupide*, and crying, crying, crying.

She had recourse to the torn off strip of petticoat again, and blowing her nose with an air of determination, sniffed back the tears.

A sudden knock at the door startled her. Gerald?
But could he be here so quickly?

She hastily dabbed at her eyes, thankful for the
darkness that she saw had come on outside un-
noticed, dimming the room.

'Come,' she called.

The door opened. A stout female stood in the
aperture, an oil lamp in her hand. She came into the
room. A middle-aged countrywoman, plump of
cheek, and a little shy. She held up the lamp.

'Beg pardon, miss, but I'm told as how—' She
broke off, her eyes widening, her jaw dropping
open.

All at once Melusine remembered Pottiswick,
and the errand he had run.

'You are Mrs Ibstock, I think,' she said eagerly.

Pottiswick's daughter found her tongue. 'Lawks-
a-mussy! It's Miss Mary. Miss Mary to the life.'

CHAPTER NINE

As she devoured the simple meal of bread and cheese, and several slices of cold roast beef, the whole washed down with a poor sort of coffee, Melusine listened with avid interest to the details of her mother's life as revealed by the exclamatory conversation of Joan Ibstock. This forthright dame was so excited, she could not keep still, but paced about the parlour much as Melusine had done earlier.

'Well, what was I to think, miss? Martha never wrote nothing about you, and I did ask.'

'You see,' Melusine explained between mouthfuls of food, 'poor Marthe had promised to my father that she will say nothing. She broke this promise when she told me that my mother was this Mary, and not Suzanne Valade at all.'

'But she must have known I'd longed to hear of you. When mistress took and died—' Joan broke off and sighed, moving away to the window. 'Well, water under the bridge is that, miss. Anyhow, it were me as got you down to the wet-nurse. Come every day to see you was flourishing. On the orders of Mr Jarvis, that were. But I'd have done it without, though it weren't my place. Only an under-maid I was then. But Miss Mary and me—'

Melusine looked up as the woman broke off again. She smiled encouragingly, laying aside her plate and turning her chair from the table.

'You knew her well, Miss Mary?'

Mrs Ibstock turned at the window. 'We was of an age, you see, miss. Used to play together, we did, all over Remenham House. Miss Mary and me, and Martha too sometimes. Oh, Mr Jarvis paid no mind,' she added hastily, as if expecting disapproval. 'That there governess didn't like it, of course, me being the lodgekeeper's girl, and Martha just a country wench like me. Her pa was only the smithy. T'weren't fitting, we knew that. But Mr Jarvis said as how Miss Mary not having no brothers and sisters like, it were good to have friends.'

'I see now how it was that Marthe knew of the secret passage,' Melusine said.

'Oh, we was always in there, miss,' admitted Joan, moving closer. She shuddered, adding confidentially, 'You wouldn't get me in there now, mind. Nasty, damp passages. Rats and things crawling all over. Horrid!'

'Yes, but it has been extremely useful for me,' argued Melusine, 'so that I am very much pleased with this passage.'

'Fancy my old pa thinking you was a French spy. Though he never seen so much of Miss Mary as I did. Mind, when we were all growed up, it were different. And when she took and married that Mr Charvill, we didn't think to see her at Remenham House no more.'

'But you say that I was born here,' objected Melusine. 'Certainly you must have seen her.'

Mrs Ibstock's lips tightened and she looked away a moment. 'Yes, miss. She come home within a few months of the wedding. She were that miserable.'

Melusine rose from her chair in sudden irritation. 'Oh, *peste*. I know why. For that my father so *stupide* was in love with this Suzanne Valade, is it not?'

'Well, miss,' temporised Mrs Ibstock, 'we didn't rightly know that then. For he come after her, did Mr Charvill. And a right set-to there were betwixt him and Mr Jarvis, I can tell you. Miss Mary being his only child 'an all, he were in a right pelter.'

Melusine could not suppress a smile. 'And with my grandfather Charvill also so very angry, it was not perhaps so very comfortable for my father.'

'Between the devil and the deep blue sea, he were,' agreed Pottiswick's daughter. 'Small wonder in a way that he found hisself consolation elsewhere.'

Melusine sobered, sitting down again. 'Yes, only that this consolation he had found before he married my mother. This I know for at the Valade estate it was talked of very much, even that they supposed me there to be the daughter of Suzanne.'

'But you don't look anything like her,' burst out Mrs Ibstock.

'*Comment*? You have then met this Suzanne?'

The woman turned a deep red. 'It weren't my wish, miss, I can tell you that. Only your pa knew as how I were the one as saw to you at the wet-nurse's cottage, and he got a-hold of me and made me bring him to you.'

'*Eh bien?* And so?'

'He says as how he's going to take you with him to France with his new wife.' Joan sniffed. 'Well! I hadn't no notion as he'd got hisself married again. I didn't believe him and I said so. I said as how I'd tell Mr Jarvis as he wanted to take you away. So he bring me to see this Suzanne, who were staying at an inn nearby.'

'But it is *imbecile*,' interrupted Melusine, struck by the impracticalities of her father's scheme. 'To take a baby all the way to France without a wet-nurse.'

'That's just it,' said Joan Ibstock shamefacedly. She went across to the little window again, her back to Melusine. 'He arst me to find him someone who might go with you. I'm that shamed to confess it, miss, but it were then I thought of Martha.'

Melusine stared. 'Martha was my wet-nurse? But she is unmarried.'

Joan nodded, her face still averted. 'Aye, that she was. Fell to sin, did Martha. Took and ran away when she got herself with child. Only she sent me a message, and together we found a cottage for her to stay at. An old woman took her in. She were brought to bed a few days after Miss Mary. Only her babe died. And so—'

'And so she was able to become my—' Melusine did not say it, for wet-nurse no longer seemed appropriate. Martha had been more to her than that.

'It was a good chance for a new life,' Joan explained, venturing to face Melusine again, 'and Martha took it. Small blame to her. But we were both pledged to secrecy, and I couldn't reveal my part for fear that I would lose my place. For Mr Jarvis was beside himself when the letter come from Mr Charvill and he knew he'd lost you as well as Miss Mary.' Tears glistened in her eyes. 'He'd have been that happy if he'd known how you're the spit of her, miss.'

Melusine jumped up, full of new hope, all the earlier clouds vanishing from her horizon. 'But this is altogether a chance of the luckiest. You will be my witness, Madame Joan. When I shall go to the lawyers that have the interest of this estate Remenham, you will come with me.'

'Me, miss?' uttered Mrs Ibstock doubtfully. 'Who'd believe me? And I'd have to tell my part in it all, too.'

'What matters it?' cried Melusine impatiently. 'Who is to be angry with you now?'

'Miss Prudence, that's who,' stated Joan bluntly. 'What's more, I wouldn't blame her.'

Arrested, Melusine eyed her with interest. 'Prudence? This name I have heard it spoken. It is a very good English name, no? But who is she?'

'Mrs Sindlesham, I should say,' said Mrs Ibstock, correcting herself. 'And she's——' She broke off, a sudden light in her eyes. 'Why, that's it. That's who you ought to go and see, miss.'

'Who, Joan, who? Of whom do you speak?'

'Mrs Sindlesham. Mr Jarvis's sister, that was. Leastways, she'd be your great-aunt, wouldn't she?'

Astounded, Melusine was just about to demand further information, when a commotion outside the room interrupted her. She turned towards the door, and had taken a pace towards it when it was flung open.

Captain Roding strode into the parlour. He was no longer in military uniform, and it was evident from his suit of brown brocade that he had been disturbed while preparing for an evening engagement.

Without preamble, in a voice of extreme exasperation, he demanded, 'Now what the devil's to do? What in God's name do you mean by sending Gerald such a ridiculous letter? Never read anything half as crazy. What do you mean by it, eh?'

'But I did not send it to you,' Melusine rejoined instantly. 'Where is Gérard?'

'Out of town,' Hilary said briefly. 'And I'd like to know what the devil—'

'Out of town?' repeated Melusine, stupefied. '*Parbleu*, is this a moment to be out of town? What is the matter with him that he is out of town when I need him?'

'Famous!' uttered a new voice from the doorway. 'I knew you would be furious. Did I not say so, Hilary?'

Melusine's glance shot across to the newcomer, and found a petite blonde standing there, very fashionably attired in a velvet mantel over an apple-green robe, the furred hood framing a face alive with mischief. She came quickly into the little parlour, which now seemed inordinately crowded, and coming up to Melusine, seized her hands in a warm clasp.

'How do you do? I am so happy to meet you. I am Lucilla Froxfield, you must know. I am betrothed to Captain Roding, which is why you can't have him, you see.' She smiled on the last words, adding, 'Oh, I don't blame you for trying. He is delightful, is he not?'

'That will do, Lucilla.'

Melusine found her tongue. 'If you mean this *capitaine*, he is on the contrary altogether the least delightful person I have met.'

'What, even less delightful than Gerald?' enquired Lucilla, her eyes dancing.

'As to that, I am at this moment altogether displeased with Gérard, you understand,' Melusine temporised.

'I rather gathered as much,' said Miss Froxfield, releasing her hands. 'And I do understand. Quite trying of him not to be there when he is wanted. But that is men all over.'

'Yes, and it seems to me a very strange thing that he interferes all the time in my affairs when I do not want him to do so,' Melusine said aggrievedly, 'and the very first time that I wish him in truth to rescue me, he is not there. *Parbleu*, but I will certainly kill him this time.'

A peal of delighted laughter greeted this threat. 'Yes, do,' approved Lucilla. 'Will you—what was it? —"blow off his head"?'

Melusine eyed her, a little uncertain. 'You make a game with me, I think.'

'No, no,' the other lady assured her with a twinkle. 'I can't tell you the times I've wished for a gun to point at Hilary's head. Perhaps I may borrow yours one day?'

'Lucilla, you wretch,' burst from the captain.

'But she will not shoot you,' Melusine told him flatly. 'One does not blow off the head of a man with whom one is in love, *en effet*.'

'Don't be too sure,' said Miss Froxfield darkly, with a mischievous glance at her betrothed.

'I can't help but be sure,' he returned shortly. 'You wouldn't know one end of a pistol from the other.' He turned to Melusine, ignoring the indignant protest that greeted his words. 'And it may interest you to know, mademoiselle, that the first thing Gerald must needs do on reaching town is to rush off to that convent of yours to make sure you were safe.'

'Truly?' asked Melusine, warmth lighting her bosom. 'But I was not there.'

'Of course you weren't there,' snapped Hilary. 'Knew you had the lad with you, and thought you were merely delayed. So he made his dispositions and went off on some other fool's errand.'

'But what dispositions?'

'Posted the men I had brought back with me all about Golden Square to watch for Valade.'

'Ah, that was well done of him,' exclaimed Melusine. 'In this case, I will not kill him at all, even that he should have remained to wait for my letter.'

'Well, I am glad he did not,' intervened Lucilla, forestalling another withering comment from the captain. 'For your messenger was obliged instead to come and find Hilary, and it has given me the opportunity to meet you. And I have wanted to so very much.'

'But why?' asked Melusine, astonished, and somewhat overwhelmed by the other girl's volubility.

'Don't be silly. Such a mystery as you have set up. Anyone would be intrigued.'

'Yes, but I do not wish to have a mystery.'

'It cannot be helped now. Oh, and only look at those stains,' cried Miss Froxfield, gesturing at the blood on the ruffles to the sleeves of Melusine's riding-habit, and on the chemise she wore under it.

Melusine shrugged. 'It is nothing. One little minute with soap and water, *voilà tout*.'

'Glad you're so sanguine,' interrupted Captain Roding. 'Gerald had to change both shirt and breeches.'

The reference to Major Alderley's wounds reminded Melusine all at once of the fight they'd had, and its consequence. *Peste,* she had forgot the sword. What was to happen now? She turned to Roding quickly.

'You have come to me in place of Gérard? But how is it you will help me?'

'That's all right and tight. We've brought a carriage to take you back to London, and I've settled with Trodger, who has just given me a coherent account of the affair. You're neither of you any longer under arrest.'

'Ah, then indeed I thank you,' said Melusine on a sigh of relief, moved for once to smile at the captain. 'But my poor Jacques is wounded and—'

'All taken care of,' interrupted Hilary. 'There's a surgeon on his way, and my men are under orders to do whatever is needful. When the lad is fit to be moved, we'll bring him home.'

Melusine blinked at this competence. 'But—'

'Nothing at all for you to worry your head over,' said the captain, moving to try and usher her forth. 'You'll come with us and get yourself safe back home to your convent, understand?'

'But wait,' begged Melusine, hanging back. 'First I must see Jacques, and—'

'No need for that,' intervened Roding, grasping her arm and trying to drag her to the door. 'Come along. Where is your hat?'

'*Parbleu*, is this a way to rescue me?' Melusine demanded, digging in her heels and wrenching her arm out of his hold. 'I have first some affairs to finish.'

'Yes, Hilary, do stop hustling the girl,' put in Miss Froxfield, much to Melusine's relief and approval. Shoving between them, she confronted the captain herself. 'For my part, I am in no hurry to end this exciting little adventure.'

'Adventure!'

But this sally was not attended to, Lucilla turning at once to Melusine. She put back her hood in a determined way. 'Go on up to the boy, my dear. I will hold Hilary in check, never fear.'

'*Merci.*'

About to hurry from the little parlour, Melusine remembered Mrs Ibstock. She whipped round suddenly, and discovered the woman wedged into the corner by the window, keeping out of the way.

'Ah, Madame Joan. This woman knows me—' throwing the remark at Lucilla '—and that I am the daughter of Mary Remenham. It is very important because I have lost my proof. She will tell you all the story while I am gone.'

Then she whisked from the room, hearing Lucilla utter a delighted squeal as she closed the door behind her. This Joan would hold them for a little. Enough to let her find out a piece of information most urgent.

Trodger was lying in wait at the bottom of the narrow stairs. 'Now then, missie, where do you think you're going?'

'I must see Jacques only for one little minute,' Melusine told him prettily, fluttering her lashes. 'It is to say goodbye, you understand.'

'Is it, now? Well you won't, then, for he won't hear nothing, missie. Fast asleep, he is.'

Melusine spread her hands and sighed. 'But you do not understand, *mon ami*. Even that he sleeps, I must give to him my thanks, for he has been excessively brave for me.'

The sergeant's air became positively avuncular. 'Ah, trying to be the young hero, I take it, which is why he near got hisself killed. Many's the young 'un I've seen get hisself into just such a knuckleheaded mess all on account of a pretty wench.'

'But I find it was extremely kind of him,' protested Melusine, 'and since it is that he is not any more under arrest—'

'No, he ain't,' interrupted Trodger in some dudgeon. 'And I don't mind telling you it goes agin' the grain with me to let you go free and all, missie.'

'But I have told you that your *capitaine* would not like it that you arrest me.'

'Now that's where you're wrong. Left to Capting Roding, as he told me hisself, you'd be in prison this moment. Only the major won't have it, and we've to bide by what the major says.'

'*Merci*, Gérard,' Melusine muttered under her breath, adding aloud, 'And the major, he will also wish that you let me go to see Jacques. Please to let me go there.'

Grudgingly, the sergeant shifted aside and allowed her access to the stairs, grumbling to her retreating back, 'If I'd me way, missie, I'd send you back to France where you ought never to have come away from, if you arst me.'

Melusine might have responded that she had not asked him, but she was too intent on her mission. She must speak to Jack. If he was asleep, then she much regretted that she must wake him up.

In fact, Kimble was drowsily awake when she entered the little bedchamber, the state of which left a good deal to be desired, even without the added debris arising from tending a wounded man. It was dusty, with dirty clothing strewn about, a cracked basin thick with grime on the rickety dresser, and a film of grease on the leaded casement.

Melusine, intent on the luckless Kimble, did not care. At sight of his wan features, she forgot the urgency of her need for a moment, and fell to her knees at his bedside, placing her hands on his slack ones where they lay on the soiled coverlet.

'Oh, Jacques, I cannot forgive myself!'

'Never you fret, miss,' he uttered at once in a faint voice. 'Ain't no call for you to go a-blaming of yourself.'

'I thought you were dead,' Melusine confided. 'And all to help me.'

'Not dead, miss. And I'd do it again for you if needs be.'

'Do not say so. You are to remain here until you are well. That *capitaine* has arranged it all. *En tout cas*, I will not permit that you endanger yourself again for me.'

'I chose to come with you, miss,' Jack interrupted more firmly. 'And I wouldn't be no sort of a man if I'd heard what I heard, and gone off and left you.'

That arrested her. 'You heard Gosse—I mean, the man you know as Valade?'

'Clear as day, miss,' he uttered. 'Brung the lantern, I did, and opened the door again in case you was ready. Heard voices. Knew something was up. You were only one room removed from the library, see. Saw the villain through the keyhole. So I come round the other way and—Lordy, miss, I'm that sorry I made a mull of it.' He shifted unguardedly, and hissed a breath, wincing.

'Do not speak any more for you give yourself pain,' said Melusine fearfully.

'I must. Something to tell you.'

'And do not say you made a mull. I find you were excessively brave, *mon pauvre*.' Then she frowned. 'You wish to tell me something? *Parbleu*, I have nearly forgot once more. Me, I have a question for you first. The sword, Jacques.'

Jack blinked at her. 'Just what I was going to tell you, miss. It's on the horse.'

'The horse?' echoed Melusine. 'But it is not on the horse at all, Jacques. That is why I ask you. I have forgot all about the sword until the *capitaine* has come. But I have remembered the horse and have asked this sergeant that a soldier fetch him. I told the soldier how he must go by the passage, and he found it and brought it here. But he did not find the sword of *monsieur le major*, for this sergeant would have recognised it and told me that I am arrested again.' She stopped, for Jack was feebly laughing. 'But what is it that amuses you, Jacques?'

Kimble's grin spread wider. 'I'll wager that militiaman never rode the animal, then.'

'I do not think so,' Melusine agreed, still puzzled.

'If he had, he'd have found the sword, see. Or felt it. It's well hidden, miss. Wasn't easy, I can tell you. But I wrapped it in that nun's gear you give me. Then I tucked it nice and snug under the saddle-bag. Couldn't fit it inside, but the horse's blanket lay over it, and, like I said, as long as no one rides him and don't remove the blanket, I think it'll stay hid.'

'But you are excessively clever, Jacques,' cried Melusine, relief flooding her. 'Certainly no one will find it. I must have this beast brought to London with me, that is seen. He must be tied behind the carriage.'

She put in her request for this requirement immediately on returning to the little parlour downstairs, and instantly fell foul of Captain Roding again.

'Tie a horse behind the carriage?' he echoed incredulously. 'What the devil for? I'll have one of the men ride the creature up tomorrow.'

'But, no,' cried Melusine anxiously. 'It is excessively important that the horse comes with us.'

She saw suspicion darken his gaze. 'Why?'

Melusine eyed him dubiously. 'Pray you, do me this one little service, and do not ask me why.'

'Are you off your head? Think I don't know you're up to some mischief or other?'

Melusine feigned innocence. 'What mischief?'

'I don't know, but I'll go bail you're at something. I'm not Gerald, remember.'

'It is well seen you are not Gérard,' Melusine said, but thankful now that he was not. Gerald would certainly have demanded back his sword. Captain Roding either did not know, or did not remember that she had it. She turned to Lucilla, a plea in her face. 'Pray you, mademoiselle, can you not—'

'No use trying to enlist Lucilla's aid,' snapped Roding. 'Either you tell me why you want the wretched animal, or it stays here.'

'But, Hilary—'

'Don't you begin, Lucilla, for I won't stand for it.'

'I beg your pardon?' said Miss Froxfield frostily.

'Do not beg his pardon,' intervened Melusine quickly, coming between them. '*Eh bien*, I will tell you. You see, the horse it does not belong to me, nor to the nuns. It is the horse of the priest, you understand, and—and he does not know that I have borrowed it.'

Captain Roding stared at her, his jaw dropping, while Lucilla hastily turned away, although Melusine caught the laughter in her face.

'Do you mean to tell me,' enquired the captain at length, 'that you have had the infernal audacity, the —the gall, the—the— Gad, it's an outrage! You've stolen a horse from a *priest*?'

'I did not steal it,' protested Melusine hotly. 'I have only borrowed it.'

'Without permission.'

'*Oui, mais*—'

'You are, without exception, the most unprincipled, the most unscrupulous, the most shameless, immoral, devious—'

'Pardon me, sir,' burst in Mrs Ibstock suddenly, her tone belligerent, bringing the captain's tirade to an abrupt halt as he turned to glare at her. 'Ain't my place, I know that. But stand by and hear such things said about my late mistress's daughter, I won't.'

'Bravo,' applauded Lucilla, clapping her hands.

'*Merci*, Joan,' cried Melusine, moving to her and seizing her hand which she clasped between both her own for a moment, as she turned to the others. 'Now you see why it is I no longer require the proof of which I have spoken.'

'What is all this about your proof?' demanded Roding, diverted.

'This was a picture of Mary Remenham that I have found today. I thought it was a mirror at the first, for it was so very like myself.'

'So that was it. Couldn't make head nor tail of that note of yours. Barring that the Valade fellow had sneaked back. And I'll have that story off you as we journey back to town. How the devil did you break a picture?'

'Don't be obtuse, Hilary. She hit the villain with it. She said that in the note.'

'It's no use you being superior,' said Roding severely. 'You didn't understand it any better than I.'

'Well, I do now,' Lucilla said firmly, and turned back to Melusine. 'What did you do with the portrait then? Not that I suppose it is much use any longer. Was it ruined?'

'But yes, it was entirely ruined. And I think also that Gosse—I mean that one who calls himself Valade—stole it. Only now it does not matter at all because Joan has come and has seen me.'

'Yes,' agreed Lucilla excitedly, 'and she has been telling us how much of a friend she was to your mother. How fortunate that she recognises the resemblance.'

'Couldn't help but do so, ma'am,' said Mrs Ibstock. 'Knowed it the instant I set eyes on her. Miss Mary to the life, I said, and so she is.'

'I suppose you want to take her along as well as that infernal stolen horse?' said Hilary sarcastically.

'I have said it is not stolen,' snapped Melusine indignantly. 'And certainly I wish that Joan will come with us.'

Miss Froxfield intervened quickly as her betrothed showed signs of erupting again. 'I don't think you need do that, Melusine—if I may call you so. After all, you may easily come to fetch Mrs Ibstock when you need her. It must be some days before you can arrange for her to make an identification.'

'Yes, that is reasonable,' agreed Melusine, nodding.

Lucilla shoved Roding out of the way so that she could take hold of Melusine's hands again. 'And you know, my dear, I do think you must make up your mind to beard this wretched grandfather of yours. After all, if Valade—or no, what did you say was the villain's name?'

'Gosse,' Melusine supplied.

'Well, if the fellow Gosse is still at large, there's no saying what he will be at next, is there? I see nothing for it but for you to see General Lord Charvill at once. After all—'

'Yes, but I do not wish to see him,' Melusine protested. 'And it is perhaps not so necessary that I do so, because Joan has told me of another who

may like to say I am the daughter of Mary Remenham.'

'Who is that?' demanded Lucilla eagerly.

'I do not remember the name,' Melusine said,
turning to Mrs Ibstock. 'You said?'

'Mrs Sindlesham, your great-aunt, miss.'

Roding started. 'Sindlesham? But Gerald has
gone out of town to visit that very person.'

CHAPTER TEN

'I am come on a mission of some delicacy, ma'am,' Gerald said calmly to the old lady.

'Oh, you may come to me on any mission you like,' uttered Mrs Sindlesham roguishly. 'It is seldom enough I am visited by anyone at all, let alone a personable young redcoat.'

Gerald could not suppress a grin. 'Is that why you allowed me in, ma'am?'

A dimple appeared in the faded cheek. 'I allow anyone in. I am quite indiscriminate, I assure you.'

Mrs Prudence Sindlesham, a widow of several years' standing, so she told Gerald, was a scarecrow of a female, long and lank of limb in a figure that had once been willowy. She looked more than her sixty odd years, in spite of a still lush head of black hair, streaked with a little grey, which was visible under her cap and of immediate interest to Gerald.

'Forgive my not rising to greet you,' she said, holding out a claw-like hand. 'I have an arthritic complaint, which is why you find me retired from fashionable life. I rarely set foot in London these days.'

If she suffered from dragging pain in her joints, Gerald thought it explained why her features were prematurely lined. He noted an ebony cane laid close to hand, which suggested she was able to get about. He bowed over her hand, venturing to drop a kiss on it's leathery surface.

'It is London's loss, ma'am.'

Her features broke apart in a laugh. 'Oh, I do love a flatterer. But you must not imagine me wrapped in melancholy.' The sharp eyes twinkled. 'I have an excellent excuse to remain comfortably ensconced in my parlour here, able to indulge in my favourite pastime.'

She waved towards a handy table to one side which was piled high with so many volumes, it looked in imminent danger of crashing to the floor. Gerald raised a questioning eyebrow.

'You are an avid reader, I take it.'

'Voracious. And not a worthy tome in sight. My poor son despairs of me, for I have primed every member of the family to bring me the latest novels whenever they choose to visit.'

Gerald laughed. 'No doubt accompanied by the latest *crim con* tales.'

Mrs Sindlesham's lips twitched. 'But of course. Do sit down, dear boy. I have no intention of allowing you to depart in a hurry.'

Taking the chair she had indicated with a careless wave of one stiff-fingered hand, Gerald felt hope burgeoning. He had not thought to find a lady so ready of humour and willing to give him a hearing.

'You give me an excellent excuse to have in the Madeira,' said his hostess, reaching for a silver hand bell and setting it pealing.

'Do you need an excuse?'

'Oh, you know what doctors are. They will insist upon a catalogue of things one must not do, which does nothing but fill one with the greatest desire to do them.'

Gerald laughed. 'You are a born rebel, ma'am, and I can see now where she gets it from.'

Mrs Sindlesham's alert glance found his. 'She?'

'Damnation!' He saw her frown, and added at once, 'I beg your pardon, ma'am. It slipped out—as did that "she".'

'Well, sir? Who is "she"? Not my granddaughter, I take it. Much too young for you.'

'I don't even know your granddaughter, ma'am.'

'You wouldn't,' agreed Mrs Sindlesham. 'She's little more than a schoolgirl, just out. But come, sir. You intrigue me.'

To Gerald's relief, the entrance of the butler interrupted them, relieving him of the necessity to explain himself. He had meant to come at his business in a roundabout way, but for that little slip.

It was evident the lady's servant knew his mistress, for he had come equipped with a tray upon which reposed a decanter and two glasses. The business of serving gave Gerald a few moment's grace, for he was dubious about the effect on an elderly female, not in the best of health, of raking up old memories.

She lived, he noted, very carelessly. The parlour was cluttered but cosy. Mrs Sindlesham occupied a large padded armchair to one side of a corner fireplace, which gave out a heat more than adequate for September to one of the major's robust constitution. Beyond was a chaise longue, covered with cushions and shawls laid anyhow across it, together with a discarded tapestry in the making, and a scattering of woollen threads about it. Besides the table close by loaded with books, there was a central table with upright chairs around, covered in a multitude of papers, inks and quills, and assorted unrelated items such as playing cards. There were sidetables and a writing table, similarly buried in bric-a-brac, and the chair by the French doors could hardly be seen for blankets.

Accepting his glass from the butler, Gerald glanced at Mrs Sindlesham and saw a dimple peep out. 'Dreadfully untidy, is it not? Can't abide bare rooms.'

A trifle discomposed at being caught examining his surroundings, Gerald was provoked into retort. 'Then I don't advise you to visit Remenham House.'

Too late he saw his error. A swift frown brought the still dark brows together for a moment.

'So now we come to it.'

Her gaze followed the butler, who was moving towards the door. She waited for him to leave the room, and turned back to Gerald. Abruptly the sterner look vanished and she twinkled.

'Tell me, my boy. You are not with the Kent militia, are you?'

'West Kent, yes.'

'Dear me. And what took you to Remenham House?'

'I shall come to that presently,' said Gerald cautiously. 'Am I right in supposing you to have been a sister to the late Mr Jarvis Remenham?'

'Quite right.'

She sipped at the liquid in her glass, but her eyes remained fixed, rather unnervingly, on Gerald. Following her lead, he fortified himself with a swallow of the excellent Madeira before responding.

'I recall my father speaking of you as a Remenham.'

'Perfectly correct, my boy. Prudence Remenham.'

'Prudence,' repeated Gerald unguardedly. 'Why, that's one of the names with which she tried to fob me off.'

'She again?' enquired his hostess, her delicate brows rising

'I beg your pardon, ma'am. I spoke a thought aloud. So you are Prudence Remenham.'

'Was. Almost the last female to bear the name, too,' muttered the old lady. 'There are no Remenhams left.'

'But there is still Remenham House.'

'Oh, a ruin,' exclaimed Mrs Sindlesham, throwing up a hand. 'Not but what it was near that before Jarvis died. Half the rooms empty. Paintings sold off the walls. And all to satisfy a succession of rapacious lightskirts.'

'Lord,' Gerald murmured, awed more by the outspokenness of his hostess than by what she had said.

The old lady clearly read his state of mind, for the apparently irrepressible dimple peeped out. 'Shocked you, have I? We weren't mealy-mouthed in my day, my boy. You didn't see me fall into a swoon when you cursed just now, did you?'

'I'm beginning to doubt if anything less than a sledgehammer would send you into a swoon,' Gerald retorted.

She let out a delighted laugh. 'When you're my age, you'll be just as hardheaded. I often wonder why the young always take us ancients for namby-pamby creatures.' She gave him a straight look. 'So now you may safely cease your roundaboutation, and tell me what took you to Remenham House.'

'I was called in, ma'am, to catch a French spy—at least, that is what Pottiswick thought.'

'That old fool? Why my brother kept him on I shall never know. Except he was the only idiot who would stay.' She shook her head sadly. 'Went to the dogs, did Jarvis, after Mary died.'

'His daughter, ma'am?' Gerald asked.

'That's right. Nothing anyone could say or do would change him. I tried. Sindlesham tried. My late husband, I mean.' All at once Mrs Sindlesham looked across at him, a sharp question in her eyes. 'How did you know that Mary was his daughter?'

Gerald hesitated. Was this the right moment? After what she had said about Jarvis Remenham's habits, he could do with more information before he revealed his purpose.

'Come, come, ma'am,' he said smiling. 'I live in Kent. One is always familiar with the business of one's neighbours.'

She set down her glass with a snap. 'Don't fob me off, boy. You don't know about Mary because you live in Kent. It was years before your time.'

Gerald capitulated. 'You are too shrewd for me, ma'am. Very well, then. I have a special interest in Mary Remenham because I believe I have discovered her daughter.'

For a moment or two there was dead silence in the parlour. Mrs Sindlesham's wrinkled cheek had paled, and her eyes were fixed upon Gerald in a look that wrung his heart. Distress, deep-rooted, and age old. He had thought it might have that effect.

But then the features changed. The eyes left him, searching beside the chair for her cane. Her hand grasped it firmly, and she pushed herself forward. Gerald at once rid himself of his own glass and leapt to her assistance.

'Thank you,' she said, leaning heavily on his arm for a moment. Then she slowly straightened, releasing him. 'I can manage now.'

Gerald stood back, and watched her cross the room to the closed French doors. She turned there and beckoned. He came to her and stood before her, waiting, the morning light dazzling his eyes.

'Now,' she said, in an imperious manner that so much reminded him of Melusine that he was obliged to suppress a grin, 'I can see you properly. Tell me that again.'

'I have found Mary Remenham's daughter,' he repeated.

Slowly Prudence Sindlesham nodded her head, her eyes never leaving his face. 'You're speaking the truth.'

'As far as I know it, ma'am. Unfortunately, I have little detail of the circumstances which surrounded the birth of the girl, and her subsequent removal to France.'

'Ah, you know about that, then?'

'That much, yes. As I understand it, Remenham House devolves upon Melusine, in default of her mother, the actual heir.'

'Melusine, did you say?' Mrs Sindlesham sighed. 'That would have grieved Jarvis. He wanted her named Mary. Of course Nicholas was bound to give her a French name.'

Gerald smiled. 'I assure you it suits her as Mary would not. She is extremely lovely, but for her to have borne the name of the Blessed Virgin would have been nothing short of sacrilege.'

For the first time since she had heard the news, Mrs Sindlesham's features relaxed and a tiny smile appeared. 'Would it so? What sort of a girl is she, then?'

'She's a consummate devil,' Gerald declared roundly. 'But with more courage in her little finger than in many another female's entire body. She's naïve, and yet uncannily shrewd at times, and you daren't rely on anything she says. She's as stubborn as the proverbial mule, and—' with a sigh that felt wrenched out of him '—utterly captivating.'

Mrs Sindlesham shook with laughter. 'What a catalogue.' She gestured at his hand, on which Roding's makeshift bandage had been replaced by a more efficient one. 'Dare I suppose that to be of her making?'

Gerald flushed. 'Yes, but quite my own fault.'

'Was it?' Her lips twitched. 'I take it that you like this great-niece of mine?'

'One cannot help but do so.' A reluctant laugh escaped him. 'She gave me four separate identities for herself, you must know, including Prudence, before I managed to get at her real name.'

'Ah, that explains your surprise. I may say she does not sound in the least like Mary,' said Mrs Sindlesham bluntly. 'Mary was indeed naïve, but there I should say the similarity ends. She was a merry creature, it is true, and quite beautiful. But a biddable girl.' She drew a heavy breath. 'Else she would not have married that ne'er-do-well only because Jarvis proposed him to her.'

She sagged a little suddenly, as if the painful memories in her mind had exhausted her body. Gerald instantly took her arm and guided her back to her chair. A little Madeira seemed to recover her enough to resume the discussion.

'Poor Mary had no idea about the elopement Nicholas had undertaken,' she told Gerald. 'He had run away with a Frenchwoman, you see, but Everett Charvill—I refer to the general—took care to conceal the matter. Though, to be fair, he did not know of it until after the wedding. It would have been very well if she had been some common creature who might have been bought off. But this was a vicomte's sister. How much Mary knew is a mystery. I suspect she knew something, for she came home to Remenham House when she was increasing, and report has it that she was very unhappy. Certainly, we—that is Jarvis and I—knew nothing of it until after Mary's death.' She stopped, her lips tightening.

'What happened, ma'am?' enquired Gerald gently.

The old lady's face was stiff with anger. 'The wretch said nothing to anyone. He left Remenham House immediately after his wife died, giving birth to their daughter. His absence was thought by the charitable to be from grief. He returned to attend the funeral. His demeanour then was sober enough to lend colour to that belief. Immediately after it, he was off again, and that, let me tell you, was the last anyone saw of him.'

'What?' gasped Gerald, shocked. 'But he must have—'

'Nicholas Charvill never did anything he must do,' Mrs Sindlesham said evenly. 'He lacked moral fibre, did Nicholas. Later Lord Charvill told Jarvis that it had been precisely the same at the outset. Nicholas had not dared to tell his father about the Valade girl. So he obeyed Everett and married Mary, and kept the woman as his mistress.'

'Did no one know, then?'

'No, for the vicomte, we learned later, wrote to General Lord Charvill in pursuit of his sister. Too late, alas, to stop the disastrous marriage. Naturally it all came out then. The general did what he might to hush it up, and paid handsomely to manage it, I daresay. What he told the vicomte I was not privileged to learn.'

'How was it then that Nicholas Charvill was known to have gone to France. And with his daughter?'

'He wrote to Jarvis from an inn in France, saying that he had married Mademoiselle Valade, and that his baby naturally belonged with her father. Until that moment, Jarvis had imagined the child to be safe in the wet-nurse's cottage.' Mrs Sindlesham sighed deeply. 'I think that was what began his downfall. Had he had the child to think of, he might have recovered from his grief at Mary's death. But he...simply lost all hope.'

She was silent for a space, and it was evident that this part of the story was still too painful to be recalled with ease. But it was of vital importance to Melusine, and Gerald felt he must pursue it.

'Forgive me, Mrs Sindlesham, but do you tell me this inheritance that Melusine has fought so hard to recover is completely wasted?'

The old lady gave him a sharp look. 'That is what she wants, is it?'

'Do you blame her?' he said stiffly. 'The poor girl was thrust into a convent to become a nun. How she learned of her heritage I do not know, but you need not imagine that it is greed that drives her.'

'Well, don't bite my head off,' protested Mrs Sindlesham, clearly amused. 'I am far from imagining anything of the kind. I know nothing about the girl, save what you have told me.'

Gerald shrugged. 'I know her, ma'am, but I know next to nothing of her story. She will not confide in me. But she has let fall enough for me to understand that she knows about her father's misdeeds.' He grinned. 'Her purpose, if you will believe me, is to get herself a dowry so that she may marry an Englishman.'

Mrs Sindlesham laughed lightly, but her eyes quizzed him. 'Does she need a dowry for that?'

'Melusine believes so, and that is what counts.'

'Melusine,' repeated the old lady. 'It is pretty. But it does not sound as if the girl that wears the name resembles either of her parents.'

Gerald frowned. 'You don't believe her?'

'My dear Major Alderley, I do not know her,' Mrs Sindlesham pointed out. 'Bring her to me and we shall see.'

For a moment Gerald said nothing at all. His gaze remained steady on the old dame's face, as he thought about it.

'Is it worth it?' he asked at last. 'Assuming she can prove her identity, does Remenham House belong to her?'

Mrs Sindlesham shifted her shoulders. 'That is a matter for the lawyers. Jarvis did not leave a will.'

'What?' Appalled, Gerald could only gaze at her. In the circles into which he had been born, the passing on of land was of vital importance. To die intestate was unforgiveably irresponsible.

'I know,' said Prudence Sindlesham, sympathy in her tone. 'Unheard of, ain't it? To tell the truth, I half expected him to leave everything to one of his doxies.' She grimaced. 'They lived with him, one after the other, for all the world as his wife. My son went down after his death. To settle things, you know. He said the place had gone to wrack. The last of Jarvis's harlots must have departed in a hurry, for she had apparently left a roomful of clothes.'

'Yes, I know,' Gerald put in with an irrepresssible chuckle. 'Melusine was making herself mistress of them when we met.'

Mrs Sindlesham's mouth dropped open. 'She's wearing a lightskirt's clothing?'

'Nothing obviously so, I assure you. A riding-habit is all I have seen.'

'Of course she could not have known to whom they belonged.'

'Believe me, she wouldn't have cared. I dare say anything seemed better to her than the nun's habit she had been obliged to use.'

He saw that Mrs Sindlesham, for all her vaunted freedom of speech, was honestly shocked by this revelation. Whether it was the nun's habit or the harlot's clothing that distressed her more, he could not begin to guess. She would stare if she knew the full sum of Melusine's activities.

'It was your son who left the place empty then?' he asked.

'What else was there to do? He paid off the servants and left old Pottiswick in charge, saying that the place would have to remain empty until the heir was found.'

'What heir?'

'Exactly. There was none. Only the next of kin. That would be myself, or if she lived, Mary's daughter.'

'Not, I trust, Nicholas Charvill?'

'Hardly. That would be an unkind twist of fate.'

'Grossly unfair, too.'

'Have no fear. Since Mary predeceased Jarvis, Nicholas could scarcely argue himself to be my brother's next of kin. But his daughter might well have a claim.'

'Why did you not claim it yourself?' asked Gerald.

'I had no need of the place, and there was no money, of course.'

'Ah.' Gerald sighed. 'I feared as much. Still, I suppose Melusine can always sell the house.'

A twinkle crept into Mrs Sindlesham's eye. 'That will be a matter for her future husband to decide.'

Gerald started. He had not considered this aspect of the business. Until this instant, he discovered, he had thought of Melusine's plan only in a nebulous fashion, a naïve girl's dream. But what if she were to marry? He glanced towards the elderly dame and found her watching him, the dimple very much in evidence. What was the old tabby at? Unaccountably embarrassed, he cleared his throat. There was more to be told, and this was as good a time as any.

'Before she can think of marriage, Melusine must prove her identity. You see, the trouble is that the matter is in dispute.'

'How can it be in dispute?' frowned Mrs Sindlesham. 'There is no question of a dispute.'

'I am afraid that there is,' Gerald told her evenly. 'And it is not only a question of her identity, but a matter of her life as well.'

The full story—or as much as Gerald knew—of Valade's machinations shocked the old lady so much that she was obliged to recruit her strength with a refill from the Madeira decanter. She listened with growing apprehension to the tale that Gerald told, omitting any mention of pistols and daggers, and at the end delivered herself of various expletives highly unsuited to a lady of her advanced years.

'Yes, ma'am,' agreed Gerald with a grin. 'The so-called Valade is an evil person, and should certainly be got rid of in the manner you describe. However, he has already presented himself to the Charvills, and passed inspection. It is only a matter of time before he presents himself to whoever has the deeds to Remenham House—a lawyer I presume—and claims that property for his wife's.'

'I shall stop him,' declared the old lady furiously.

'But can you? You don't know Melusine for Mary Remenham's daughter, any more than I do.'

'A pox on the creature,' swore Mrs Sindlesham, clenching and unclenching her stiff fingers.

'I trust you are cursing Valade, and not Melusine.'

'Of course I am, imbecile,' she snapped, unconsciously echoing her great-niece. 'But you said she was looking for proof. What sort of proof? There are no papers at Remenham House.'

'I don't know,' confessed Gerald. 'She would not tell me. But it must have been something that could show her to be Mary's daughter. Think, ma'am. What might it have been?'

Mrs Sindlesham shook her head helplessly. 'I have no idea. Unless it was a jewel or locket of some kind.'

'No, for that would have had to be in Melusine's possession to start with.'

'Very true.'

Gerald sat back in his chair, thinking hard. 'I dare say the best plan will be for me to bring her to see you, after all. Hang it, there must be something about her that will give it away.'

Mrs Sindlesham abruptly sat up straighter in her chair. 'You said she was beautiful. What does she look like?'

'Black hair. Very dark, like yours, ma'am. But she does not resemble you in any other way. She has blue eyes, and her figure is more full.'

'It could hardly be less so,' said Mrs Sindlesham tartly. She pointed. 'See that writing table? Go and look in the drawer there.'

Obediently, Gerald rose and walked to the other end of the parlour. He opened the drawer of the writing table. It was a mass of knick-knacks.

'What am I looking for?'

'A miniature. Rummage, my boy, do. You will not find it else.'

He did as she bid him, and was very soon rewarded by the discovery of an oval miniature, encased in gold. He stared at the woman depicted thereon for a long moment, awe in his head. Then he looked across at Mrs Sindlesham.

'Well?' she said. 'Is there a resemblance?'

'This is Mary Remenham?'

'That is my late niece, yes.'

Triumph soared in Gerald's chest. Returning to Mrs Sindlesham's chair, he held up the miniature so the face depicted there was turned towards the old lady.

'Your niece, ma'am. And your great-niece. It might as well be Melusine herself.'

Martha sniffed dolefully, scrubbing at her reddened eyes with a large square of damp linen. She was sitting on the mean straw mattress that was placed on the iron bedstead in the makeshift cell, while Melusine stood with her back to the door, confronting her old nurse with the truth.

She was clad in fresh linen, but still wore the riding-habit she had appropriated, having sponged out the spots of blood late last night and left it to dry in the kitchens. She had been obliged to wait all morning for the opportunity to talk to Martha, who chose always to retire to her cell for the period of recreation that preceded afternoon prayers. Last night there had been no time. Not with the unavoidable explanations, and the need to secrete the sword and hide it before returning the priest's horse to its stable—which had been her excuse for running from Martha's protestations.

But today Melusine's new-found knowledge put Martha at a disadvantage.

'Hadn't meant you to know,' said the nun gruffly. 'That's why I never told Joan Ibstock that you were still with me when I wrote.'

'But Marthe, this is *idiot*. Certainly as soon as I have found my right place at Remenham House, I must find out everything.'

'Who was to know if you would find your place?' countered Martha. 'Odds were against it. Why open my mouth if there might not be a need for it when all's said?'

Melusine acknowledged the logic of this. 'Yes, that is reasonable. But still you have told me of my real mother when I thought it was Suzanne Valade.'

Martha looked up, belligerence in her tone. 'Would you have me face my maker with that on my conscience? If I'd died, there'd have been no one to tell you, for your father would not have done.'

'Certainly that is true. And Suzanne, even that she has behaved to me not at all like a mother, would also not have said.'

'She?' scoffed Martha. 'Couldn't even trouble to make a pretence of motherhood.'

Of which Melusine was only too well aware, for her stepmother had done nothing to save her from the convent.

'What's more,' went on Martha, 'I knew something Mr Charvill didn't, or he wouldn't so readily have left it behind him.'

'You would speak of the house?'

'Many's the time little Miss Mary would say her papa meant for her to have it, she having no brothers and sisters at all—when we played together I mean, she and me and Joan Pottiswick.'

Melusine could not regard this view with anything but scepticism. 'You think my father would not have married Suzanne if he had known? Me, I do not agree. He did not even care for his own inheritance at this place in Wodeham Water.'

She paused, holding her nurse's eyes.

'Don't look at me like that,' Martha begged. 'Oh, dearie me, you make me feel a traitor.'

'Only because you did not tell me entirely the story? That is silly. I would not think so of you, Marthe. You have been to me like a mother, not only a wet-nurse.'

'Poor sort of a mother,' Martha said with bitterness. 'No, Melusine. You're a lady. Me—I'm nothing but a country wench, and one who went to the bad.'

'But this is *idiot*. Have you not given your life to God? Do you not repent?' Coming to the bed, Melusine sat beside her old nurse and took hold of one of her hands. 'And I am very glad you did this bad thing, because if not, who would take care of me?'

Martha shook her head, and Melusine spied wetness again in her eyes, although they met hers bravely. 'You don't know the whole, child. I'm ashamed to confess it, but I didn't want the charge of you—a too close reminder of my own lost babe.'

Tears sprang to Melusine's own eyes, and she clasped the hand she held more tightly. 'But do you think I can blame you for this, Marthe?'

'I blame myself. Oh, I grew fond of you as the years went by. But it's love you should've had when you were tiny and I didn't give it to you. Even though I knew you'd no one else to care. For that worthless father of yours—'

Melusine let go the hand only so that she might throw her own hands in the air. 'Do not speak of him. Me, I prefer to forget that I have such a father.' A thought caught in her mind and she turned quickly to her old nurse. 'But there is something still I do not understand. Why did he take me?'

Martha's damp eyes were puzzled. 'Why?'

'Why take me to France? Why trouble himself with me, when so easily he could leave me to this Monsieur Remenham to keep?'

To Melusine's instant suspicion, Martha bit her lip, drew a breath, and avoided her charge's gaze.

'You were his daughter. He loved you.'

'Pah! Am I a fool? Have you not this moment past said how he did not?'

Agitation sent her to her feet. How she hated talking of the man who was responsible for her being brought into the world. She paced restlessly to the door and back again, biting her tongue on the hot words begging to be uttered. But they would not be denied.

'This is not love, Marthe. To love in such a way, it is excessively selfish.'

Leonardo had taught her that. Leonardo had taught her pretty well everything she could have need to know, when they had talked long at his bedside. His stories had enchanted her, even if in some deep corner of her heart she guessed they were not entirely true. But his life, ruled by chance and the fight to survive had appealed strongly to Melusine's rebellious spirit. As Leonardo had himself pronounced, who better than a mountebank to teach of the perils awaiting the unwary? Who better than a wastrel to demonstrate the worth of thrift? And who could instruct better in the matter of affections than one who had thrown them away?

'If he had loved me,' she said, in the flat tone she had learned to use to conceal her vulnerable heart, 'he would have left me at Remenham House to live a life of an English lady.' The questions that had long haunted her came out at last. 'Why did he make me French, Marthe? Why did he give me this name of Melusine, and say I am born of Suzanne Valade?'

Martha looked at her, but her lips remained firmly closed.

'*Dieu du ciel*, but answer me!'

Martha's eyes were swimming again, and she reached out. Melusine felt the calloused hand grasp around hers. 'I'm only a poor country wench, child. I don't understand the workings of a gentleman's mind.' A grimace crossed her face. 'But you know. You know, Melusine.'

The familiar hollow opened up inside Melusine's chest, and she could not prevent the husky note that entered her voice.

'Yes, I know.'

She dropped to her knees before her old nurse and hugged the work-roughened hand with both her own, looking up into Martha's face where slow tears were tracing down her cheek.

'It is that he needed me for his lie, no?' Melusine said, striving to control the quiver in her voice. 'That he can say he was married only to Suzanne all the time. This way there will be not so much shame, and the vicomte will let them remain.' The core of hurt rose up, tearing at her insides. 'I am not a person, Marthe. I am a thing to be used. And when there is no longer any need to use it, why then, enough you say—and throw it away.'

There was no denial in Martha's face, though Melusine longed to hear her words contradicted. Her old nurse's hands returned the pressure.

'God loves you, even if your father didn't.'

Melusine fought down the raw emotion that threatened to overwhelm her and drew a steadying breath. She disengaged her hands and stood up.

'You are wise, Marthe. A true nun. God must love me, for he has guided me here.'

'In a somewhat roundabout fashion, if you ask me,' came in a mutter from her old nurse, very much in her usual style. 'What are you going to do now, child?'

Melusine sighed away the last of her distress. 'I must see the lady who is my great-aunt. You have spoken her name, I think, Marthe. Or perhaps my father once. For when this Joan said it, I had a memory.'

Martha frowned. 'All so long ago and my memory ain't what it was. Wait, though. Prudence? Mr Remenham's sister that was.'

'*Exactement*. Prudence. It is she that I must see.'

'You won't go to the general then?'

'There is no need.' The one ray of light lifted Melusine's gloom a little and she smiled. 'You do not know how I am like my mother.'

'Oh, yes I do,' Martha said, getting up off the bed. 'Why do you think I told you about the portrait? I'd not seen it, of course, but I'd seen Miss Mary just before she got married, which is when it was painted. Joan told me it was hung somewhere in the house, only I couldn't remember where after all this time.'

'I do not care any more about the portrait,' Melusine said, opening the door to the attic corridor that gave off onto the row of little rooms that served as private cells for the senior nuns. 'I have Joan to tell me how much I look like Mary. And also I have this Prudence.'

'Yes, but how are you going to find her?'

'I will ask—'

She broke off. She must not tell Martha about Gerald. Better to remain silent. As silent as she had remained about who had brought her home last night. She knew Martha would not ask anything that she did not wish to know. It had ever been her policy, much to Melusine's relief, for she was apt to complain that it only made her mad and there was nothing she could do about it.

Although she had said a great deal when she heard about the shooting that had left poor Jack so badly injured. Martha had grumbled at being obliged to report the matter to Mother Josephine, who had decreed that Melusine must confess to Father Saint-Simon.

Melusine had confessed this morning, that she had borrowed his horse, that Jack had met with his accident through her fault. But to confess about Gerald—no, a thousand times.

En tout cas, why had he not returned? She pondered the question as, later, she paced about her favourite retreat. Where was the expected message from this captain, who had promised to send her word at the instant Gerald returned to town. He had been gone entirely one day, for yesterday afternoon he had departed from Remenham House, and she had waited with patience like a saint, and now it was again the afternoon. The late afternoon, *en effet*. Where was the message? Where was Gerald? Until he came back, what was there for her to do? *Eh bien*, it made no sense to do anything. For if Gerald had indeed gone to see this Prudence, it was better to wait for his report.

At least here she was safe. Without Jack, it was certain that she faced danger if she went outside Golden Square. Besides, the sun had gone in and it looked like rain. And who knew if the men that Gerald had posted there would follow her to protect her somewhere else? In truth, where were these soldiers? She could not see them, although she assiduously searched the mist-shrouded square from

the vantage point of the bay window in the large
first floor room which had become her headquar-
ters.

It was an odd room, used principally for the re-
ception of guests and visiting dignitaries, packed
from end to end with ill-assorted sofas and padded
chairs. Every movable mirror had been placed here,
to discourage vanity, and since no whitewash
covered the brocaded purple wallpaper, its pervas-
ive hue gave an added sense of heaviness to the
crowded chamber. Melusine, starved of colour for
years, revelled in it.

But not today. Nothing could occupy her attention long today, unless it concerned her situation.
Yet there was nothing for her to do. She had
thought of the lawyer who conducted the Remenham business, but she knew not where to find him.
Gerald perhaps would know how to find him.

A new thought checked her steps and she froze.
If Gerald knew, what should stop Gosse from finding out? Perhaps he was even now at the lawyer. He
would take with him that traitress Yolande, and
claim to the lawyer that this was Melusine Charvill.

Pig and brute! Yet calling him hard names would
not help her. *Dieu du ciel*, but where was Gerald? On
the move again, she found herself standing before
one of the mirrors, gazing into her own countenance without seeing it.

Automatically, she glanced at the slight red graze
left on her neck that marked the point where Gerald's sword had nicked her. She touched it, and her
gaze lifted.

Critically, she stared at her own features. Her long incarceration at the convent in Blaye had taught her to be dismissive of her own appearance. Like the nuns, she hardly ever looked in a mirror. Vanity was a vice not just to be deprecated, but effectively strangled at birth. Only Leonardo, and then Jack, had shown her that she might be admired. Now, as she stared at the image of her own face, she recalled something Major Alderley had said. Her name, he said, was as pretty as its wearer. And he liked her. Her heartbeat quickened.

In truth, she liked Gerald also. Too much, perhaps. For it was not a good thing to like one man too much when one was going to marry another. She could not say who, not yet. But there must be an Englishman who would like to marry her to get Remenham House. For she knew that men married to get something. So it was with Gosse, who had wanted to marry her. Leonardo would not have married her. He had said so. He was not in love with her *en désespoir* which, he said, was necessary if a man would marry without getting a dowry from his wife. And Gerald—

Melusine swallowed on an unaccountable lump in her throat. Gerald would not marry her even with a dowry. Had he not said so? Not that she wished him to marry her. Not at all. Was she a fool to wish a person of a disposition altogether not pleasing to marry her? Was it not true that he made a game with her very often? Had he not been extremely interfering from the beginning? And had he not kissed her, just when—

Her thoughts skidded to a stop. She closed her eyes and felt again an echo of the swamping warmth that had attacked her when his lips met hers. Dizzily, she grabbed at the mantel for support and, resting her head on her hands, paid no heed to a betraying sound behind her—until an unexpected arm encircled her.

As she started, rearing up her head, a hand stole about her mouth and closed down hard.

'*Silence,*' hissed a voice in French.

CHAPTER ELEVEN

Melusine's limbs nearly gave way beneath her. Gosse! *Dieu du ciel*, but how did he get into the convent?

She had perforce to obey his command, for speech was impossible. The arm about her was steel hard, and she felt the weapon that was placed at her heart, which thumped uncomfortably in her chest. So often as she had herself manipulated a dagger, she could not mistake the shape that pressured across her chest, or the sharp point that dug below her bosom.

Her mind jumped with questions as fear raced through her and hardened into a bid for retaliation. Did he intend to kill her now, this instant? Or had she a moment or two to try to save herself? Recalling Leonardo's dictum, she did not struggle, for that would only tighten the trap about her, and perhaps even spring it. Then she would be dead, and that was no use. She tried surreptitiously to reach her own dagger, in its cunning hiding place in her petticoat. But Gosse began to drag her towards the door.

Hope reared. He meant to take her out of this room, perhaps even out of the house. He was a fool. Why not kill her here, and leave silently, the way he must have come? Could it be that he had not the intention to kill her? *En tout cas*, it gave her a chance.

'You will keep yourself utterly quiet,' he instructed, a growl in her ear as they headed for the door. 'The sisters here will not save you. They are all at prayer at this hour.'

Melusine knew it to be true. He had chosen his time well. Even were she to get an opportunity to scream, it would be some time before such a call, unprecedented though it might be, brought the nuns so much out of their absorption that they interrupted their prayer to investigate. Time enough for Gosse to shut her mouth forever, as he did not hesitate to point out to her.

'Scream and you are dead,' he snapped, and released her mouth so that he might open the door.

'Where are you taking me?' she asked, assuming a fearful accent.

'Think I'm fool enough to do my business in a convent?' he said scornfully. 'I don't want a hue and cry after me, I thank you.'

'Where, then?' Melusine asked again.

She was thinking fast now, all her senses on the alert. If he got her outside, surely the soldiers would see her and intervene. Only how had they missed him? Were they *imbecile*? Or perhaps the mists had concealed him from them. Then Gosse spoke again, answering the question in her mind.

'Never mind where. But don't think your heroic *milice* will save you. I came in by the vestry, and we will go out that way again.'

Joy rose in Melusine's bosom. Now she knew why the soldiers had not caught him. The vestry door opened to the mews behind, and not to

Golden Square. It had been a part of the vast domain of the servants in the house's earlier incarnation. The chapel was situated in the old ballroom, and from there, down a few stairs, the vestry had taken the place of the pantry next to the kitchens. And in the vestry was the sword of *monsieur le major*.

Her mouth was once more covered as they left the second floor guest saloon and headed for the back stairs. Melusine did not try to fight her captor, for that would only make him angry. But she made a pretence of struggling a little, for it would be out of character for her not to do so and she did not want to arouse his suspicions.

He had made himself master of the layout of the house, that was plain. He led her unerringly, pushing her down the narrow stairway that had been the servants' access to the upper floors, and thence through a small door that led into the chapel.

It was the largest room in the house, which was why it had been given over to the main business of the convent as a house of God. Pews had been brought in and set in two rows before the huge table, covered in white cloth, that formed the altar at the far end. All the precious paintings and statues of the divine family were here, as was the enormous wooden crucifix set above the altar. No one could take the place for anything but what it was, and even Gosse hesitated in the doorway.

Go in, go in, Melusine prayed, hoping desperately that he would not change his mind and take another route. She must get to the vestry.

The delay was only momentary. Emile Gosse must know his only chance was to be rid of Melusine. Had he not said as much at Remenham House?

She allowed him to march her through the chapel without resistance. She knew that the stairs they had to negotiate to the vestry were extremely narrow, and she had made her plans. Gosse had to release his clamp on her mouth, for the awkwardness of the position made it impossible to negotiate the little stair.

'*Silence,*' he warned again, with a prod of the dagger at her heart.

Melusine did not attempt to speak. She gulped for air merely, for it had been difficult to breathe with his hand almost cutting off the supply to her lungs.

They negotiated several steps, and then the stair turned a corner. As Gosse pushed her around it, she felt his hold about her of necessity loosen slightly. Her elbows were ready. Jerking forward, she jabbed backwards. He grunted, and his grip gave. Melusine flung herself down the rest of the steps and through the doorway. Turning, she heaved at the bottom door and slammed it in his face just as he came leaping forward to grab her.

She heard him crash against it, and turned the key in the lock. She was breathing hard, dragging for air, half in fright and half because the sudden effort had used up what little air she had managed to draw so briefly.

Then she was turning, ignoring the muttered cursing and the rattling that immediately ensued at the door. Darting quickly to the chest that contained the priest's vestments, she leapt onto it and reached her arm down to scrabble behind it on the floor. Her fingers found the lump she sought and, with a little effort, she dragged out the black-wrapped foil.

Grace à Leonardo, she could defend herself now!

Gosse was still attempting to manhandle the door, when she turned the key and wrenched it open. Then Melusine jumped back into the fencer's pose, on guard, the point of the wicked blade directed towards her enemy. Washed in light from the vestry window, she held her ground, all thought at bay, bar the steel determination long ago instilled in her by her unconventional tutor.

For a stunned moment, Emile did not speak. He looked from the sword to the dagger with which he had brought her down here, and grimaced. Then he relaxed back a little, and let the weapon dangle from his fingers.

'Very clever, Mademoiselle Melusine.'

'The tables, they are turned, I think,' she returned.

'Do you think I am afraid of a sword in the hand of a slip of a girl?'

For answer, Melusine lunged at him. He jumped back, cursing. She resumed her on guard position, and glaring steadily at him, waited again.

'*C'est ridicule*. That I should be challenged by you of all people.'

'*Hélas*, poor you,' Melusine rejoined sarcastically.

He growled in his throat and, thrusting his coat open, revealed his own buckled sword-belt. No surprise, for Melusine was aware no Frenchman in his situation would dream of walking abroad unarmed. He thrust the smaller weapon into a scabbard that hung from his belt. Taking hold of the hilt of his own foil, he drew it forth.

'Very well, mademoiselle, so be it,' he snapped. 'The outcome, I think, is in very little doubt.'

Again, Melusine did not waste words. She lunged without warning again, and Gosse, just catching her blade on his own, was obliged to retreat backwards up the little stair. She advanced, stabbing at him. He could not possibly lunge in the confined space, and so had nothing to do but back himself into the chapel as fast as he could.

Melusine ran up the stairway after him, her point flailing to frighten him into allowing her access to the chapel.

Gosse backed, not even attempting to parry so unorthodox a use of the foil. In seconds, they faced each other before the altar. If he had imagined Melusine would be hampered by her petticoats, he was disappointed. She had learned this art in skirts, and knew well how not to be disadvantaged. The slack of her riding-habit and full under-petticoats was gathered into her left hand, and her booted ankles were visible as she held the skirts well out of her way.

Nevertheless, she was no fool, and she knew that they could easily break loose and cause her to fall. She had no intention of fighting fair. Leonardo had not taught her to do so. She was naturally weaker, she would tire quicker, and she need not concern herself with the peculiar obligations of honour obtaining amongst gentlemen. Play foul, and win. That was Leonardo's motto.

Melusine circled her adversary only far enough to give herself the aisle between the pews behind. Gosse must now fight with his back to the altar, and a dais at his heels.

'*Alors*, pig!' she cried and lunged in quarte.

He parried without apparent effort. '*Eh bien?*'

She thrust again, from the same place. 'Take this.'

'With ease, mademoiselle,' he countered, catching her blade.

Bon. Now he thought she was so foolish that she knew only one stroke. Melusine feigned a displeased frown. And lunged once more.

'Again?' Another simple parry. Gosse sneered. 'You do not try.'

'Ah, no?' She saw his guard relax and lunged again.

This time she feinted as his point came up to deflect her own, and disengaging, passed under and cut at his cheek. Panic leapt into his eyes as he brought his wrist up just in time to parry the blade.

'*Sapristi*,' he gasped.

Melusine made no reply. She ought to have leapt back on guard. Instead her point disengaged, dropped, and then the sword came up again and banged, flat-bladed, onto Gosse's wrist with such force that his own blade dropped from his grasp. In a flash, Melusine had jumped forward and clamped it to the floor with one booted foot.

Panting with effort, she held her point menacingly at Gosse's chest. 'That is better, no?'

'*Dieu.*' He stared at the point, glanced at the fallen sword imprisoned by her foot, and only just looked back at her weapon in time to see it thrust at him again.

He flung himself backwards, hit the dais and fell heavily before the altar, losing his low-crowned beaver. Melusine did not pause, but reached down to grasp the hilt of his sword and lift it. Swinging her arm in an arc, she let go of the foil and it flew across the chapel towards the main door, crashing down between the pews, and clattering onto the floor.

'*Eh bien*, pig. And son of a pig,' she grunted, baring her teeth.

'You are mad,' Gosse uttered, and only just had time to get himself up from the floor.

For Melusine was on him again, the point of her sword lunging so that he backed up onto the dais. She thrust at him, following, almost spitting him as he crashed against the altar, rocking the huge candlesticks and the vessels that stood on it. Gosse twisted his body to avoid another thrust, and the heavy candlesticks fell, rolling with a noise like thunder, and falling with a thud to the floor.

'How is your plan now, *mon brave*?' Melusine taunted. 'Who kills who?'

'Rot in hell,' he snarled, panting, and managed to push himself forward and leap off the dais, running for the safety of the far aisle by the wall.

Melusine flew after him, the sword held out before her and pointing directly at his retreating back.

'Pig! Pig, a thousand times!'

Running footsteps could be heard now, and she knew that the commotion was bringing the nuns, just as she had hoped. But she must stop him getting away.

Too late she realised that Emile was not trying to escape. He was shifting to reach his own weapon, which had fallen in between the pews at the back. Before she knew what had happened, Gosse turned suddenly, and vaulted one of the pews into the gap behind.

Balked, Melusine halted.

'Coward,' she threw at him, brandishing the sword.

'Madwoman,' he screamed back, as he climbed over the next pew, eyes darting down briefly to check for his sword.

Melusine shrieked an imprecation, and ran the length of the aisle, searching for the weapon she had thrown. She saw it, and checked without thinking.

Emile looked at her, then down, and clearly caught the bright gleam on the floor.

'*Alors*, I see it.'

Baring his teeth in a smile of triumph that was every bit an animal snarl, and leaping up onto the seat of the pew he was in, he jumped hazardously to the next.

In the distance a bell clanged, and chattering broke out in the doorway as several nuns came crowding in. Melusine, intent upon preventing Gosse from securing the fallen weapon, paid no attention. Vaguely she heard the distinctive sound of male voices as she saw Gosse dive towards the fateful pew.

'You will not, pig,' cried Melusine.

She pushed between the pews, hoping to reach the sword first, while desperately holding on to her petticoats to keep them up, as her sword arm wavered.

'You are dead, you,' he yelled back, leaping into the seat of the final pew.

Melusine tried to squash down, still trying to maintain her guard. The slack cloth of her habit caught on a curlicue in the carved back of the pew in front, pulling her suddenly about. She could not move.

'*Peste*,' she wailed, as Emile dropped to the floor, ducking down.

With a cry of triumph, he rose, the sword hilt grasped in his fingers, the point swishing up towards her.

A male voice, vibrant with terror, yelled out hoarsely.

'*Melusine!*'

Distracted, Gosse blinked and his eyes flicked away from Melusine's just as she flung the fullness of her gathered petticoats in the way of his blade.

ELIZABETH BAILEY

There was a tearing sound and the cloth of her habit ripped apart as the smothered point drove through it, missing its intended target.

Next instant, Melusine's blade sank into Gosse's flesh. His sword-arm fell useless at his side and she knew herself safe. He glanced at it, and saw the bloodied blade. Clearly dazed, he stared, whispering an oath.

Melusine, her breath coming in short bursts, heard a sudden flurry of several heavy footsteps and harsh commands exchanged.

'Get the swords!'

'I'll see to him. You deal with her.'

She saw the weapon wrenched from Emile's hand and he dropped to the bench of the pew and sat there, grasping helplessly at the welling blood on his arm. Then he was surrounded by black-clad nuns, and Melusine felt an unknown hand grab away her own sword.

She released her clutch on it as, dizzy with exhaustion, she leaned against the back of the pew and closed her eyes, her fingers grasping out automatically for support. Her shoulders were gripped hard and a familiar voice spoke.

'You damned little fool! How dared you steal my sword?'

Her eyes flew open. 'Gérard!'

'Yes, it's I,' he said, and grinned. 'Can I not leave you for a day without you getting yourself into trouble?'

'*Imbecile,*' she uttered faintly. '*Grace à vous,* I am compelled to rescue myself.'

264

'Yes, it's all my fault,' he agreed soothingly, 'and you may rail at me presently as much as you please.'

Melusine began to sag, and felt his strong arms catch her up and lift her bodily into a comforting embrace.

'But for now, I'm taking you home.'

Melusine's arm crept up around his neck. 'Home?'

'To your family.'

'*Merci*,' she sighed and, surrendering at last to his oft-proffered aid, allowed her head to droop onto his chest. 'I am done, Gérard. Me, you may have.'

There was a chuckle in his voice. 'May I, indeed? I'll take you up on that.'

CHAPTER TWELVE

In the elegantly appointed blue saloon, Melusine sat disconsolate, gazing out of the window at the dull sky. She was quite tired of the stream of visitors and heard with relief the words of her newfound great-aunt, addressed to her son's butler.

'No more, Saling, no more,' said Mrs Sindlesham in accents of exhaustion. 'Not another caller will I receive this day. Deny me, if you please.'

'Very good, ma'am.'

'Unless it is Captain Roding,' put in Lucilla Froxfield from the curved back sofa on the other side of the fireplace.

'Except Captain Roding,' agreed the old lady, nodding at the butler. 'Is he meeting you here then, my dear?'

'He had better,' said Lucilla. 'I left a message at home that he should do so as soon as he returned from Kent.'

Saling coughed. 'Will that be all, ma'am?'

'Yes, yes. Go away,' came fretfully from Prudence Sindlesham, and Melusine heaved a sigh as she looked towards the butler, who was making his stately way to the door.

To her consternation, the sound drew her great-aunt's attention and she threw out a hand. 'Stay, Sa-ling!'

The butler halted, looking round enquiringly. Melusine glanced towards the elderly dame and found that sharp gaze directed upon her. But her words were not addressed to Melusine.

'If Major Alderley should happen to call, you may admit him also.'

A hand seemed to grip in Melusine's chest and she hit out. 'Pray do not trouble yourself, Saling. The major will not call.'

She turned quickly away that her feelings might not be obvious to Lucy and her great-aunt. She had reason enough to be grateful to Prudence Sindle-sham and it was not fair that this horrible feeling of loneliness should be made known to her. Also Lucy, who had been so much her friend. Melusine could not wish either to know how their kindness served only to emphasise the lack in her life ensuing from Gerald's continued absence.

The events that had initially followed in the wake of her triumph over Emile Gosse had quite confused and dazed her. That day Gerald had brought her to this excessively careful house, where she had felt very much alone and very unlike herself. The arrival of *la tante* Prudence late next day had changed all this, it is true. For she and this old lady became at once friends. Gerald had himself told her that this Prudence will present her to society as Melusine Charvill. Also he had said—laughing in that way with his eyes which made a flutter in her chest —that Prudence will find an Englishman to marry her.

It would be the culmination of her plan. But why this part of the plan now seemed to her quite unattractive was a question she did not care to examine too closely. She had the dowry she needed for the lawyers were working to give her Remenham House. This was good. She was very satisfied about this. But about the unknown Englishman she was not so satisfied.

She was no longer certain that she desired an Englishman, if she must judge of one in particular. Had he come to see her to find if she needed something? No. The son of Prudence instead was obliged to take her back to the convent on Sunday to see Martha and tell her the good news, and to fetch her meagre belongings. And Gosse had been still there, so Martha said, and not in prison.

To be no longer with Martha was strange. They had cried a little, both. But it was not *adieu*, so she promised her old nurse. Only *au revoir*. All her life Martha had been there. Without her, it was lonely. Melusine was loath to admit how much more lonely since Gerald chose not to visit her. He had brought her here to this place—where her freedom was curtailed even more than at the convent so that a cavalier was very much needed—and only on Monday came again. And not on Melusine's account, but to see Prudence, who had no use for a cavalier.

Although Melusine had taken care to trouble herself about the hand she had cut, and was glad to find it healing very well. But did Gerald trouble himself about her? No. He says only that he must tie up all the loose ends. But days had now passed. How many ends had he?

Well, she must cease to trouble herself for this *imbecile*, whom it would give her very much pleasure to shoot. And she had not dressed herself in this habit of a blue so much like the sky just for his sake, no matter that Lucy had said how much this colour suited with her eyes. It was a habit she had taken from Remenham House, but could not wear because of the colour which must draw attention. She had thought to wear it now, since she must look more the *demoiselle*. But of what use to wear it when there was no one of importance to see and admire?

'For shame, Melusine,' protested Lucy, as the butler bowed himself out of the room. 'Poor Gerald has been very busy about your affairs this last week.'

'This is not a new thing,' Melusine snapped, goaded. 'Always he is busy about my affairs. But he does not come to see me since three days, even that these are my affairs and one could think that he would tell it to me if there is news, no?'

'When he has news to tell he will come, child, trust me,' the old lady assured her.

Melusine gritted her teeth. 'It does not matter to me if he comes or no, madame. Soon I shall make my *début*, that it will be known that I am the real Melusine Charvill, and then I shall not require the services any longer of this *imbecile* of a Gérard.'

'It's already known,' said Mrs Sindlesham, 'judging by the number of callers we have had these two days.'

'Yes, indeed,' agreed Lucilla enthusiastically. 'The whole town is talking. And I, I am happy to say, am in the delightful position of being in the know. I am sure I never enjoyed so much popularity in my life.'

The dimple that so fascinated Melusine peeped in her great-aunt's cheek. 'So yours is the rattling tongue, is it, young madam?'

'I should say so. I have held people spellbound —in confidence, so that we may be sure of its spreading like wildfire—with an account of all Melusine's activities, and—'

Horror filled Melusine and she jumped up. 'Lucy, do not say that you have told everyone all that I have done?'

'Well, yes, but—'

Consternation filled Melusine's breast. 'But you are *idiot*. This is not the conduct of a *jeune demoiselle*. This I know, for the Valades have taught me so, and the nuns also. How will I get an Englishman to wed me if they know that I behave not at all *comme il faut*?'

'Perhaps the Englishman in question will not care,' suggested Prudence, with a twinkle in her eye for which Melusine was quite unable to account.

'Not care? For this he must be an Englishman *tout à fait sympathique*, and—and I know only...'

Melusine's voice petered out. Fearful that she had given herself away, she sank back down onto her stool. Despair engulfed her at the horrid remembrance that the one particular Englishman she knew to be *sympathique* did not at all wish to marry her.

Lucy's bright tones pursued her. 'Never fear, my love. I've made no mention of guns and daggers or, indeed, any of the more exciting aspects of the business.'

Melusine turned her head. 'But you have told them that I have been disguised, no? That I have broken into Remenham House, and—'

'No, no, child, don't be alarmed,' said her great-aunt, her tone soothing. 'Why, you have heard yourself all that is being said. Have we not received Lady Bicknacre just this morning? Not to mention the Comtesse de St Erme.'

'And was not she put out?' demanded Miss Froxfield with a tinkling laugh. 'How she pouted, and tried to make out that she had been imposed upon. As if it were she, and not Melusine, who had been hurt by the imposters.'

'In a way she had been,' said Prudence. 'She has constituted herself leader of the *émigrés* here, and feels justifiably slighted by having taken the pretend Valades under her wing.'

'Lady Bicknacre too,' said Lucilla, a delight in her voice that grated on Melusine. 'Both of them so wise after the event. The comtesse always felt Madame Valade to be not of her class, of course. While Lady Bicknacre had never trusted Valade. What a treat to see all the old tabbies taken at fault for once!'

'You are a dreadful child,' scolded Mrs Sindlesham, with which Melusine could not but agree, despite the dimple rioting in her great-aunt's cheek. 'You see, Melusine, that none of our visitors were as informed as they would wish to be. They know only that the Valades have practised an imposture which affects all society, and some will think your adventures excessively romantic.'

'Pah! How can it be romantic? That is silly.'

'People are silly. They cannot imagine the discomforts involved, and they see only mystery in your fight to recover your lost heritage. But the factor of overriding interest is that they have all met and approved the said imposters. I dare say it will be chattered about for weeks.'

The idiocy of it all irritated Melusine. 'I begin to ask myself why it is that I wish to become of these people.'

'We are not all of us so empty-headed, Melusine,' pleaded Miss Froxfield.

A rare moment of amusement lightened Melusine's mood for a moment. 'You are extremely empty-headed, Lucy. So says your *capitaine*.'

Lucy giggled. 'Hilary is a darling.'

'This is what you say of him? Me, I find he is growling all the time like a dog.'

As if to bear her out, the door opened at this precise moment to admit Saling, who barely announced Captain Roding before the man himself strode into the room.

His eyes swept the company, and fell upon Melusine with a glare.

'Ha! Just the person I want. Where the devil have you hidden all those weapons? Don't tell me you've got 'em with you.'

Annoyance sent Melusine leaping to her feet. 'Certainly I have them with me. But what affair is this of yours?'

But Captain Roding was not attending. Instead, he was bowing to her great-aunt. 'Beg your pardon, ma'am, but she's enough to try the patience of a saint.'

'*Eh bien*, you are not a saint,' Melusine snapped.

To her chagrin, he ignored her, and turned a venomous eye on his betrothed. 'And what the devil do you mean by demanding that I wait on you here? D'you think I haven't enough to do handling that caper-witted female's affairs, without dancing attendance on you?'

'Don't be cross,' begged Lucilla, much to Melusine's disgust.

She watched her friend rise and go towards her affianced husband, a look of mischief in her face.

'Do you think I could bear to be without you for a moment longer? I am quite jealous of Melusine taking up all your attention.'

It was immediately evident that Lucilla Froxfield was not as silly as Melusine had thought, for the face of her captain immediately changed and he took her hands, a look on his face that caused Melusine an instant pang. Would that a certain major might cast upon her such a look.

'Didn't mean it, love. Know that, don't you?'

'Of course I know it,' Lucy told him, and Melusine read the whisper in her mouth of those precious words, 'I love you.'

Melusine watched with a tightness in her chest as Captain Roding kept hold of Lucy's hand, even as he turned back to Prudence.

'Truth is, it's Gerald who's put me in the devil's own temper, ma'am. Gone off, cool as you please, and left me to manage everything.'

'Gone off?' repeated Melusine, her wrongs rising up to tear into her chest. 'To where has he gone off?'

'No use asking me,' shrugged the captain. 'That fellow of yours is a deal better, by the by. Should be home soon.'

The shift threw Melusine's attention off the errant major for the moment. 'Jacques? Oh, that is news of the very finest. You saw him? You have been to Remenham House?'

'Remenham House? I wish I'd been only to Remenham House. Feels as if I've been dashing back and forth about the whole country, if you want to know.'

'But tell,' demanded Melusine impatiently.

'Yes, tell us everything at once,' instructed Lucilla, pushing him towards the sofa she had vacated, and obliging him to sit beside her.

Mrs Sindlesham raised her brows. 'Dear me. If you two are examples of the modern miss, I don't know what the world is coming to.'

Noting the twinkle in her great-aunt's eye, Melusine forebore to comment, grateful to Lucilla for adjuring Captain Roding to give an account of himself. Melusine fetched her stool and plonked it down next to her great-aunt's chair.

'Well,' began Captain Roding, looking at Melusine, 'you know those nuns of yours took up Valade—I mean, Gosse—and put him to bed to mend his wound, and I posted a guard outside his room so he couldn't escape, for Gerald told you all that. I went off to round up his wife. What the devil is her name, now we know she isn't you?'

'Yolande,' supplied Melusine. 'She is a maid only, and I do not believe she has married Emile.'

'Had a certificate for it,' argued Roding. 'Signed by a priest at Le Havre, so it must be true. But it was under false names, so I dare say it ain't valid. In any event, I brought her to the convent and we had her locked up separately, and told 'em both they'd be taken into custody as soon as Valade was fit to go.'

'Gosse,' corrected Lucilla. 'He isn't Valade, and the Comtesse de St Erme is absolutely furious.'

'Never mind the comtesse,' adjured Prudence.

'Yes, don't interrupt me,' said Captain Roding severely.

'But you cannot expect that we will any of us remain altogether quiet,' objected Melusine. 'And me —'

'You, mademoiselle, are more trouble than you're worth, and I'll thank you to—'

'Hilary, don't,' said Lucy, and Melusine's rising temper cooled a little.

'The major thinks she's worth it,' put in Prudence quietly.

Melusine's heart jumped and she felt heat rising into her cheeks. She tried for her usual confident tone, but only succeeded in sounding gruff, even to her own ears.

'I have not asked for this trouble from anyone. Always I have said I will take care of myself, and I have done so.'

To her surprise, Captain Roding backtracked. 'Didn't mean to say that. Only I'm so incensed with that crazy fool Gerald that—oh, well, never mind.'

'Get on, Hilary, do,' begged Lucilla.

He frowned. 'Where was I? Oh yes. Well, I was all for dragging in Bow Street there and then, and getting the pair of those fraudsters thrown in gaol. But Gerald wouldn't hear of it. Made me fetch up Trodger and a couple more men, and together we searched his luggage and got hold of every single paper the man possessed. Gerald, meanwhile, was off hunting up these lawyers, together with your son, ma'am—' turning to Mrs Sindlesham '—and you know the outcome of that. Fellows are drawing up the necessary papers, but gave Gerald a letter of authorisation for you, mademoiselle, to use in the interim.'

'But where then is Gosse?' demanded Melusine. 'Do not tell me he has escaped.'

'I'm coming to that. Gerald went through all the papers in front of Gosse and that woman of his, one by one. His French is better than mine, so he knew exactly what he was handling. Gather he found stuff belonging to the real Valade, and the vicomte, as well as your own letter. He kept that, but the rest...'

He paused, but Melusine caught the inference.

'He destroyed the papers?'

'That's right,' Roding said, throwing her a glance of frowning surprise, as if he had not rated her intelligence so high. 'Burned them, one by one, right before that fellow's eyes. Gosse cursed him finely, of course, but there was nothing he could do. Our men had him fast, held down in a chair.'

'*Bon*,' exclaimed Melusine, triumph soaring. 'I find this was excessively clever of Gérard.'

'Then what?' demanded Lucilla in a hushed tone.

Hilary threw up his eyes. 'Then he went stark staring crazy, if you ask me. Gave me a purse, and told me to take both of 'em up to Harwich and put them on a packet for Holland.'

'He let them go?' asked Miss Froxfield incredulously.

Melusine was silent, revolving this outcome in her mind as she stared at Roding, who was frowning at her in a puzzled way. But her great-aunt was nodding, as if this was what she had expected. Lucilla broke across Melusine's thoughts.

'Melusine, don't sit there. Say something.'

'Ain't you in a rage?' asked the captain. 'Rather thought I'd have to disarm you when you heard of it. That's why I wanted your weapons. Looked all over that dratted convent of yours—or at least Trodger and the men did so—but no sign of them.'

'I fetched them with my clothes when the son of madame took me to see Marthe,' Melusine admitted. She drew a breath, and sighed it out. 'I am not in the least in a rage. On the contrary, I am altogether satisfied.'

The couple on the sofa stared at her blankly. Prudence twinkled at them, and reached out to pat Melusine's hand.

'Well said, my dear. Now tell them why.'

Melusine shifted her shoulders. 'As to Gérard, I do not know why he does this.' She closed her mind on the possibility of finding out, and went on, 'But me, I have been in a war, and I have won. Gosse would have killed me, and perhaps in the fight I might kill him. But to make an arrest to be like a revenge? No, a thousand times.'

'But what of justice?' asked Lucilla, evidently dazed.

'I have justice. I have Remenham House which is my right. It is known that I am Melusine Charvill, which is also my right.' Her breath tightened and she was obliged to control an inner ferocity. 'Do you think I would do to him as he made a threat to do to me? No. This is not honourable.'

This was Leonardo's philosophy. Those who lived outside the law might squabble among themselves, even unto death, Leonardo told her. But never would any so dishonour himself as to hand a fellow rogue over to the authorities.

'I rather suspect,' added Prudence, 'that Major Alderley's motives were somewhat different. A trial always brings those involved into public notice, and I dare say he feels there will be scandal enough without adding to it. A nine days' wonder is soon forgotten. But with Gosse and the woman in prison here, there is always the chance that the whole affair may be raked up all over again.'

There was sense in what she said, Melusine was obliged to concede. But next moment, Captain Roding put up her back.

'You've cause to be grateful to Gerald, then.'

'Grateful? Certainly I am grateful,' Melusine snapped, knowing full well she sounded anything but gratified. 'Still more would I be so if he had come himself to tell me this.'

'How could he when he didn't even handle it himself? Went off, I told you, and left it all to me. I'd to go to Remenham House as well, and show Pottiswick your letter of authorisation. And, incidentally, check on that unfortunate young fellow Kimble.'

'But where? Where has he gone? Always he goes off, and he says no word to anyone. I shall know what to say to him when he comes.'

The door opened and Saling entered again.

'Major Alderley, ma'am, and General Lord Charvill.'

Melusine's heart leapt, and as swiftly clattered into dead stillness as the implication of the second name hit home. She flew up from her stool and faced the door. The figure she had longed to see came into her line of vision, but at this crucial moment of hideous realisation, Melusine barely took it in, her eyes fixing blankly on the man behind. An old man with a bent back who limped in, slow and stiff, leaning heavily on a cane.

A slow heavy thumping started up in Melusine's chest, and she scarcely took in the astonished silence in those present in the room.

Gerald vaguely noted that his junior leapt to his feet at sight of his former commander, and that Lucilla sat with her mouth at half-cock, dread in her face. His attention was focused on Melusine's transfixed stare and he forgot to say any of the things he had planned to say. He had known she would be shocked, but he was equally certain Melusine would have refused to see her grandfather had she been forewarned. To his relief, Mrs Sindlesham stepped into the breach, grasping her cane and rising painfully from her chair.

'Good God! Everett Charvill, as I live. I suppose you have come to see your granddaughter.' She moved to Melusine's side as she spoke. 'Here she is.'

'Don't need you to tell me that, Prudence Sindlesham,' barked the old man, his glance snapping at her briefly, before resuming his study of Melusine, who, to Gerald's intense admiration, was standing before him, glaring and stiff with defiance. 'I've eyes in my head, haven't I?' He grunted. 'No mistaking you this time. Spit of your mother.'

'*Parbleu*,' burst from Melusine indignantly. 'I do not need for you to tell me this. I also have eyes, and I have seen the picture.'

Gerald drew his breath in sharply as Lord Charvill took a step towards his granddaughter, thrusting out his head.

'What's this? Impertinence! French manners, is it?'

'*Grace à vous*,' Melusine threw at him fiercely.

'She means thanks to you, General,' Gerald translated automatically, forgetful of his old commander's fiery temper.

Predictably, Charvill turned on him. 'I know what it means, numbskull! Didn't spend years in the confounded country without picking up some of their infernal tongue.' His head came thrusting out at Melusine like a belligerent tortoise from its shell. 'What in Hades d'ye mean, thanks to me? Want to blame anyone, blame that rapscallion who calls himself your father.'

'He does not call himself my father, for he calls himself nothing at all,' Melusine told him, her tone violent with fury.

'Dead then, is he?'

'If I could say that he is dead, it would give me very much satisfaction. But this I cannot do. I do not know anything of him since I have fourteen years, and that he sent me to Blaye to be a nun.'

'Ha! You're Catholic, too, damn his eyes,' growled the general.

'Certainly I am *catholique*. I say again, *grace à vous*.'

'How dare you?' roared the general.

'And you!' shrieked Melusine. 'You dare to come to me? What do you wish of me? Why have you come? I do not want you!' She swept round on Gerald abruptly and he braced for the onslaught. 'Now I see that you are mad indeed. You bring me this grandfather, whom you know well I do not in the least wish to see, for I have told you so.'

'I didn't bring him,' Gerald returned swiftly. 'He just came.' He gestured towards the fulminating general. 'Can't you see he is not a gentleman with whom one can argue?'

'You think so?' Melusine said dangerously, and her eyes flashed as she swept about again and confronted her grandfather once more. 'I can argue with him very well indeed.'

'Pray don't,' begged Mrs Sindlesham, one eye on the general's embattled features. 'I don't want him having an apoplexy in this house.'

'Don't be a fool, woman,' snapped Charvill, thrusting himself further into the room.

At this point Lucy, in an effort perhaps—foolhardy, in Gerald's opinion—to pour oil on troubled waters, rose swiftly to her feet and came towards the old man, her hand held out.

'How do you do, my lord? I am Lucilla Froxfield.'

'Tchah!' He glared at her. 'What has that to say to anything?'

'Nothing at all,' smiled Lucy nervously. She indicated the captain who had retired behind the sofa. 'I think you know my affianced husband.'

'Captain Roding, sir,' put in Gerald, adding on a jocular note, 'Another of the green whippersnappers you had to contend with some years back.'

'None of your sauce, Alderley,' rejoined the general, shaking hands with Hilary who came forward to greet him. Then he looked towards his granddaughter once more, who had flounced away to the window at her great-aunt's interruption. 'Now then, girl.'

She turned her head, eyes blazing. 'Me, I have a name.'

'Melusine, sir,' Gerald reminded the general, exchanging a frustrated glance with Mrs Sindlesham. Her efforts were vain. There was going to be no quarter between these two.

Lord Charvill champed upon an invisible bit for a moment or two, closing the gap between himself and the girl, and muttering the name to himself in an overwrought sort of way. 'Melusine...Melusine. Pah! Damned Frenchified—'

'If you say again,' threatened Melusine, moving to meet him like a jungle cat poised for the kill, 'this scorn of a thing French, *monsieur le baron*, I shall be compelled to give you this apoplexy of which she speaks, madame. I am entirely English, as you know well. If it is that I am in the least French, and that you do not like it—'

'I don't like it,' snapped the old man. 'And I'll say it as often as I choose, you confounded impertinent wench! Who do you think you're talking to? I'm your grandfather, girl.'

'Pah!' rejoined Melusine, apparently unconscious of echoing him. 'You and Jarvis Remenham both, yes. *Parbleu*, but what grandfathers I have!'

It was stalemate, Gerald thought, irrepressible amusement leaping into his chest. They confronted each other, barely feet apart, neither apparently any longer aware of anyone else in the room. An old man and a young girl, the one as stubbornly offensive as the other.

'I'm damned if I see what you have to complain of,' uttered Charvill, a faintly bewildered note underlying his irascibility. 'What could either of us have done?'

To Gerald's acute consternation, Melusine's lip trembled suddenly, and her eyes filled. In a voice husky with suppressed despair, she answered.

'You could have *fetched me home*.'

Pierced to the heart by the poignancy of this utterance, Gerald could neither move nor speak. It was a moment before he recognised that the effect had been similar on all those present, including General Lord Charvill. With astonishment, Gerald saw a rheumy film rimming his old commander's eyes. Swiftly he looked back to Melusine and found she had whisked to the window, dragging a pocket handkerchief from her sleeve and hastily blowing her nose.

For an instant, Gerald wished the rest of the world away that he might go to her and administer appropriate comfort. But the general was turning on him, the hint of emotion wiped from his lined features.

'I wish you joy of the wench. If you ask me, you'll have to beat her regularly if you don't want to live a dog's life.'

'Nonsense,' said Mrs Sindlesham loudly, casting an anxious glance upon Melusine.

Well might she do so, Gerald thought in irritation. He caught the elderly dame's eye, throwing her a desperate message. To his relief, she nodded.

'The truth is, Everett,' she said brightly, limping up to the general and tucking a hand in his arm, 'that the girl is you all over again. I've been wondering where she got her dogged will, and that hotheaded adventurous spirit, for it wasn't from either Mary or Nicholas, that's sure. No one seeing you together could doubt that she is your granddaughter.'

Gerald was relieved to hear the loud guffaw issuing from the old man's lips. 'You think so? Well, if that's so, I know where she gets her impudence, Prudence Sindlesham.'

'Do you indeed?' rejoined the old lady, twinkling at him, and urging him towards the door. 'Let us go elsewhere and discuss the matter. I loathe this room. Much too formal for a cosy chat between old friends.'

So saying, she threw a meaning look over her shoulder at Lucilla, much to Gerald's approval. Then she passed from the room on the arm of General Lord Charvill, chatting animatedly to him.

Gerald realised Lucy had taken the hint, for she dragged her betrothed towards the door. 'Come, Hilary. Mama will be expecting me. I will come later to see you, Melusine.'

'Yes, but I need a word with Gerald,' protested the captain, hanging back.

'Oh no, you don't,' said Gerald in a low tone. 'Talk to me another time.'

'What?' Hilary glanced from Gerald to Melusine, and coloured up. 'Oh, ah. Yes, of course. Later.'

The door closed behind them both and Gerald was alone with Melusine.

From the corner of her eye, Melusine saw Gerald move towards her and she turned to confront him, the confused turmoil in her mind causing her chest to tighten unbearably. She gave tongue to the most urgent of her plaints.

'Why did you bring him? I hate him.'

'Yes, that rather leapt to the eye,' Gerald said, and the faint smile sent a lick of warmth down inside her. 'I went to see him because I thought he ought to know about you, having already been imposed upon by our friend Gosse. He had to know the truth, Melusine.'

She eyed him, all her uncertainty surfacing. 'And this is where you have been all the time?'

'I would have been back in a day, I promise you. Only your horror of a grandfather insisted on coming with me, so I had to wait for him to be ready and travel at his pace. What could I do?'

'Anything but to bring him to me,' Melusine threw at him. 'If you had told him that I would rather die than see him, he would not have come.'

Gerald grinned. 'You don't know him.'

'No, and I do not wish to do so,' Melusine pointed out.

His face changed and she saw, with a stab at her heart, the dawning of irritation in his eyes.

'Hang it all, Mrs Sindlesham is right! You are two of a kind.'

Melusine took refuge in defiance. 'But I find you excessively rude, Gérard. First you do not come to see me since three days, and me, I know nothing of what happens with Gosse until this *capitaine* of yours has come today. And now, when you come at last, you bring me this grandfather, and you dare to tell me I am like him.'

He sighed elaborately. 'I know, Melusine. I am altogether a person of a disposition extremely interfering, as you have so often told me.'

'Do not make a game with me,' she interrupted, gripping her underlip firmly between her teeth to stop the threatening laughter.

'But I am perfectly serious,' he returned in a voice of protest. 'Here were you patiently waiting, without uttering one word of complaint the entire time, which of course you never do, being yourself a female altogether of a disposition extremely sweet and charming without the least vestige of a temper —'

'Gérard,' Melusine uttered on a warning note, desperately trying to control the quiver at her lip.

'—and what do I do? Well, we know what I do. Yes, yes, there is no doubt about it. I see that I am a beast—I beg your pardon, *bête*—and an imbecile, and an idiot.'

Melusine stifled a giggle. 'Certainly this is true,' she managed.

Gerald shook his head. 'I can't think how I've tolerated myself all these years. And I suppose it is too much to expect that any entirely English young lady would be prepared to tolerate me for the remainder of my life.'

'You say—what?' gasped Melusine. Her amusement fled and she stared at him, as a slow thump began beating at her breast.

There was question in Gerald's gaze as it met hers, and apology in his voice. 'You see, I had another reason for visiting your grandfather.'

Melusine hardly dared believe she had heard him aright. He was apt to play so many games, she was afraid she might have misunderstood. *Eh bien*, why did he not repeat it? What was she to say?

'Prudence,' she began hesitantly, pronouncing the name in the French way, 'has said that she will help me to—to marry an Englishman.'

'Yes, that's what I'm talking about,' Gerald said. 'I, on the other hand, want to help you to marry this Englishman.'

Melusine's heart leapt, raced for a moment, and suddenly dropped again. Just this? *Parbleu*, did he think this was enough? She did not wish to marry him—at least, not just because he was an Englishman.

'You have said you do not wish to marry me,' she accused.

'Oh, I don't *wish* to marry you. I'd need to be out of my senses.'

Quick anger flared, surpassing the fluttering hope.

'*Dieu du ciel*, is this a way to have me say yes? If it is that you do not wish to, why do you ask me?'

'Ah.' Much to Melusine's chagrin, Gerald folded his arms and leaned back, as if wholly at his ease. 'I can answer that. Of all the entirely English women I know, you're the only one with a French accent.'

She was too distressed to bear this. '*Imbecile*. Is this a reason?'

'Not good enough? Now I had every hope that it would appeal to you. I'll have to think of something else.'

'Do not hope it,' returned Melusine, snapping uncontrollably. 'I do not wish to hear any more reasons so foolish, so do not trouble to think of them. I see now that you make a game with me indeed. You do not wish to marry me at all, that is seen.'

Gerald unfolded his arms and threw his hands in the air. 'But I have been perfectly honest about that. I don't wish to marry you at all.'

'In this case, I do not at all wish to marry you,' Melusine threw at him furiously. 'And I have a very good mind to kill you.'

'But you must,' Gerald said, quite as if he meant it. 'Not kill me, I mean. Marry me.'

'I will not.'

'But the general gave his permission.'

'*Je m'en moque.* And it is not at all his affair.'

'But it's my affair, Melusine. You have to marry me.'

'Why should I?'

'Because I can't live without you!'

'That is your own affair, and—'

Melusine broke off, staring at him, shocked realisation kicking in her gut. Reaction set in and she
leapt at him, beating at his chest with her fists.

'This is the way you tell me that you love me?
You English *idiot*, you!'

He seized her wrists to hold her off, actually daring to laugh, much to Melusine's increased fury.

'What else do you expect? It's the penalty you
pay for marrying an Englishman.'

Melusine wrenched her wrists out of his hold
and stepped back, digging into her skirts, which she
had adequately prepared some days ago. 'But I do
not pay this penalty.'

'Uh-oh,' came from her infuriating suitor and his
eyes dropped to the weapon she was dragging from
the holster under her petticoat. 'Here we go again.'

Both hands about the butt of her unwieldy pistol, Melusine glared at him.

'If you love me, you will say it, or else I will blow
off your head.'

'Will you indeed? Truly?'

His smile held so much tenderness, she was
tempted to surrender at once. But, no. This she
would not endure. She infused menace into her
voice.

'Say it.'

Gerald remained infuriatingly calm. 'I've never
before made love at pistol point.'

'But you do not make love,' Melusine pointed
out.

'I kissed you once, didn't I?'

Her pulses jumped and she stared. 'You would say that already then you love me?'

His glance was a caress and Melusine's resolve weakened.

'When we met probably, and you threatened me at the first. But it was only when that damned scoundrel nearly spitted you in the chapel—' He broke off and, to her intense satisfaction she saw he was not as much in command of himself as he would have her believe. 'It must have been so, Melusine, or I wouldn't have kissed you.'

A tiny giggle escaped her, and she lowered the pistol a trifle. '*Eh bien*, you are not like Leonardo.'

His face changed, all the humour and tenderness leaving it in an instant. Something like a snarl crossed his face, and ignoring the pistol, he moved forward, seizing her shoulders.

'Leonardo again,' he growled. 'What was Leonardo to you?'

Melusine was instantly on the defensive. '*Laisse-moi.*'

'Damn you, answer me!'

Her eyes flashed. 'It is not your affair.'

'Was it yours?'

Insulted beyond bearing, Melusine lost her temper. '*Dieu du ciel*, for what do you take me?'

'I don't know,' he threw at her. 'That's why I'm asking.'

The fury welled. 'You wish a reason for jealousy? *Eh bien*, you may have it. Leonardo he was my—'

'Don't say it,' Gerald cut in hoarsely. There was a pause, while the steel grey eyes sliced at her. Then pain entered their depths. 'You wound me to the heart, Melusine.'

Releasing her, he turned and walked swiftly towards the door. For an instant, Melusine watched him go. Then instinct took over. With a cry of distress, she dropped the pistol and flew after him, racing past him to the door. Flinging her back against it, she put her hands out, barring his way.

'Gérard, do not go,' she cried, breathless. 'Me, I am *tout à fait stupide*. You make me angry, and I lie. *Voilà tout*. Leonardo was to me nothing at all.'

There was a kind of aching hunger in Gerald's gaze. 'Do you swear it? There's no knowing if one can believe you.'

'I do not lie to you now,' she said, near frantic at the thought of losing him. Yet her hands dropped, and she sighed deeply. 'You do not understand, Gérard. Leonardo was to me perhaps like a father, not a lover as you think.'

'I don't want to think it,' he said, and she thrilled to the savagery in his tone.

'You are jealous!'

'Yes,' he agreed simply. 'Because I love you. I can't help it.'

Melusine's eyes misted. 'You said it. And I have no more the pistol.'

She was seized by two strong hands and drawn close. Gerald's gaze bored into hers.

'Tell me the truth, Melusine.'

'Of Leonardo? Yes, I will tell you.' She spoke with difficulty, holding down the rising emotion that threatened to overwhelm her. 'He was very kind to me. Not like my father. Nor my grandfathers both. To them all I am nothing. They do not come for me, to find me and bring me home. And for Suzanne and the vicomte, I am nothing. I am no one, Gérard.'

Gerald did not speak, but there was a look in his face that made Melusine glad she had at last had the courage to confide in him. The jealous burn at his eyes subsided and his finger came up. She felt the softest touch caress her cheek, and a wave of tenderness engulfed Melusine. Her hand came up and she laced her fingers with his.

'That is why I have come to England, you understand. To—to find myself. Because Leonardo, he made me see that I can be someone.'

'You were always someone, Melusine. Even if you didn't know it.'

The gentleness in his voice nearly overset her. 'It did not seem to me that it was so. Until Leonardo.' Then all at once remembrance made her smile. '*En tout cas*, it is not reasonable that I could be at all in love with him. He is extremely old—forty at least—and he has a belly excessively fat. Also he is ugly. And I was altogether disgusted when he kissed me.'

'How shocking,' Gerald returned. 'I trust you were not altogether disgusted when I kissed you.'

'But I have told you not. And if it is true that you love me, I do not know why it is that you do not kiss me again at once.'

'I would have done, only you threatened to blow off my head,' Gerald reminded her, laughing.

'Do not be *imbecile*. Do I blow off the head of a man with whom I am in love?'

'That,' said Gerald, disengaging his hand and at last drawing her into his arms, 'deserves a reward.'

Melusine drowned in his kiss. Her heartbeat raced, her limbs turned to water, and it was only by a miracle and the strength of the arms that held her that she remained standing on her feet.

It was some time later, after a series of these devastating assaults, that Melusine found herself seated on the sofa lately vacated by Lucilla and Captain Roding, cuddled firmly in the arms of a major of militia reduced quite to idiocy.

'—and I love your raven hair, and your bright blue eyes, and your very kissable lips—' suiting the action to the words '—and I love the crazy way you speak English, and the way you curse at me. I love you calling me Gérard and *idiot*, and I love you when you threaten me with every weapon under the sun, and—'

'Pah!' interrupted Melusine, scorn in her voice. 'I do not believe you. You make a game with me, *imbecile*.'

'And I love the way you call me *imbecile*,' finished Gerald.

Melusine giggled, and tucked her hand into his. 'Certainly you are *imbecile*. If I did not love you *en désespoir*, I would assuredly blow off your head.'

'That's exactly what I'm afraid of. Why do you think I'm indulging in all this very un-English love talk?'

'But you are *idiot*, Gérard. The pistol, it was not loaded.'

'You mean I need not have said it? Damnation.'

'But I have still a dagger,' Melusine warned.

'Oh, have you? Well, in that case, I love your little booted feet, and your ridiculously long eye-lashes, and—'

The End

THANK YOU!

Thank you so much for buying and reading my book.

If you enjoyed it, please consider leaving a review. It does help us indie authors so much to have lots of reviews because it tells readers the book is worth their time and it makes it much easier to get good promotion opportunities.

You can find out about me and my books on www.elizabethbailey.co.uk

I love to hear from readers. Contact me on elizabeth@elizabethbailey.co.uk

As you have just read one of my traditional Regency and Georgian romances, I would love to introduce you to my Brides by Chance series. This is the first.

www.elizabethbailey.co.uk/brides-by-chance

Orphaned. Abandoned in a house of strangers.

Forced into ladylike conduct. Berated for mistakes. Unhappy and lonely, Isolde turns to her guardian for support. Is Richard's kindness enough?

Struggling with his father's legacy. Appalled to find his ward related to his worst enemy. Will Richard save Isolde or use her for his own ends?

And what of his jealous sister? Will her vicious machinations prevail?

Destiny may fail both hearts before the spark between them has a chance to catch fire.

BRIDES BY CHANCE TITLES

In Honour Bound, Book One
A Chance Gone By, Book Two
Knight for a Lady, Book Three
A Winter's Madcap Escapade, Book Four
Marriage for Music, Book Five
Damsel to the Rescue, Book Six
Widow in Mistletoe, Book Seven
His Auction Prize, Book Eight
Disaster and the Duke, Book Nine
Taming the Vulture, Book Ten

Have a look at the titles already out here:
www.elizabethbailey.co.uk/brides-by-chance

Why Brides by Chance? If you care to call them Cinderellas, you won't be far wrong.

Think of all the many women of the Regency who could never hope to marry. Orphans, poor relations with no dowry, no social expectations. Existing in genteel poverty, or living on the bounty of others. Or perhaps with a place in Society but too dull or too poor to attract a suitor.

Such are my heroines. And the Brides by Chance series contains their stories, some linked with recurring characters.

Regencies in the traditional style and all different. We have adventure, scandal, suspense, romps, runaways, mysterious fugitives, vanishing memories, hidden secrets and bluestocking blues. Heroes to die for, bucket loads of romance, and heroines destined far beyond their wildest dreams.

Elizabeth Bailey grew up in Africa on a diet of unconventional parents, theatre and Georgette Heyer. Eventually she went into acting and trod the boards in England until the writing bug got to her, when she changed to teaching and directing while penning historical romances and edgy women's fiction. Her 8 year apprenticeship ended with publication by Mills & Boon, and 18 historical Regencies.

Latterly she had two historical mysteries published by Berkley which are being re-released by Sapere Books, along with the third Lady Fan novel. And there are more of these mysteries in the pipeline. Look out for *The Gilded Shroud* and *The Deathly Portent*.

Meanwhile, Elizabeth says it is wonderful to be able to return to her first love, historical romance, and put out new and old releases in e-book. She is thoroughly enjoying writing the Brides by Chance series.

www.elizabethbailey.co.uk

Printed in Great Britain
by Amazon

44809093R00172